A Small C

On the Road to Santiago

Sky Clad Journeys – Volume 1

Other books by Robert G. Longpré

Healing the Soul series (Autobiographical):

Volume 1 - A Broken Boy on the Broken Road, 2014
Volume 2 - On the Broken Road to a Magical Other, 2013
Volume 3 – Healing a Broken Man, 2016

Skyclad Poetry series:

Volume 1 - By the Sea and on the Prairies, 2013
Volume 2 - At Home and in Nature. 2014
Volume 3 - She, He, We, 2015

Skyclad Journeys series:

Volume 1 – A Small Company of Pilgrims, 2014

Crazy Emigrant: The story of Nicholas Berdowitz, 1979

A Small Company of Pilgrims

On The Road to Santiago

Skyclad Journeys: Volume 1

Robert G. Longpré

Retired Eagle Books

December, 2014

"We long to have some reliable, comfortable ground under our feet, but we've tried a thousand ways to hide and a thousand ways to tie up all the loose ends, and the ground just keeps moving under us."

Pema Chödrön,

"Whatever reality may be, it will to some extent be shaped by the lens through which we see it".

James Hollis

All rights reserved. No part of this publication may be reproduced, stored in a retrieval system, or transmitted in any form or by any means, electronic, mechanical, recording or otherwise, without the prior written permission of the author.

This book is a work of fiction, and as such, the characters and events in the story are products of the author's over-active imagination. Any resemblance to actual human beings, living or dead, is entirely coincidental.

Copyright © 2014 by Robert G. Longpré

ISBN: 978-1506137322

Retired Eagle Books
Box 423
Elrose, Saskatchewan
Canada S0L 0Z0

Table of Contents

Foreword – A Gathering of Archetypes
Prologue
Chapter One – The Call To A Pilgrimage
Chapter Two – Touching Landmarks
Chapter Three – A Small Company of Pilgrims
Chapter Four – Saint Jean Pied de Port
Chapter Five – Crossing The Threshold
Chapter Six – Peeling Off Layers
Chapter Seven – What is Real?
Chapter Eight – Meditation on the Path
Chapter Nine – A Place of Spirits
Chapter Ten – Meditation Among the Ruins
Chapter Eleven – A Journey Defying Common Sense
Chapter Twelve – Being One's Own Worst Enemy
Chapter Thirteen – On Someone Else's Path
Chapter Fourteen – Our Ladies of the Way
Chapter Fifteen – A Bump On The Road
Chapter Sixteen – Changes On The Journey
Chapter Seventeen – Taking Risks, Being Vulnerable
Chapter Eighteen – Loses Along the Way
Chapter Nineteen – Challenges, Temptations, Trust
Chapter Twenty – Illusions of Control
Chapter Twenty-One – Tired, Dusty and Falling Apart
Chapter Twenty-Two – It Comes Down To Trust
Chapter Twenty-Three – Between Heaven and Earth
Chapter Twenty-Four – A Pile Of Rocks On The Way
Chapter Twenty-Five – Trust And Intimacy
Chapter Twenty-Six – Picture Worth a 1000 Words
Chapter Twenty-Seven – Shadows and Light
Chapter Twenty-Eight – Skin is Just Skin
Chapter Twenty-Nine – And Two Become One

Chapter Thirty – Portal To Spirituality
Chapter Thirty-One – Coming Clean on the Camino
Chapter Thirty-Two – Endings and a New Beginning
Epilogue
Afterword
Acknowledgements

Foreword

Jacques banged on the oak table with a repeated hammering as he tried to get the attention of the assembly gathered in the attic. There were at least twenty-four of them in attendance at the meeting – twelve men and twelve women. Trying to get any of them to pay attention was next to impossible. Each one in the group saw themselves as the most important member present and believed that the others should attend to them as though at the foot of a guru.

Jacques stood above the assembly and went silent. As others began to sense Jacques' presence glowing and radiating to touch all of them, a quietness began to descend. He glared at each of them for the briefest of moments. His piercing eyes told them who the true boss was in the gathering, like a principal staring down a bunch or rebellious high-school students. Then, his face became one that was lined with centuries of age and wisdom, the face of a man who has seen too much and lived too long.

"We need to get started," he spoke when a rare silence finally filled the small room at the top of the house. "We need to make this happen now or we will lose him. We have lost too many souls to the darkness. The idea has been planted in his head to begin his journey.

Nodding to Sid, Jacques continued, "Sid has used his skills to have our subject believe that the idea of a pilgrimage was his own. We have been debating this long enough. It is time to now act. Since we can't overwhelm the subject with all twenty-four of us, only a small company of us can accompany him on his pilgrimage."

Taking a deep breath before continuing and looking again at each of the assembled group, Jacques continued, "Of course, I can't compel anyone here to leave well enough alone with the plan. However, I do hope that if you make an appearance while the pilgrimage is in play that you won't get in the way of group's goal, the goal that all twenty-four of us have already agreed upon. We must … must not lose his soul."

Prologue

This story, like most accounts of reality, seems too impossible to be factual truth. And since I am treating my story as a fictitious tale, it gives me liberty to say things that I would otherwise have had to leave unsaid. My name is the only real name used in the story though some of the people in it are real enough. However, just to make it interesting, and to somewhat play by the rules of fiction, most of the characters are fictitious – well at least their names have been changed.

The setting is real. The Camino de Santiago de Compostela is a real pilgrimage route that has been walked for more than nine hundred years. For whatever reason (it will be explained in the story), I found myself walking the Camino. Rather than create a world of fictitious places for the Camino, I used my real-life experiences for the hostels, cafés, sights, and the trail itself. I walked the pilgrimage route in late summer and the beginning of autumn, and have used this time frame for the story to be told. Since I don't have any knowledge of the trail in other seasons, it seemed pointless to change the season in the story.

But, I'm getting ahead of myself here. I need to get back to the task at hand, giving you some background so that you can understand the context from which the story emerges. I am a psychotherapist, not a novelist, a Jungian psychotherapist; I guess I had better clarify that, I was a psychotherapist. In the distant past, I was an aspiring musician and poet. That was back in the days of Flower Children and hippies. Like most of the others from that era, I grew up and entered into the mainstream of life–I fell in love, got married, had a career in the civil service, and raised a family. And then, it all fell apart.

I won't talk about who or what I was in previous lifetimes as that really doesn't have much, if any, bearing on the story I am about to tell you. It is enough to simply say that in this lifetime I got to the point in time where I was forced to make the journey back into a conscious being. The first half of my life, like all humans, was basically a life lived unconsciously and instinctively. Until, if ever, one falls into a living nightmare, there is no reason to become a more conscious being.

I am so thankful that it all fell apart for me, as it forced me to finally become a more authentic person and begin a new career that gives my life meaning. It wasn't just the new career that gave me a renewed confidence in life, I have to give credit to the role that meditation played in the healing. I had been a closet Buddhist and decided to acknowledge my need for meditation and structure.

As for relationships, my relationship to my children, and now my grandchildren were all that I needed. I was fortunate to have remained friends with my ex-wife. Somehow, all that was enough for me. I didn't need another woman in my life. I was happy with the status quo. At least, that is what I had come to believe. But so much for what I believed.

The truth is to be found in the pages to follow.

                René Beauchemin

Chapter One – The Call

Jacques was sitting in René's living room in his favourite chair waiting for René to bring him a fresh cup of tea. Over the past eighteen years, he had been René's mentor, analyst, and friend. Jacques had come into René's life soon after René had suffered a mental collapse that had sent the young man in search of analysis. René knew Jacques as a Jungian analyst. He had no real idea of just who Jacques was outside of their relationship. And that was as it should be.

René returned with a tray carrying a Wedgewood teapot with a matching cup and saucer for Jacques, a tea mug with an eagle motif, a small dessert bowl with sugar cubes, a tiny pitcher of condensed milk, and two English scones. René had learned long ago, Jacques preferences. The old man was set in his ways and resisted change. As he set the tray on the side-table next to Jacques, René thought of how resistance to change the octogenarian was, as he wore the same kind of corduroy jacket with leather patches on the elbows and herringbone tweed pants as when he had met him.

"There you are," René offered, "Proper tea, not some tea bag rubbish as requested. Help yourself to the scones, there's more of them in the kitchen."

Jacques waited while René poured him a cup of tea. It wasn't fitting or proper for Jacques to pour his own tea when he was a guest in someone else's home. "And yes, I will indeed have a scone, thank you."

For the next twenty minutes the two men made small talk while sipping their tea. Finally, Jacques brought up his reason for visiting.

"So you are determined to go on this long-distance hike. Couldn't you just get a membership at a local gym to work on your fitness? You know, this isn't going to do your therapy practice any favours, don't you?"

"Jacques, we've been over this all before. I can't really explain why I have to do this, I only know that I have to do it now or I'll regret it for the rest of my life."

Jacques smiled inwardly. The idea had been well planted and was going to be realised.

René continued, "I've let me clients know that I'll be gone about six weeks. And, I've given them the names and contact information for counselling work with either Esther or Harold. Six weeks isn't too long."

"So, you leave tomorrow? Paris first?"

René sat back relieved that the grilling was done. "Yes, to both questions. I will likely be in Paris for a night before I take the train to south-western France. I have a few places I want to visit first before leaving the city, places with pilgrimage history."

"I imagine that you're children and grandchildren will be over this evening to celebrate and wish you well in your travels," Jacques added with a smile. "Isn't it one of your popcorn-and-a-movie nights?"

"Yes, it is," René admitted proudly. For the past number of years, he had made his Friday evenings almost sacred time for his family. His children would bring their children over for a movie, or games and suitable treats. Even his ex-wife's two children born following their divorce were included in the gatherings. The only exceptions were on those Fridays when he was either at a conference or travelling away from home.

"I'm going to show them some photos I found on the Internet, pictures from other people's Camino."

"Well, since you are still determined to go," Jacques acceded, "I will wish you well. Walk carefully and with confidence, René. I will be there with you in spirit."

Jacques left soon after, still a few hours yet before the arrival of his family. René decided to go over his backpack and its contents one more time, checking what he had packed against recommended lists and his carefully prepared list. The backpack weighted in at just over seven kilograms, well within the recommended ten percent of his own body weight.

With time to kill until his family arrived, René took out his journal:

> *Two years ago, I watched a movie called <u>The Way</u>, out of boredom. I was filling the empty hours with sitcoms, movies and wandering through malls though I had nothing to buy nor any desire to possess anything. However, that movie touched a tender spot within me and stirred up things that had long been buried. The call to my own journey came as I watched the movie. 'This is what I have to do,' I thought once the movie came to an end. So, I bought some new shoes and a backpack, reserved a plane ticket to Paris, and dreamed of walking the Camino. Tomorrow I finally being that journey. It might be an act of foolishness, but it is a very important act for me. I remember reading one of Jung's books where he said, "if you don't live your nonsense you will never have lived at all, and the meaning of life is surely that it is lived, not avoided." I am done avoiding my hero's journey*

~

As he took off his black backpack, a small forty litre pack, René settled into one of the comfy chairs that were grouped in pods of three around a pedestal that supplied electrical outlets for those who were addicted to their tablets and laptop computers. A few other people were already seated, busy staring at their smartphone screens. René resisted getting out his own tablet as he sat back to enjoy the large cup of coffee he had purchased at Starbucks. He was addicted to their Café Mocha. He didn't want the distraction of Facebook or Twitter. He simply wanted to breathe and savour his coffee, hoping that the anxiety he felt at attempting the Camino would dissipate with the soothing sips of sweet coffee laced with chocolate. He did, however take out his journal and wrote:

> *Today, I am sitting in the tiny space that passes as a lounge at the Macdonald-Cartier International Airport in Ottawa. Surprisingly, the lounge near Starbucks is comfortable. I'm early for the flight to Toronto as I hate leaving things to the last minute. I'm always worried that some road accident or detour or road construction would cause me to be late.*

So began René's journey which he was to document in a new journal that his daughter, Élise, had bought for him along with a set of coloured pens. His son, Jérôme, had given his father a Patagonia runner's cap to replace the Tilley that had seen better days. René was sad to retire the Tilley, yet he was enthusiastic about how light and cool the new hat felt. The hat was tucked into his backpack along with the collapsible set of walking poles. A smaller pack held the camera and tablet which he would use for posting to a blog site created for his pilgrim adventures.

René lived in a suburb of the city about an hour from the airport. He had a private practice in his home and had begun to piece his life back together and rebuild his practice since making the commitment to walk the Camino. Of course, I did a lot of training and learning since watching the movie. He had a son and a daughter who had come to accept their father's imperfections. It's always hard for children to learn that their hero wasn't perfect. It is also hard for a parent to lose that aura of being his children's hero.

René had taken the time before leaving home a few hours earlier, to do his daily meditation. Because his flight to Toronto was to leave at two in the afternoon, there wasn't the usual early morning rush that he usually experienced when flying. Living alone since his divorce, he had learned to meditate within a room served both as his sacred sanctuary, and his office and library. Often he would have incense burning and some very soft music playing in the background, tactics he used to help quieten his mind which would otherwise run rampant with thinking.

René sipped his coffee slowly as his attention began to wander through a chaotic minefield of images and thoughts. In only a matter of moments, his breathing began to settle down. Finally able to regain his focus again, he asked himself for the umpteenth time why he was leaving his comfortable home, his friendly and tolerant neighbours, and his family scattered throughout the city and neighbouring towns, to walk almost a thousand kilometres in Europe. To tell the truth, he still wasn't sure that this was something he really wanted to do.

Yet, in spite of his doubts, here he was sitting in the airport lounge while his ex-wife drove his car back to his home. René felt guilty about leaving his clients and the life that finally had begun to piece itself back together. But the guilt didn't change the fact that he knew he needed, somehow was even compelled to do this long walk across the northwestern corner of Spain. Perhaps he would figure it all out somewhere along the way.

René looked around the lounge and noticed that it was beginning to fill up. With more people arriving, it began to be noisier as well, too noisy for him to think anymore. He moved his backpack from the seat beside him to sit on the floor between his feet in case someone needed the chair. It wasn't long before another person sat in the seat and smiled at René.

"Going to Toronto?" asked a man who was at least twenty years older than René. Though this man was a stranger, René had a niggling sense that he should know the man.

"Yes, it's the first stop on a longer journey," offered René in a friendly response. "And you?"

"Same here. As for myself, I am connecting on to Québec City before joining a group headed to Saint Anne de Beaupré. Have you ever heard of the place?"

"Yes," answered René as he smiled in remembrance of a childhood memory. "My grandmother used to go on a pilgrimage to Saint Anne de Beaupré every few years when I was a kid."

"From the looks of your backpack, I see that you are going to walk the Camino, that you're headed on a pilgrimage of your own," noted the other man.

"What gave my secret away?" asked René in surprise.

"The patch on your backpack. I recognise it as belonging to the Canadian Company of Pilgrims. It used to be called the Little

Company of Pilgrims back in the nineteen nineties. Your backpack doesn't quite look new. It looks as if it is waiting for an adventure to be continued," added the man. "Let me introduce myself, I am Father Federov. And yourself?"

"Name's René. René Beauchemin. Have you walked the Camino?" asked René with genuine curiosity.

"No. I've kept all of my pilgrimages here in Canada with the exception of one I walked for a week in Mexico," responded Father Federov. "So, have you discovered the reason, your reason for going on a pilgrimage, the pilgrimage of the Camino in particular?"

"Honestly? No," was all that René could offer for an answer.

Father Federov laughed and patted René's arm. "Perhaps the answer will come while you are walking. But then again, perhaps not. For now, it is enough to honour the Call."

"What do you mean, honour the call?" asked René.

"That's Call with a capital C." clarified the priest. "The Call is that inner voice that comes from the soul, a voice that is asking you to recognise your soul and its needs."

"I don't know as if I could say that I am following a Call," mused René. "It feels more like I am giving in to some sort of obsession, following some sort of New-Age fad. It seems that the movie, "The Way" has brought a lot of misfits such as myself, out of the woodwork to make this improbable trek."

"Hmm," commented the priest. "I guess you could say that the Call becomes an obsession when it gets deferred for too long. Something for you to think about, René," he added.

René looked at the priest quizzically. After just a few moments, somehow this stranger had pierced through layers of armor the expose the tender nerve of truth. At that moment, the woman standing at the Air Canada desk announced the first call for boarding the plane. With no sense of being in a hurry to board, René thought it would be the perfect time for a stop in the public restroom before boarding. He hated disturbing people once he was seated on the plane. It was only an hour and a half hour flight, two hours counting the time spent in preparing for takeoff and the taxiing in for landing at the terminal in Toronto. A bathroom stop now would mean no stress on his body later. Taking a moment to thank Father Federov for his company, René excused himself with a final wish to the priest for a safe journey to Saint Anne de Beaupré.

~

The flight from Ottawa to Toronto went well, if any air flight can be said to go well. As always, René couldn't find a comfortable position because of an old injury to his hip. He had been seated beside a younger woman who spent the entire journey watching the in-flight programs on the small screen built into the back of the seat in front of her. It was just the way René wanted it to be as he had no desire to make small talk. He had spent the first half hour of the flight glancing at the En Route magazine in the pocket in front of him before taking out his small tablet in which he had loaded a meditation timer program. He had pre-set the timers to ring every ten minutes with a final three bells to mark the end of his meditation after thirty minutes. A second meditation was just what he needed. Plugging in his earphones and then closing his eyes, René entered into meditation.

As usual, meditation was a mixed bag of sensations, thoughts, silences and chaos. It took some patience and more than a bit of self-forgiveness to bring himself back to his breath, tracking the in-breath and out-breath until his mind once again stilled for a short while. It seemed that the thirty minutes disappeared quicker than normal when the final three chimes signalled the end of his meditation. René had begun meditating thirty years earlier when he was attending classes at Carleton University in Ottawa. Cécile, had joined him in that initial experience of meditation along with two of his classmates who were close to the same age. René had started university after a two-year hiatus following high school, a period of time he had spent wandering around Canada like a gypsy. Those travels had allowed him to meet Cécile in Montreal where he had played in a folk-music bistro. The two of them had been inseparable, with her being his gypsy queen. After two years of travelling together, they decided that it was time to to get married, build a career in the Federal government as a civil servant, and raise a family.

Both René and Cécile had been baptised as Catholics though neither of them had found a home in the Church. Cécile's church was in the world of nature. René was slower in finding his church. It was only with the purchase of a small Buddhist book, The Book of the Dead, and a small statuette of Buddha that sparked an interest in things spiritual for René, a spark that was soon followed by the search for a class on meditation during his first year at university.

René's attention was brought back to the present moment as the stewardess asked him to put his seat back in the upright position, as they were preparing to land at Pearson International Airport.

The Air Canada flight to Paris was scheduled to leave Toronto later in the evening with arrival in Paris in the next morning, a flight lasting seven and a half hours if all went well. René had a long wait for the flight. He opted to go through security early in order to spend the wait time in the passenger area where there were enough coffee shops and fast food options to satisfy any hunger and thirst. With no luggage other than his backpack to take care of, René found himself walking down the various passages simply to keep moving. The plane ride from Ottawa had left him restless and he needed to be moving. René knew that he had another eight hours of confinement to a plane seat coming up, so he took advantage of the opportunity to walk.

René had stopped along the way to buy another Starbucks coffee, not because he was particularly thirsty, but because of the memories that the brand brought back to him. During the last years of their marriage, René and Cécile had little money to spend on dinners out or expensive entertainments as raising a family had left them little money left over for splurging. One of their rare treats was to go downtown for a Starbucks where they would imagine themselves as free as they used to be in their lives before kids. They laughed a lot back then as they made an effort for bringing romance back on those Starbucks' dates.

With a coffee in hand, another Café Mocha, René sauntered along checking out the various shops along the way. However, it wasn't the shops that interested him, rather it was the people who moved in and out of those shops. As he walked along, he began to invent all sorts of stories about them–where they were from, where they were going, and even why they were travelling. Since René was in the international flight wing of the terminal, he knew that the other passengers waiting for planes, were bound for other countries.

Eventually, with his restlessness eased, René found a seat at a small restaurant where he ordered a salad. He had thought for a moment about perhaps eating some pizza or even a burger and fries, but somehow he resisted that urge for fast, greasy food – it was more about guilt than it was about the urge to eat healthy.

Later, with his hunger eased, René found a seat in the section of the departure. He opened his tablet with the intention of sending Cécile an e-mail of thanks for driving him to the airport and returning his car to his home. He also thought of posting on Facebook for everyone else who might be interested in following his journey. It didn't take René long to connect to the Internet and take care of the tasks he had set for himself. Rather than stay online, he closed the tablet and opened the new journal that his daughter had given to him for this journey. The journal included a red ribbon to mark his last entry. He had already taped in photos of his three grandchildren and their parents, as well as a larger photo that included all of them taken just two weeks earlier in the backyard of his home. Taking out one of the new pens that she had included with the journal, he made wrote:

> *The journey has begun, I should say my journey has begun. Like Lao Tzu said once centuries ago, "every journey of a thousand miles begins with a single step." My steps so far, have been only in airports and onto and off of planes. But even these were not my first steps on this journey. I have already walked more than a thousand kilometres of Canada as I prepared for this day. The real walking on the Camino trail will have to wait for a few more days. For now, it is enough to know that the journey has begun.*

Chapter Two – Touching Landmarks

The plane had settled into its berth at Charles de Gaulle airport just outside of Paris on time the next morning. René waited his turn to disembark from the plane. With no luggage to pick up from the assigned carrousel, he soon found himself walking through customs, and then on to the RER, the train that would take him into the city. His destination was a hostel near Basilique Sacre-Coeur. The RER would take him as far as the Gare du Nord where he would then have to switch to the Metro line that would take him to the Anvers station which was the closest he could get to the Basilica. From there, he would have to walk a few blocks to the hostel he had booked on Rue D'Orsel, called Le Village.

René had it all planned out long in advance and had made reservations for the hostel weeks earlier. The last thing he wanted to do was to waste the little time he had in Paris wandering around in search of a bed for the one night he was going to spend in the city. Having studied the maps many times while at home, including a map of the airport which showed him where to catch the RER train, René soon found himself on a seat on the train next to a man in a suit. The man wasn't staring about with curiosity. It was evident that the man was at ease in the environment and was used to the journey from the airport into the city.

René knew how to speak French. Unlike most French-Canadians, René's French was not the usual Québécois that most of the people in his extended family spoke. Cécile was a French teacher and had taken groups of her students to Paris and other locations in France as part of their senior year program, an option that many of her students took advantage of over the years, and a journey that René sometimes took part in as a chaperone. René had taken a second undergrad degree in French, both to ensure that his children learned French at home, as well as for professional reasons. Many of his clients in Ottawa spoke French. When the man beside him asked him a question about being from Canada, an obvious deduction considering the Canadian flag René had sewn onto his backpack, René replied with friendly politeness.

Before too many more minutes had passed, two buskers passed by down the aisle of the train car playing their instruments and singing an old Edith Piaf song. René felt embarrassed at not having any spare change to give to the buskers. With their disappearance into another rail car, silence became the rule as everyone had become focused on their own upcoming agendas for the day.

The transfer to the Metro line M2 was uneventful, and René soon found himself at the Anvers station. He was early, too early to check into the hostel. So, for the next hour, he found himself wandering through the grounds of the Basilica remembering the last time he had been there with Cécile and her students. With that thought, a new wave of guilt and regret washed over René. So many good memories with Cécile and he had blown it. Of course, he wasn't here as a tourist, but the guilt was there regardless. Knowing it still was too early to check in, René headed to the hostel anyway to see if he could at least store his backpack there until he returned later in the afternoon to get his bed for the night.

The young woman at the front desk of the hostel showed René where he could store his backpack but warned him that he needed to wait until two that afternoon, at the earliest, to check in. With an expression of thanks, René left his backpack in the designated spot, and set off to find La Tour Saint Jacques, built in 1509. It had been the landmark that had been the gathering point for pilgrims intending to walk to Santiago de Compostela. René knew the route to the tower as he had been there before and he had plotted out the route he would walk to it before he had left home.

René took his small, lightweight camera that had a combo telephoto lens and wide angle lens, with him. With any luck, he would be able to get someone to take his photo at the monument. He also had plans to go to the Notre Dame Cathedral, then walk along Rue Saint Jacques to a nondescript church called Saint Jacques de Haut Pas.

Though he wasn't walking to Santiago from Paris, René felt the need to make these connections while he was in the city. He hoped to get his pilgrim's passport stamped at both the Cathédrale Notre Dame de Paris and at the Church of Saint Jacques de Haut Pas. He had received his credential, his pilgrim's passport, from the Canadian Company of Pilgrims based in Ottawa, several months earlier in the spring, along with the patch on his backpack that identified him as a Canadian pilgrim bound for Santiago.

René walked along the Boulevard Magenta and then along Rue St. Martin which took him to the famous tower of Saint Jason, la tour Saint Jacques. René remembered how he had almost missed the tower in its tiny park at the corner of Rue St. Martin and Rue de Rivoli when he was in Paris the last time.

René looked at the tower with some curiosity and a bit of disappointment. It took a moment for him to realise that nearby construction had made access to the park-like setting difficult. What was missing was a crowd of people. The tower seemed somehow invisible to the few passing pedestrians and even the few who walked through the small park itself. It seemed no one was aware of the sacredness of this spot in the heart of Paris.

With more than a bit of agitation, René explored as best he could, the tower from behind a fence barricade, taking a few photos hoping that at least one of them would be worth keeping. Then, he found a bench along one of the paths and sat. He needed to clear the agitation from within before going on if he was going to have any hope of enjoying the rest of his mini-pilgrimage through Paris. It took only a few moments of mindful breathing for a calmness to return.

Finding some measure of peace, René got up and was pleased to see a young couple near the tower taking a selfie of themselves with their cell phone. They quickly accepted his offer to take their photo for them and then take one of him with his camera.

A few blocks later, René walked across a bridge to the island that was home to the world famous, Cathedral of Notre Dame. As with every other time he had visited Paris and the cathedral, there were crowds of tourists everywhere. The heat of the mid-August sunshine in the city, was welcome though René felt he was perhaps wearing too many clothes for the oppressive, city heat that rose in waves off the pavement.

Entering into the cathedral, a welcome coolness wrapped itself around him. René slipped into a pew and sat still. In spite of the crowds within the cathedral, there was a respectful quietness, disturbed only by the sounds of shuffling feet and muted voices whispering. For some unknown reason, a tear moistened the corner of an eye. It wasn't time for such nonsense in René's opinion, so he got up and made his way to the cathedral office where he stood in line in order to get the church's stamp in his credential.

Leaving the cathedral, he continued south across another bridge, le Pont au Double, René found himself walking along the Quai de Montebello, which paralleled the Seine River, to return to Rue St. Martin. The first thing he saw was another park, the Square René Viviani. It was a busier park than at la Tour Saint Jacques. He stopped to take a few photos of the bizarre structures in the park before continuing on.

Back at the corner of Rue St. Martin, René had noticed that the street had changed its name to the Rue du Petit Pont, rather than what he had expected would be Rue Saint Jacques. Worried that he might have taken a wrong turn, René took out his map and studied it carefully, comparing it to the Cathedral, the bridge and other landmarks visible all around him. This was the right spot, so he risked turning to walk down this unexpected street. It wasn't long before he saw another street sign which told him he was indeed walking on the Rue Saint Jacques. It felt strange and even exhilarating to be walking on the same route that had been walked by millions of pilgrims in the past. They had made their way to Tours then on to Santiago.

Signs along the street told him that the Université de Sorbonne was close by. René soon found himself passing by the university, as well as the Collège de France. At the corner of Rue Gay-Lussac and Rue Saint Jacques, he saw a bookstore flying the Quebec flag. It was called the Librairie du Québec. Normally he would have stopped to check out the bookstore, but he was on a mission. Only one block remained to reach the church that was his destination.

René reached the corner of Rue Saint Jacques and Rue de l'Abbé de l'Épée, and stood in front of a non-descript white building. It didn't look in the least like a church with the church's entrance set at the edge of the sidewalk. However, the sign on the wall confirmed that it was indeed the church Saint Jacques de Haut Pas. He tried the door and found that it opened. He slipped quietly inside and saw that he was alone in the church that was hidden behind the street wall. There on a wall, was the image of Saint Jason dressed in pilgrim's clothing. This is what René had been searching for. He realised that he had found the right portal that would now allow him to enter onto the path of transformation, the path of his pilgrimage. He didn't know why finding this portal was important, but he instinctively knew that it was.

~

Back at the hostel, René noticed that he had somehow acquired a blister, something that surprised him. For the past four months he had been walking between six and twenty-five kilometres each day in preparation for the Camino. It had taken a good month for him to find the right hiking shoes, and the right socks. Since he had been walking with the new shoes and socks, blisters had become a non-issue. Then it dawned on him that he had walked that afternoon in his sandals rather than his trusted shoes. It definitely wasn't a good way to begin a pilgrimage. Threading a needle through the blister to relieve the pressure, René took care to treat the blister properly and turned his attention to his evening meal spread out in front of him in the dining room of the hostel. He had purchased a few slices of pizza and a bottle of orange juice, along with a couple of bananas for his meal.

There were others in the dining room, mostly young people eating salads or sandwiches. René studied them with interest trying to guess at their stories, what had persuaded them to wander far from their homes and families. René was the oldest person in the room, older by at least two decades of life; and he was in his own opinion, the most unremarkable person in the room as well, dressed as he was in his hiking clothing that was built for durability rather than as a fashion statement. A few of the others looked at him and smiled encouraging him to return their smiles.

René had taken his camera and tablet with him as there was Wi-Fi reception in the dining room and lobby of the hostel. His camera was able to upload photos to the tablet which would then automatically upload the photos to his Flickr account. He also chose a few of the photos to post to his Facebook account for his children, Cécile, and a few colleagues. He had promised to post when he could so they would be able to follow his journey as it unfolded.

René had previously decided, before he left home, that he would go through the photos when he was back in Canada in order to write up the story of his pilgrimage. He didn't want to try culling the photos beforehand. He realised that if he spent too much time with the photos, he would miss out on the reality of the Camino in front of him. He promised himself to be present as much as possible on the pilgrimage.

Before turning in for the night, in his room that was shared with four others in the hostel, René took out his journal as well as the paperback book that he had put into his backpack at the last minute, a book that he had bought at a second hand store. <u>When Things Fall Apart</u>, by a Buddhist nun called Pema Chödrön was one of those unintended purchases. He opened the book and began to read:

> "Embarking on the spiritual journey is like getting into a very small boat and setting out on the ocean to search for unknown lands. With wholehearted practice comes inspiration, but sooner or later we will also encounter

fear. For all we know, when we get to the horizon, we are going to drop off the end of the world. Like all explorers, we are drawn to discover what's waiting out there without knowing yet if we have the courage to face it."

The words had him think about his previous attempts to face the darkness within himself that lay like a festering wound, waiting for a weakness to appear. Closing the book, he took out his journal and wrote:

> *I got a blister today. I hadn't paid attention and then it was there. I guess that this is a reminder that I have to focus on the little things on this journey, things if ignored will bring this attempt to a crashing halt. Mindful, I can't get lost in my head where reality and illusion become inseparable. I don't want to find myself back home having failed because I wasn't aware enough to spot the dangers that could bring it all to an end. Mindfulness – I have to remember that – Mindfulness.*
>
> *I have just read a bit from Chödrön's book. Will I have the courage to confront my wounds hidden in darkness on my journey?*

Chapter Three – A Small Company of Pilgrims

René had woken early even though the train he had booked to Bayonne wasn't to depart until 10:25. There was just the first hints of dawn to be seen out of the dorm window though he could hear the first signs of a city waking to begin a new day. He had already showered and shaved and taken care of the blister on his right big toe, draining it before applying a blister bandage. Dressing quietly, then packing the silk sleeping back liner that had served as his sleeping bag for the night, René checked to make sure everything was in the pack where it was supposed to be. Satisfied that he was ready, he made his way down the tight, narrow and twisting stairwell to reach the dining room where breakfast was available as a self-serve option. He chose coffee and a couple of croissants for breakfast, along with an orange juice and a few strawberries.

René checked his email and Facebook account while he drank a second cup of coffee. There was no immediate rush to be out the door. He had plenty of time to make to the Austerlitz station and the train to Bayonne. Finally, unable to sit still, he packed away his tablet and went out the door of the hostel en route to the train station.

It seemed that René's time in Paris had disappeared too quickly as he was wanting to see more of the city. Perhaps it was a last attempt to find a way to test his resolve, or even to abandon the journey for a less challenging adventure. The last days of August in Paris held a rare quality of light, especially at early morning and before sunset, in this city of love. René could spend years in the city and never exhaust his sense of wonder.

The journey to the Austerlitz train station via the Metro on the M12 line was crowded with morning commuter traffic, something René had expected. Once at the station, he was able to buy his tickets for the ten twenty-five train. Even buying the train ticket had been a risk, as he would have had to wait until twelve twenty-five if the train had been fully booked. He took his seat on the train when the doors opened for boarding. It appeared as though there wasn't anyone booked into the seat beside him which meant that for a while, at least, he would have some quiet time, perhaps even some meditation time before the next stop.

Good intentions aside, René took out his guidebook for the Camino thinking that he would once again trace the route and the expected overnight stops. The book had been stripped of all the unnecessary pages in order to keep his backpack weight down. It had been a long process to finally arrive at a carrying weight of just under seven kilograms including a filled water sack that held two kilos of water. Sighing, he returned the guidebook into his pack and took out his Nexus tablet which was loaded with more books that he would likely find time to read at the end of each walking day.

René chose <u>The Heart of the Buddha</u>, by Chögyam Trungpa, which he hadn't yet begun. He had added the book to his reading list because of the title of the first part of the book, the "Personal Journey." It didn't take long for René to figure out that this personal journey was about "waking up and shedding our covers." René furrowed his brows upon reading those words. Somehow this business of shedding covers sounded a lot like the transparency and vulnerability that was the mantra of various people who held a naturist view of life. Of course, Trungpa was referring to an inner journey and not about stripping off clothing during an outer journey. Closing the tablet, René leaned back and stared out the window. There would be time later for more of Trungpa's book. For now, he only wanted silence and the scenes that passed before his eyes.

After a while, feeling as if he was being hypnotized by the constantly flashing scenes outside of the window, René decided it was a good time to meditate, He didn't open his tablet to the meditation program. He wanted simply listen to an inner voice which would let him know when the meditation session was done rather than depend on timers and chimes. With hours to ride on the train, keeping track of minutes seemed irrational.

When his eyes again opened, René saw a man looking at him. 'Strange,' thought René as he hadn't heard anyone approach or sit down. Usually when he meditated he could hear better, sense better the world around him. After all, that is why it was called Mindful Meditation. Perhaps he had fallen asleep while meditating, but he doubted it as he was still sitting upright with his hands resting appropriately on his lap.

"I see I have disturbed your meditation," smiled the old, bearded man opposite him.

"How did you know I was meditating?" René questioned.

"It was your meditation that drew me here," replied the smiling man.

As René looked at him, there seemed to be something vaguely familiar about the man, as if somehow he was supposed to know who this man was. Before he could follow that thread of thought, the man spoke again.

"Yes, you know me, René."

With a look of utter surprise, René blurted out, "How do you know my name?"

All he got for an answer to his question was a smile and a slight nod of the stranger's head acknowledging that truth.

"Who are you?" asked René with some frustration.

"Obviously, you already know that answer. Be still for a moment and just listen to your breath and you will remember," counselled the smiling stranger.

Following the wise advice while keeping his eyes open, René realised that the man in front of him wasn't really a man. Somehow, René had reached deep inside of his own psyche to awaken the Buddha within. After all, according to Buddhist belief, everyone was Buddha and had Buddha nature.

"Okay, so I am talking to myself, is that what you are trying to tell me?"

For an answer, all he got was a widened smile and another slight nod of the stranger's head.

"Great! So now I am hallucinating," muttered René. "I sure hope people don't see or hear me talking to thin air otherwise . . ."

The sentence went unfinished as it finally dawned on René that he was in a different reality at the moment, not the same reality that had his body sitting in a train car on its way to Bayonne. He thought about what he knew of inner world characters that exist within each person. What was it that his friend Daryl Sharp had written so long ago? Something along the lines that the ego was only one among a whole boarding house of characters found within the human psyche.

Each of these characters had archetypal references such as the Shadow, the Anima, the Mage, the Guide, the Warrior, the King and the Fool. It seemed that his wires were crossed somewhere between depth psychology and Buddhist psychology. Perhaps, what he was experiencing was something shared between both approaches to the human psyche? Catching himself in an ever-expanding train of thoughts, René brought himself back to the situation at hand.

"So, you are a part of me?" he offered to the man. "Perhaps my inner guide, an archetype?"

"Ah!" beamed the stranger appreciatively. "I told you that you recognised me. Yes, I am one of your guides for the journey we have begun."

"So, since you are supposed to be my guide, can you tell me more about my journey?" quizzed René with an air of disbelief.

"I can only tell you what you already know," the guide responded. "And to be sure, all the answers are already inside you. Bit by bit over the weeks to come, you will uncover bits and pieces of those answers. And when we have arrived at the end of this journey, the answers will stand before you without disguises and masks and riddles to hide behind. In your words, they will stand naked and proud."

"What's with this nakedness?" René demanded with a bit of upset with yet another reference to naturism.

"A good question," replied the guide. "Like you, I am interested in the answer that you will find. For now, it is time for me to make myself scarce. Your time for meditation is done. I will be back. But, before I go, I have a small gift for you."

With those final words, René found himself blinking with surprise at finding himself once again alone with no one else sharing the seat across from him. Checking his watch, he saw that he had been meditating much longer than usual. That knowledge would have allowed him to dismiss the imaginary visit from his guide with the exception of a curious egg-shaped small stone that was now clasped in his hand. He looked at the stone which was dark green with light flecks of white softening its appearance. He knew he had been given a talisman which was to protect him from unknown dangers on his journey. René held the stone within his palm, closing his fingers over it and felt its warmth. It felt real, too real.

~

The train pulled into the station in Bayonne in the southwest corner of France on time. Once off the train, with a few hours to kill, and a need for some coffee and lunch, René crossed the street and easily found a suitable place called "Le Longchamp," a typical bar and restaurant that was popular in every French city and town. He saw an empty table in front of the small café and waited for someone to come so that he could order his coffee and something to eat. The waiter arrived after a suitable period of time to ask what "Monsieur" would like. René ordered a café au lait and asked for a menu. The coffee arrived in short order and René requested a croque-monsieur, a glorified grilled ham and cheese sandwich for his lunch. He anticipated a better meal for supper once he was in Saint Jean.

While waiting for his sandwich, René got out his journal:

> *The train ride to Bayonne was interesting to say the least, and perhaps a bit too interesting. I am not sure what to make of visualising my guide. I kind of expected to meet a guide, so to speak, on this journey. However, I did think that it would be a real person. Perhaps the real guide is yet to make an appearance and the visualisation was more about my being over-stimulated by my travels and with reading some of Trungpa's book. I don't know what to make of the stone that was in my hand when I finished meditating on the train.*

Perhaps it's just one of the stones I had packed for the Camino, a forgotten stone, one that is destined to be placed at the end of the world. Oh well, it's already in the past. In another two hours I will be on the last train to SJPP.

Satisfied with what he had written, and accepting that the incident on the train was simply all about his over-active imagination, René closed the journal and began to study the constant flow of people in front of the restaurant. He checked the clock on the tower of the train station to make sure that his watch registered the same time. Assuming he had enough time after eating, he wanted to stroll around a few streets of Bayonne and take a few photos. He had the sense that this would be the only time he would ever find himself in this picturesque little city in Southern France.

A few minutes before departure, René settled into a bench seat on the small train, actually it was just a single car with its own engine, with a bit of time to spare before the train was to leave for Saint Jean Pied de Port. He noticed that there were other passengers, obviously pilgrims, who were sitting in a group; as well as other passengers on the train who were likely locals and not pilgrims. Their lack of backpacks and hiking clothing were the clues that gave René that impression.

It didn't take long for the other pilgrims to reseat themselves closer to each other. René heard their animated chatter and smiled. Somehow the idea of just foisting himself on that small group, uninvited, just didn't feel right. However, it didn't take long before what appeared to be the oldest person in the group, a bearded and dark-haired man, invited him to join the group of pilgrim hopefuls, beckoning with his hand once he had caught

René's attention. Not wanting to appear stuck-up, he rose from his seat to move closer to the other pilgrims.

"Bonjour! Please join us. It looks like we are all headed off on the same adventure," welcomed the man who had beckoned him over to the group.

René studied the old man thinking that somehow, '*I should know this man.*' It was a sensation that had cropped up a lot in the past two days. That sense of unconscious familiarity continued to nag at him, as he joined the group.

"Merci, thanks," replied René while nodding his head. "It appears as if we are all headed to begin a Camino adventure," René confirmed. "I think our backpacks are a dead give-away of our intentions, especially on this train heading to Saint Jean Pied de Port."

"We were just going to begin introducing ourselves," added the disturbingly familiar stranger. "It will help pass the time until we get to Saint Jean. I will begin. My name is Mark."

"My name is René, just plain René though there is the odd person who tries to call me Ray."

"René it is then," confirmed Mark who then turned to face a younger woman sitting across from him. She was likely in her early forties and in excellent physical shape, she was beautiful in René's opinion, perhaps the most beautiful woman he had ever seen. She had long blond hair and a rich natural, golden tan. "This young beauty here is Freya who hails from Norway. Oh, by the way, I forgot to mention that I'm from Egypt," Mark added as though an afterthought.

"Hi," said the Freya.

René couldn't take his eyes off Freya. She looked up into his eyes and he felt a surge of energy race through his whole being. She smiled and then lowered her eyes a bit as though to release him from a spell she had cast upon him.

"And sitting beside Freya is Sid, who comes from India," grinned Mark.

"Hello, René," smiled Sid.

"And this is Gabriel," Mark introduced while speaking about the middle-aged man who was sitting beside him. "Gabe was telling us he's from New York."

"That's New York State," corrected Gabe. "Hi René"

"And finally, this is Miryam who is going to walk the Camino with me. She's from Israel."

"There, we now have the important stuff taken care of – René, Sid, Freya, Gabe, Miryam and myself, Mark. I guess that leaves us just to tell each other more about where we are coming from; place, career, you know anything that will give us a peek at more than a face with a name."

Mark continued to talk, "I'll begin. My home for the last two years has been here in France in Bordeaux. Before that I lived in Spain for a few years, in a small town called El Paraiso, not too far from Algeciras. For most of my adult life I have been living on the road, in more countries than I care to remember. To make a long story short, I am originally from Egypt."

Gabe spoke up next. "As I said, I'm from America where I have spent almost my whole life. I did spend some time in France and Germany when I was going to university in my youth, in order to study and learn some French and German. Now, I am a retired university teacher."

"I'm from Canada," offered René. "I guess I have been a sort of gypsy my whole life travelling back and forth across my country and into the States, the U.S.A.," he added correcting himself so that the others would understand what he meant. "I have been to Europe six times now, China a few times, India, Laos, Vietnam, and a few other countries found in Indochina and Malaysia. I have also been to Mexico a few times as well as Belize and Costa Rica. As I said, I am sort of a gypsy – a French-Canadian gypsy."

"Cool!" grinned Sid. "I am from India! Where did you go when you were in India, René?"

"Mostly touring through Rajasthan with side trips to Accra and Varanasi, and a week in India at Goa, on the beach."

"Cool!" exclaimed Sid. "I was born in Lumbini. This is my first trip out of my homeland. However, like you, I have wandered all over my home country, almost always walking. I guess you could say I was on a never-ending speaking circuit."

Before Miryam or Freya had an opportunity to talk about their places of origin, Mark cut off the topic with another question. "I wonder if anyone wants to tell us why they are making this journey."

"For me," said Sid, "it's simple. I am curious about the rest of the world. I am hoping to make real connections with real people. I read that so many different peoples of the world could be found on the Camino and this seemed a like perfect place to start."

"What about you, Freya?" probed Mark.

"I came because, I guess you could say, I was called to come here. You know, that inner voice that won't shut up until you give in a follow its insistent demands." As she spoke her words, her eyes had again found René.

"Miryam, a few words for our new friends?"

"What can I say? Since meeting you, Mark, my life has been interesting to say the least. I have the feeling that like Freya, we are all called here, all following the same unvoiced command to appear on this particular pilgrimage at this particular time, with these particular people."

"That about says why I am here as well," René laughed. "And what about you, Mark? Care to tell us what is motivating your journey?"

With evident relish, Mark was quick to take the bait. "For one thing, it is a return of sorts for me, a return to Spain that is. I miss the language and the warmth of both the people and the land. With autumn coming, France gets too cold for my Mediterranean blood. As well, I have to admit that I basically haven't much choice. A long, long time ago my father tossed me out of the house and told me not to come back home until I had found out what home was about."

"I guess you could say that this trip will finally be my last road trip before returning to my father's house," he added without the slightest hint of anger. "It's time. Miryam here has taught me a lot about home being a state of being and not a place." If anything, Mark was almost radiating with barely suppressed joy as he expressed his feelings. "Now, René, tell us a bit more about what is motivating your journey to walk the Camino."

René took a little while to search for an answer while the others sat patiently waiting for him to begin. "To be honest, I don't know why I am here or why I am walking the Camino. It all began two summers ago when I saw a film on Netflix," he began.

"Netflix?" questioned Sid with a look of puzzlement.

"That's a computer-accessible, movie database," René explained before continuing on. "I saw a movie called *The Way*. It's a movie about a man my age, maybe a little older, who was walking the Camino following the death of his son who had died while walking the Camino. I know that isn't the best reason for walking, but it's all that I have so far. Maybe a better reason will surface while I am walking."

"I think we all will discover other reasons for walking, reasons which are lurking beneath the surface," added Gabe. **René** turn to look at him with curiosity and even respect.

Somehow, those words uttered by Gabe seemed to bring the conversation to an end as everyone retreated into a personal quietness. It was as if the talk about why each had ventured so far away from home for the Camino, had turned each of the pilgrims' attention inward. René took advantage of the quietness that descended and asked if he could have a group photo while they were still on the train. His request was readily accepted. René then asked one of the other passengers on the train if they would mind taking a photo of the group. **René then took a second photo of the five pilgrims.**

René had taken the second photo taken with his camera and with the tablet, explaining that the second photo was for his wife, his ex-wife he stated correcting himself, Cécile, and his two adult children. When the photos were taken, everyone returned into a meditative silence knowing that it wouldn't be much longer until the train would arrive at Saint Jean Pied de Port.

Chapter Four – Saint Jean Pied de Port

Jet lag was finally getting to René as his eyes closed. He leaned back against the seat-bench headrest. He was tired beyond belief and he hadn't yet walked the first kilometre. He wondered how he **was** ever going to walk twenty-five kilometres the next day, with almost all of it uphill. Perhaps he questioned himself, he had made a mistake in not booking a bed at Orrison, a shorter walk of only ten kilometres, all uphill, from Saint Jean. René wasn't sure of the distance as it had been reported as being at different lengths by so many different people. Even the maps he had studied didn't seem to agree. Before he could disappear into any further into regrets, the train began to slow down and the outskirts of Saint Jean Pied de Port appeared outside of the window.

It wasn't long before the train emptied and the six pilgrims wished each other "Buen Camino!" before walking off in search of their accommodations. René hadn't booked a room in the village yet. His plan was to go the Pilgrim office before searching for a bed for the night.

René walked into the old city through a gate that led him onto the Rue de la France. Then following that short street, he turned left onto the Rue de la Citadelle. The pilgrim office, called Les Amis du Chemin de Saint Jacques, was where he needed to register as a pilgrim and get his credential. They would let him know where he could find a room that would still be available. It had taken René about ten minutes to arrive at the pilgrim registration which was still open for business.

Inside the pilgrim office, René soon registered and was given another credential which had been pre-stamped with the official logo of les Amis du Chemin de Saint Jacques. René offered his Canadian pilgrim's passport and asked for the stamp to be imprinted there as well. René looked at the scallop shells for sale, traditionally worn by those walking the Camino, symbols that modern day pilgrims put on the backpacks. He decided against buying one. The patch on his pack was enough for him, maybe even too much. René had an aversion to labels.

Finding out that most of the beds in Saint Jean were already filled for the night, the woman who served René at the registration desk recommended that he stay in a semi-private guest house called, Tartaseni. It was rather expensive at sixty Euros per night; however, unlike the other options, he could stay there more than one night. The idea of spending an extra night in Saint Jean Pied de Port was something René began to consider as potentially necessary, as it would give him a chance to spend a bit more time getting over his intense fatigue due to jet lag.

"There was another good thing about Tartasenia," noted the woman who served him, "it's close to the end of the town on the Napoleon Route making the first day's walk just that much shorter. Your feet will thank you for it at the end of the day's hike."

René found out that it was about a fifteen minute walk to Tartasenia from the pilgrims' office. The woman at the desk had phoned ahead for René with his permission, in order to reserve a bed for him at the guest house. She also suggested that he go to the guest house first before going out for a meal at one of the local establishments. That way he could store his backpack there as well as freshen up with a shower before eating his evening meal.

Both ideas sounded good to René, so he headed off to the guest house with improved spirits and a renewed level of energy. As he walked towards Tartasenia, he noticed a restaurant called the

Cidrerie Hurrup Eta Klik which looked like a promising place for supper.

The walk to the guest house had René walking back down the hill on Rue de la Citadelle, passing the corner of Rue de la France. Though it was already beginning to be dark out, the street was bright with lights coming from the little shops, restaurants, and all sorts of doorways advertising rooms for rent. Continuing on downhill as the street turned to the left. A bit further down, he saw an arch that the woman at the pilgrim office had told him he had to go through, at the junction with the Rue de l'Église. René passed through the narrow arched gate which opened onto a bridge over a small river called La Nive de Béhérobie. He stopped to look at the water and at the view of Saint Jean at night. To the right was a scene of buildings built to the water's edge, to the left René saw that the north shore was park-like with a path following the river bank. He took a few photos including one looking through the gate which he had just passed.

Once across the bridge, the street changed names and became La Rue d'Espagne. Walking up the street he noticed a small grocery store called Alimentation that sold fruit, veggies, and cheese. 'This would be a good place to buy a few supplies for the long walk up the mountain,' René thought to himself. However, he realised, now wasn't the time to buy the few groceries he planned on getting; the first task at hand was to get to the guest house and register.

René continued on, meeting the Rue d'Uhart on the right. The Rue d'Espagne then began to climb as he walked towards his lodging for the night. He came upon an old broken wall which marked the end of the street. Crossing the Avenue du Fronton, he walked through another old gate, likely one that marked the old walls that would have protected the original, old part of Saint Jean, onto a more open and slightly more modern area of the city. He knew he had to follow along the left-hand side of the street, La Route de Saint Michel. He was already walking on the pilgrimage route that would lead south out of the city and up the side of the mountain.

It wasn't long before he came to another junction which had the Route de Saint Michel breaking off to the left and the Route Napoléon veering to the right. René followed the Route Napoléon. The guest house was supposed to be just fifty more metres up the road. He had been told that he would find a wooden gate along the stone wall that followed along the sidewalk which he would have to go through to reach the guest house. In the gathering darkness of the approaching night, not really being all that sure of his directions, as well as a few photos, and the unfamiliar terrain, it had taken René a good half hour to reach Tartasenia.

The host, Arthur was there to greet René as he entered the gate leading to the guest house. At the desk, the host wondered if René would mind sharing his room with another pilgrim who had called looking for a bed for the night. He explained that the rate for the room would be adjusted accordingly from sixty Euros to only thirty-five Euros. René was quick to agree; after all, he had never expected to have a room to himself, especially before the Camino had even begun. Arthur's gratitude radiated in his face as he led René to the room.

There were two beds in the room, leaving René to claim one of them as his bed. He been told by Arthur that his roommate was expected around ten that evening. Thanking his host, René wasted no time in taking a quick shower and gathering the few things he intended taking with him back into the old part of town. He made sure he had his cloth shopping bag for the fruit, cheese and other necessities for his meals on the trail, as well as his ever-present camera bag.

Walking with sure steps back into town, René soon entered into the small restaurant, Eta Klik, which was where he had chosen earlier for his evening meal. The restaurant exuded the pleasant sounds of good cheer for such a small place. He was clutching his small collection of provisions for the next day as he made his way into the restaurant.

He wondered if there would be a seat for him when he spotted Gabe at one of the tables with two other people, a man and a woman. There was space at their table for one more, so René entered and approached the table. Seeing René, Gabe stood up and asked René to join them as they were just about to order their own meal. René was relieved to find companions for the meal as he would feel less alone in the crowded restaurant.

Introduction were made and, as luck would have it, the other man at the table with Gabe was also staying at the Tartasenia. He was a middle-aged Swiss, whose name was Luca. Luca's backpack, looking suspiciously heavy and large, sat on the floor beside the table. The woman at the table was called Anne, a divorced French woman who was only planning on walking for two weeks as she had to return to work in Tours. By comparison, her backpack was tiny.

Anne told the others at her table that this was the fourth stage of her Camino. In each of the previous three years, she had walked almost two weeks to cover the distance from Le Pu en Velay in France. Her expectation was that she would reach Santiago in two more stages following this year's walk.

"Anne, why two weeks each year?" asked Luca.

"I have a family and a career that takes up most of my life," she explained. "I didn't want to wait until I retired as I am not sure if I will be healthy enough to walk then. Besides, with any luck, my children will get married and give me grandchildren by the time I retire."

René smiled and spoke up, "I have three grandchildren, two girls and a boy."

For the next half hour the talk surrounded their children. Like himself, Luca was also a grandfather. The food was good, the wine was even better, and the talk soon became all about the Camino. It was only after finishing a second litre of house wine and a platter of cheeses that René finally excused himself saying that the morning would come too soon. He needed some sleep if he was going to survive the walk to Roncesvalles the next morning. Luca decided to leave with René since René knew the way to the guest house. Luca was a story teller, and he talked almost constantly as they made their way through the city to the guest house, making René fear that sleep would be a long time in coming.

As they made their way up the hill towards the Tartasenia guest house, Luca asked René when he had committed to walking the Camino. René admitted that he couldn't really answer that question as he never was totally certain until he had arrived in Saint Jean. Soon, they had reached the gate to the guest house. It didn't take long for both of them to prepare for bed. Before turning out the lights, René took a few extra minutes to write in his journal.

> *I met some interesting people today, the sign of things to come for the next five weeks. Mark and Gabe are kind of interesting people. Luca seems to get on my nerves a bit, he's my room-mate for the night. He's a*

professor in Zurich, Switzerland, teaching German literature. Anne was a pleasant person to meet. She's a midwife, divorced, and an interesting person. It would have been nice to have her company for the Camino, however she is only walking as far as Burgos this year..

But of all the people I met today, it is Freya that has most captured my attention. Wow! Oh, and there's Sid. I like Sid. He smiles a lot. I wonder if I will see much of these new acquaintances over the course of this journey.

Finally, with a "Good Night!" the lights were turned out and René fell asleep.

Chapter Five – Crossing The Threshold

At six the next morning, the host, Arthur, knocked on their door and let them know that a breakfast awaited them below. It was still dark outside as both Luca and René repacked their backpacks. With a final check to make sure that the Platypus water bag was full and that nothing had been left behind, René opened the door to go down to the dining room where breakfast was waiting. A few minutes later, while René was enjoying his first cup of coffee, Luca joined him.

"So, René," questioned Luca, "How was your sleep last night. Any dreams to mark the big event of beginning the Camino? I have to say that I slept like a log with the most favourable dream."

"I've had better sleeps," admitted René not wanting to complain. "I spent most of the time when I should have been sleeping thinking about the Camino. And yes, I had dreams when I finally did manage to sleep."

Luca smiled and asked René why he was walking the Camino, while he munched on a croissant, thickly coated with some home-made jam.

"I guess I could say that the idea to walk, not the decision to walk, began to form in my head while I watched a movie on the Camino two years ago. When the idea struck me, I had a burst of inspiration that had me buy some hiking shoes and begin walking as though I was already on the Camino even though I was still in Canada. I didn't have any real plans, but the spark was lit."

"So," probed Luca, "What took you so long to finally make the commitment to walk?

"I just wasn't ready. I mean I was fit enough, almost as fit as I am now. But, my mind wasn't ready. If anything, I walked away from the idea of actually going on the pilgrimage. I distracted myself with other things such as travelling. My life seemed to accept this change of direction as it had been the pattern of much of my life – get a passion and then abandon that passion for something trivial. Well, maybe not that trivial – I focused on writing and photography. The two disciplines helped me learn to be present in the world. It was as if I was learning detachment without becoming dissociative at the same time."

"Ah, that sounds something like being an anthropologist, studying the world with the idea of not actually being a part of the world," wondered Luca. "Do you think that maybe the retreat from the Camino was perhaps more about doing some of the preparation work that would finally bring you to the right time to do the Camino?" asked Luca. "You know, like wine has to be aged before it is ready to be drunk?"

"Hmm? That's something for me to think about as I walk," considered René. "It's time to go, my friend. Care to walk with me for a while until we find our own rhythm and pace?"

After paying their bills, the two men hefted their backpacks onto their shoulders and walked out into the morning with the sky just beginning to lighten with the dawn. Standing outside the gate and bidding their host, Arthur, good-bye with Arthur bidding them "Buen Camino!" they joined a stream of other pilgrims who had already begun walking their Camino from somewhere back along the path in Saint Jean Pied de Port.

The Napoleon route followed along a narrow, and not heavily used road. Slowly, they made their way up the slope of the foot of the mountain. By the time they had covered the first three kilometres, they arrived at a junction which headed back downhill to the village of Saint Michel. The road to Saint Michele hand been the original pilgrim route back in the twelfth century when the first Camino guide was written. Other than that historical fact, it was just another paved road as far as René could see. Still, he took a photo of the original junction just in case something should come to light in the future about that particular junction. With a digital camera, there weren't any good reasons not to take photos.

In spite of being a few years younger than René, Luca found the pace a bit too fast in his opinion, at least that's what his body was telling him. Unlike René, Luca hadn't done a lot of training. That combined with carrying a backpack that was significantly heavier than René's was wearing Luca down as he tried to keep up with René.

René agreed to press on ahead with a promise that they could meet up again for a mid-morning café au lait at the Orrison Refuge which was still about four and a half kilometres further up the hill. If they didn't meet up at Orrison, they would meet up later, as both had promised to get together with Gabe at Roncesvalles. Gabe was walking the alternate route through Valcarlos with the French woman, Anne.

René picked up the pace a bit and covered the next two kilometres to reach Huntto in thirty-five minutes, not stopping to take any photographs until then. As he passed by the small refuge in Huntto and the café where a few pilgrims were already having morning coffee, the pilgrim trail left the paved road to follow a grass track for just over a kilometre before again returning to the road. With the climb beginning to take more energy that he had expected, René decided to stop at a picnic table conveniently placed beside the path before it turned onto the road. He took off his boots and socks and decided to write a bit in his journal before putting on new, dry socks and continuing on and up for the last kilometre to reach Orrison.

> *It's hard to believe it. I am finally walking the Camino. As I am writing this, I can see hills and valleys from the table where I am writing this. I love it!*

René entered the bar-restaurant in the Orisson hostel and ordered himself a café au lait. So far he had made good time, covering the approximately eight kilometres in just over two and a half hours. He noticed that the restaurant had more than a few pilgrims already enjoying coffee and what looked like a second breakfast in the roofed patio that seemed to hang over the valley below. René took his coffee to sit outside on the terrace and enjoy the panoramic scene that stretched out below him.

This seemed to be a perfect time for him to take a few more photographs to mark the spot as well as attempt to capture the morning light on the hills and valleys below. Finally, putting his camera away, he settled back to enjoy simply being present in the moment. When he was just about finished his coffee, Luca appeared at the auberge, which prompted René to order a second cup of coffee.

Luca had a lot to tell René, mostly about how heavy his backpack was and about the ungodly heat so early in the morning. When René suggested to Luca that he would have to dump some of his stuff to lighten his pack, Luca became adamant that he needed everything in his pack and that he could manage the weight. Shrugging, René said nothing more and simply smiled. With the second coffee swallowed, René promised to save a bed for Luca in Roncesvalles where they would meet later in the afternoon. With a parting "Buen Camino!" René set off again up the hill.

Again the path followed the pavement as it zigzagged up the mountain. René had already climbed more than 500 metres since he left the guest house, and there still remained another 700 metres of elevation remaining until he reached the highest point of the day's climb. René decided to walk at a more relaxed pace rather than push it, something he was prone to do when he tackled hills when he was training. This wasn't a hill he was climbing, and it wasn't just a four-hour training exercise. This was a real mountain beneath his feet. After almost four more kilometres of pavement, he reached the Pic d'Orisson at an elevation of 1100 metres. It was getting hot and René's feet were burning in his boots. He walked off the paved road to approach a statue of the Virgin Mary, which he wanted to photograph, before he gave his feet a reprieve from the hot boots and damp socks.

At last, the boots came off as did his socks. René made sure to massage his feet after pinning the socks to his backpack where they would dry while he walked the next leg. Taking out his camera, he walked barefoot on the grass in order to capture the scenes of mountains and valleys that stretched before him. When his feet had cooled off and were feeling better, it was time to put on some dry socks and boots to continue his journey up the mountain.

Another three and a half kilometres took him passed a roadside cross. The path then became a rough country trail of grass and stones for another one and a half kilometres, where another landmark appeared, the Fontaine de Roland. René remembered his study of the Chanson de Roland when he had been at university. Now here he was, at the site of the famed event that had inspired the poem.

René had entered Spain had passed a sign indicating the border between Spain and France, just a half kilometre before he reached Roland's fountain. More photographs were taken before he forced himself to continue on, up the path. He still had just over four kilometres to travel before he reached the high point of the day's travel, the Col de Lepoeder. René was about halfway to the peak when he decided to stop for another break. After taking of his boots and socks, he dug out an apple, some cheese and a petit pain he had bought in Saint Jean the evening before. His water supply was good as he had refilled the water bag while at Roland's fountain just a short while earlier.

Just as he was about to bite into his apple, he heard some excitement from other pilgrims on the trail just a bit further up the trail. Curious, he stood up, picked up his boots and backpack, and walked about seventy-five metres where he saw five pilgrims in various stages of what could best be described as shock, titillation, exhilaration, and even anger. Upon seeing René, one woman pointed to a rock about 100 metres away upon which an obviously naked man was engaged in meditation.

"It's disgusting!" the woman ranted. "This isn't the third world, this is a Christian world. That pervert should be arrested!"

René looked critically at the outline of the man. It was obvious that he was naked, but it was impossible to see his genitals as he was faced away from the trail. Really, it was hard to see why the woman had taken offense. Sure he was naked, but not in a way that suggested he was trying to flaunt himself to all passersby. As he turned back to try and calm the woman, he caught her taking photos of the nude man with her smartphone.

"Do you really think that's appropriate?" René questioned the woman who voice was almost screeching with indignation. "You can't really see anything anyway."

"But, it's against the law! He should be in jail," she protested. "What if some children saw him? They would be psychologically scarred. I'm going to show these photos to the police and get justice done."

"Relax, lady," René interrupted. "He's meditating, can't you see that? Besides, there are no children here. Hell, even you can't see his privates. Put your camera away. If anything, you are breaking the law taking photos of someone without their permission. For sure if you put that photo on the Internet, you would be breaking the law. Why don't you just continue on to Roncesvalles? I'll take care of this."

With that said, René walked across the barren hillside to reach the man who was meditating. As René got closer, he realised that the man was Sid. 'What the hell?' was the first thought that went through his mind. Closing the distance, René was taken by surprise when Sid spoke up without opening his eyes.

"I've been waiting for you, René. It's a beautiful afternoon. Why don't you join me in meditation?"

~

Luca approached René who was sitting in a meditation pose not far off the pathway that had seen a growing number of pilgrims passing by as the day advanced. A few pilgrims had stopped to take a photo of René while he was meditating. René sat barefoot and bare-chested on the grass with his backpack close, by leaning against a rock. Lying in front of René was a book, <u>The Heart of the Buddha</u>.

"René?" called Luca softly.

Hearing his name, René opened his eyes and saw Luca. A smile grew with the recognition of his new friend. "I was meditating," he explained unnecessarily. Then, with a tinge of alarm, René looked down only to find some relief. He was wearing his hiking shorts. He must have been dreaming about seeing Sid meditating naked on a rock.

"I guess it's time to get back on the trail," suggested René as he slipped his still damp merino wool tee shirt over his head. We still have about two hours of hiking left to get to Roncesvalles."

René and Luca reached the monastery in Roncesvalles at four-thirty in the afternoon, a full nine and a half hours since their departure from Saint Jean Pied de Port. Luca was struggling, mostly because of his heavy backpack. Just after the Col de Lepoeder, René had convinced Luca to switch backpacks for the last four kilometres into Roncesvalles, as he had doubts that Luca would be able to complete the remaining four kilometres before darkness would have set in.

While the two walked, René matched Luca's silence as he had a lot to think about. Had he simply been hallucinating? Probably he had simply fallen asleep after reading some more from the Heart of Buddha, and had simply blended reality and imagination in a dream. But what was all that stuff about nudity doing in the dream?

With their showers done and having taken some time to rinse out his salt-encrusted socks, René postponed his intention to go strolling around the village with his camera. He had to somehow convince Luca that his backpack needed to be lightened if Luca was ever going to complete the journey to Santiago. As the contents of Luca's backpack were spread onto his bed, René couldn't believe what Luca had managed to squeeze into the fifty litre backpack. Most of the weight seemed to be in books, electronics, and art supplies.

"Haven't you heard about e-books?" quizzed René.

"They're not the same," protested Luca.

"Damn rights they're not the same," countered René. "They're much lighter. I have more than a hundred books on my tablet that weighs less than a kilogram. These books you're carrying weigh at least three kilos, if not more. Besides, you are also carrying an iPhone, an iPad and a laptop computer. What in good lord were you thinking about when you packed all of this?"

Luca looked at the pile in front of him and knew he had too much though he was loathe to admit it. But what could he do about it now. After all, he just couldn't leave the books or his electronics behind. He had a lot invested in them, and not just money. "So what can I do? I can't just throw them away," whined Luca.

"Most of this stuff we can send on to Santiago. There's a guy there that stores pilgrims' excess stuff like yours, until they get to Santiago. We can just mail it to him and it will be there for you when you get to Santiago. How does that sound?" asked René in a gentler voice.

"Maybe the books and some of my extra clothes. I do need the electronics for reading and writing and, and I just need them. And my art supplies; if anything, they're the last to be sacrificed."

"Well, I'd suggest keeping just the iPad, but not the computer. They both do the same job. The iPad as it is lighter. What do you think?"

"The iPad is too small for me to use for writing. My fingers are too fat. I make too many errors while trying to write on the iPad."

"How about writing on paper a journal. Send both the computer and iPad along with most of your books, the extra clothing and all your shaving gear. You really do need to make your pack as light as possible," implored René, "If you're ever going to make it to Santiago."

A package was put together with each item being weighed in Luca's hand, however the sending of the package would have to wait until they got to Pamplona. Someone, another pilgrim in a neighbouring bunk, who couldn't help but hear their exchanges, suggested that they use the baggage transfer service to take the package to their next stop. Baggage transfers would allow Luca to have continued access to his books and electronics at the end of each day's hike. It was up to Luca to choose to continue the daily forwarding of the package, or to send it on to Santiago once they reached Pamplona.

Arriving at a solution to Luca's quandary, René left Luca to finish up with his packaging of extras as he headed out with his camera to learn what he could about this ancient pilgrimage site. Stepping outside, he felt the air had become a bit cooler, definitely cooler than it had been the night before in Saint Jean.

The monastery itself was large, but it was not near as interesting as a photo subject, as was the little church near the monastery. While walking at a snail's pace and taking photos of the few buildings to be found, from various angles, René decided it was time for another café au lait. He spotted a small restaurant, which also served as a small hostel, just up the road a short ways. The restaurant had a patio where he noticed that a few groups of pilgrims had already gathered to share a cup of good cheer.

"Ah there he is," exclaimed one of the pilgrims who pointed to René from the patio, "the half-naked pilgrim!" The statement was followed by some good-natured laughing as arms waved for him to join them.

"Yeah, I guess I am the half-naked pilgrim," grinned René with just a little bit of embarrassment at having already earned a nickname just hours into his Camino journey. "It sure was a hot one out there today, wasn't it?" he added as if that would explain resting in just his hiking shorts along the trail.

"So, you're a Buddhist?" asked another man who had seen him when he passed by René while he had been meditating just before the peak.

"Sort of," replied René. "More like a Buddhist wannabe instead of a real Buddhist. I just meditate to get my balance, to relax when I get a bit stressed."

"Your book looked interesting," the man continued. "I saw that it was about Buddha. I've tried doing some yoga and meditation a few times, but it was way too boring for me. I always have to be moving, be doing something. I don't sit still very well," he added with a smile.

"Unless you're having a brew, a cerveza that is!" chuckled another man pointing to more than a few empty glasses sitting on the table.

"Touché! You got me there, Frank," laughed the man. "Here, pull up a chair and have a brew with us," he offered to René.

"I'd prefer a coffee if they have some," returned René as he brought a chair over to join the group.

After an hour of listening to the varied stories of the first day's hike up from Saint Jean, René and a few others at the table left to walk back to the monastery and prepare for the evening that was being served there. Though introductions had been made while at the table, René couldn't remember anyone's name other than Frank's. René was tired, deservedly tired after the day's hike. There was little doubt in his mind that he would sleep well that night.

Back in the monastery and sitting on his bunk bed, René asked Luca how he was doing and if he was interested in going to the evening mass, at which there was to be a benediction of the pilgrims. Luca told him that he was going to go, as were Gabe and a few others that he knew. They had assumed that René would go with him. With a smile of agreement and of relief upon hearing that Luca was okay, René opened up his tablet to read from one of the eBooks he had bought for this journey.

> "What legendary travelers have taught us since Pausanias and Marco Polo is that the art of travel is the art of seeing what is sacred. Pilgrimage is the kind of journeying that marks just this move from mindless to mindful, soulless to soulful travel."

Interesting choice of words, thought René as he noted the use of mindful, a word that René had always associated with meditation – a state of mindfulness. René bookmarked those words and continued to read as he lay in the bunk for a few more minutes. Then, tired of reading, he took out his journal for a final few words about his first day on the Camino:

> *Luca is, surprisingly, turning out to be a likeable person. He fits in well with the others with whom I shared a table this evening. Gabe, Miryam, Mark, Sid and Freya were also at our table along with a few others that didn't seem to belong to a group. Strange how people find each other in spite of being solitary in disposition and not seeking to be in a group..*
>
> *I don't know how to explain what happened this afternoon. I thought I had found Sid meditating nude not far off the pilgrim trail. After that, I don't remember anything. It just all went blank until I was roused out of meditation by Luca. I was wearing only my hiking shorts, thank God, not nude, when he roused me. As I learned later once I got to Roncesvalles, I have earned the nickname as the "half-naked pilgrim." Things are getting slightly weird to say the least. It might just be a simple matter of jet lag and my not getting enough sleep. Oh well, we'll see what tomorrow brings.*

Chapter Six – Peeling Off Layers

The night was very long and sleep was hard to maintain over the cacophonic symphony of snoring that punctuated all the other sounds, which came with almost two hundred people sharing a large room. It was almost with relief that René finally got out of bed and gathered his belongings to repack them. His plan for this day was to walk as far as Zubiri. It was just a twenty-two kilometre walk, a gentler walk according to his guide book.

Most of the other pilgrims were intent on going a little further and going as far as Larrasoaña, which was the target for stage two as suggested by the guide book. It was becoming evident to René that for many, the Camino was a challenge to conquer with a proven recipe, an outer challenge. Few he had met so far, had thought of the pilgrimage as something holy or spiritual. It was interesting to him that the few he had encountered early, and now whom he counted as friends, were among those who knew that the Camino was an undertaking that was sacred, soulful.

The mass the night before, had been enjoyed in the company of Freya, Sid, Luca, Gabe, Miryam, and Mark. René had asked the others about their day. Mark and Miryam had walked alone on the Valcarlos route, and had arrived more than an hour before René and Luca at Roncesvalles. Sid, Gabe and Freya had all arrived at different times as they had walked alone from Saint Jean. They, too, had made it to Roncesvalles before René and Luca. Thankfully, Sid made no mention of his nude meditation and meeting René earlier in the day, leaving René to conclude that what he had experienced had to have been a dream, no doubt the product of the heat and fatigue.

Gabe had decided to walk with Luca at a gentler pace to Zubiri which left René free to walk on his own at his own pace. Luca's package was sent on to Zubiri where Luca would then pick it up. In a way, this pleased René as he needed some alone time. He was soon packed and out the door while it was still dark with dawn just faintly etching the hills to the east. There was just a little worry nagging at him, that of taking the wrong road out of town in the shadowy darkness, as there only the one road. Just on the outskirts of the village, a sign indicated that there were 790 kilometres to go to reach Santiago. The sign was talking about the driving distance, not the actual walking distance which was a mystery yet to be solved.

There were a few people gathered by the sign. As he approached, someone in the group asked René to take a photo of them at the sign, and offered to use René's camera to take his photo by the sign. When the photos were all taken, everyone continued on their way with René soon pulling ahead of them as he walked comfortable free.

All the months of training had prepared René, both mentally and physically, for walking the Camino. The path paralleled the paved road for about two kilometres before returning to being on the road. By the time René had reached a village called Burguete, the sun was rising over the trees, casting a beautiful light that ached to be photographed. René's first rest-stop goal was to reach Espinal, another three and a half kilometres down the road, where he would hopefully be able to stop for some breakfast and café con leche, as café au lait was called in Spain.

He was lucky in Espinal, in finding a bar-café open. He stopped and enjoyed two cups of coffee with his small breakfast before heading off back on the pilgrimage trail in full daylight. As René walked through fields and young forests, he arrived at

Alto de Mezquiriz, after an uphill climb of almost a hundred metres. At Mezquiriz, the trail began a three and a half kilometre descent into a town called Viskarret. René had hoped to take photos of an old 13th century church in the village. Viskarret was also called Gerendiain. René had noticed that almost all of the villages had two names posted on the road signs; one in the Basque language and the other in Spanish. The Church of Saint Peter in Viskarret, was quite simple and beautiful for all of its simplicity, a fact which pleased René. With no prospects of more coffee until later in the day when he reached Zubiri, René decided it was worth a short break for another change of socks and a few moments for writing in his journal:

> *Before leaving Canada, I had been reading a book by Joseph Campbell called <u>The Power of Myth</u>. I was struck by a few words that seemed to resonate with my early experiences here on the Camino: "if we live our own lives, instead of imitating everybody else's." I am not sure exactly what it is that I am questing for, but I do know that I am determined to live my own life, not the life others lead. I somehow expect that when my quest is done I will have changed and that will mark the beginning of a new life, a rebirth of sorts.*

Satisfied with his journal entry, René downed the last of his coffee, put on his dry socks and his boots, then left to carry on his walk. The next stop would be for a change his socks again, otherwise, other than moments in which he felt compelled to take photos, he had just over ten kilometres to go to reach Zubiri, at least a good two and a half hours away. He calculated that he would be there for an early lunch. Perhaps, he thought, he should reconsider his decision to stop at Zubiri and go on further. But then, upon remembering his promise to Luca before leaving Roncesvalles, he knew he would stay in Zubiri, a small village of 500 people.

The remainder of the walk to Zubiri was pleasant and filled with sunshine and forests as part of the experience. When René reached the bridge over the Arga River, called the Puente de la Rabia, he decided to leave the trail and walk along the river for a ways in search of a quiet spot where he could relax, perhaps even meditate. About two hundred metres away from the pilgrim path, he saw a small mat of grass along the river bank with a small, low bush that offered some privacy. It was perfect, the perfect place to enjoy the sun and to meditate.

René took off his socks and boots and took a sitting position for meditation. Try as much as he could, he just couldn't find a comfortable posture. He struggled, while trying to hold his meditative attention for quite a few minutes, before giving up and laying back on the grass to enjoy the heat of the sun. It wasn't long before his tee shirt was taken off so that he could feel the breeze coming off the river. He was tempted to remove his shorts and sunbathe, but the possibility of someone seeing him naked was enough to kill that idea. However, perhaps meditating half naked would work. Strangely, it was much easier to sit still, though he could still feel the strain of his shorts on his body in comparison to the freedom that he felt on the rest of his body.

As he closed his eyes and began focusing on his breathing, René heard a voice singing, a woman's voice. Rather than have the beautiful sounds become a distraction, he simply accepted the ethereal music as part of this place and time, and returned to noticing that small space between the outbreath and in breath, that in between space of nothingness. The woman's voice became stronger letting René know that whoever was singing, was coming closer.

Almost against his will, his eyes opened and he saw her on the other side of the river. She was slowly walking as she sang. Her long black hair framed her unclothed body which was glowing like dark gold in the late morning sunshine. And, as if aware of René's eyes on her, she turned her head and smiled at him and gave him a slight wave of her hand. She then turned and continued her song and her riverside stroll. René listened as he watched her. He heard the words of her song:

> "People,
> male and female,
> blush when a cloth covering their shame
> comes loose
> When the lord of lives
> lives drowned without a face
> in the world, how can you be modest?
>
> When all the world is the eye of the lord,
> on looking everywhere, what can you
> cover and conceal?"

A half hour later, René put his tee shirt, socks, and boots back on. He found his way back to the trail and walked into Zubiri while wondering if he had imagined the scene with whom he could only describe as mystical. Was she real? Or as with Sid the day before, was this simply an illusion, another product of his mind.

It didn't take too long for René to reach the Albergue Escuela in the town. It was an old school building that had been converted into a basic needs' hostel. The talk among the group from the night before had suggested that this would be the first place they would check into upon reaching Zubiri. The group had hopes of meeting up together for another afternoon of enjoyable company and of recovery from two good days of hiking. As expected, the hostel had lots of room for the pilgrims yet to come. René checked in and found that Sid had already claimed their bunks in one of the three dormitories. Then he saw her, the golden woman from alongside the river. She was talking to Sid in a manner that suggested that they knew each other. She wasn't a hallucination, what he had seen and experienced had been real. René shivered within as he tried to cope with her reality.

Walking into the dorm feeling flustered,, René claimed a bed near their bunks after greeting them with a smile and a barely voiced "Namaste!" The greeting with his hands clasped together as if in prayer, was something René had learned from a month spent in India. René always sought to honour others he met on his travels, in small ways such as with greetings in their own language if he could. In his opinion, it was all about respect.

It was obvious from their smiles, that both were pleased with his efforts. As René set his backpack down on the bed, he asked about their walk that day, as well as making small talk about the pleasant weather. As they chatted, he got out a change of clothes and his shower kit. He knew that washing his socks and tee shirt needed to be done early so that they would be able to be dry by the evening for repacking. As he headed to the shower, René asked Sid and his friend if they would join him for lunch later at one of the local restaurants. Receiving a nod of assent from both of them, René then left the room to shower, shave, and wash his few items of clothing.

In the shower, he thought again about the incident at the side of the river. He could still hear the echo of the words of the song and of the voice that had sung them. The words seemed to have been burnt into his mind, if not his heart. Wearing a clean top and a pair of light weight runners, René rejoined the golden woman and Sid as they set out to discover a place to eat. It wasn't long before they found a sidewalk café just past the nondescript square building that appeared to be the village's church. Before leaving for lunch, René had posted a note on the bulletin board letting Gabe and Luca know that he and Sid had already checked in and were out for lunch.

"Sid," enquired René, "could you introduce me to your friend?"

"Of course, René, forgive me," he apologised. "I thought you already knew Asha. Asha is from my country as you have probably guessed. Thank you for the honour you gave us with your greeting earlier," he added with sincerity.

"Pleased to meet you, Asha," smiled René. Being in your presence is like being in sunshine."

"It is an honour to finally meet you, René," she replied. "Sid has been telling me about you. He called you the half-naked pilgrim."

The conversation continued as they ate. With a bocadilla, a glorified Spanish sandwich, on his plate with some fries, and a cup of café con leche, René felt like he was in heaven. It wasn't too hot out, if that was ever possible in his mind, and it was sunny. What more could a man ask but to share this with someone.

That thought brought a small cloud over his mood . . . 'with someone' . . . he didn't have a 'someone' to share these kind of moments with anymore. Sensing his quick change of mood, Sid asked René how his meditation by the river had gone. René was jolted out of his thoughts with a start. How did Sid know he had meditated beside the river?

"Ah, my friend," soothed Sid as he noted the look of surprise on René's face. "Asha had told me earlier that she saw you meditating by the river."

"She saw me?"

"Yes, she said you were meditating half-naked, and so she finally got to know why others call you the half-naked pilgrim."

Turning a deep shade of pink, René mumbled, "Uh, yeah, I was meditating there. I didn't think anyone would see me there while I was hidden from the road and nearby buildings."

"Oh," remarked Asha, now speaking for herself. "I am sure that I was the only one who saw you. I thought that you saw me too, René?"

"Um, I guess I did see you. I, I . . . I just thought that, maybe I was imagining that I saw you," he replied softly and with a hint of embarrassment.

"Oh no!" apologized Asha, "I hope that I didn't offend you."

"No." René quickly returned. "I just thought that maybe you had hoped to have privacy while you walked and sang."

Asha looked at René with a hint of a smile and understanding. "You are so gentle, René. Yes, you saw me walking without my clothes on while I was singing one of my poems. I didn't mind that you saw me. After all, it was an honest and innocent moment that we shared by the river, don't you think?"

"Um, yes ... I guess," he spoke hesitantly. All of a sudden, what Asha had just said about singing her poem registered in his head. "You wrote that song, er, I mean, poem?"

"Yes," replied Asha, "Did you like it?"

"It was beautiful, your voice was even more beautiful that the words if that could be possible. I can still hear the words – People, male and female, blush when a cloth covering their shame, comes loose – that you were nude as these words came from within you was somehow appropriate; I mean, it just seemed so perfect."

"Yes it was perfect. For me, it was a holy moment," agreed Asha. "For me, I feel closest to the gods and goddesses when I sing to them without hiding behind clothing, as you say, it was a moment of perfection."

Sid gently interjected, "I think we should go back to the albergue and see if the others have arrived yet."

"I think I will just wander around the village a bit more," said René as he excused himself from the two. "I want to get a few photos of Zubiri and perhaps find an Internet café as I want to send a few messages to my children, my ex-wife, and some friends. I'll join you guys later."

René stayed in his seat and watched the two East Indians walk back, towards the hostel. It wasn't necessarily the need to take more photos that kept him from returning to the hostel with them; it was just that he needed time alone in order to process what had been happening. He ordered another café con leche wondering if he was becoming addicted to this incredible coffee. For some reason he had left his journal in his backpack so writing was out of the question. Fidgeting with his coffee, he decided that he might just as well go and take some more photos. Swallowing the last of his coffee, René went to the cashier and paid his bill making sure to say thank you in Spanish to the waiter.

He turned to walk in the opposite direction, south. He soon found enough things to photograph including the Zubiri Hotel, a stone building with an upper level that was painted brown and a mustard yellow. A very short block further took him to the edge of town with the paved road heading toward Larrasoaña. He knew that he was going to walk that road the next day, so he turned down a narrow road on the outskirts of the town to see what else he could discover. Soon, he had no choice but to turn back into town following another narrow street that took him past a few more restaurants and beautiful white buildings. Walking along he saw a turn to the right that led to the bridge over the Arga River which he had crossed earlier. He walked to the top of the bridge and looked back over the water. He took just one photo from the bridge, a reminder of the strange experience earlier in the afternoon with Asha. Turning back, he followed the path back to the main street where he had eaten his lunch, and then turned to walk back to the hostel.

Chapter Seven – What is Real?

Back at the hostel, René met up with his adopted family on the Camino. Strange how he had begun to think of them as family. Everyone was there, including Gabe and Luca. The group was sitting at a picnic table under the trees, just across the yard from the hostel. They were talking with a man that René hadn't seen before, a bigger man, reddish-blond and perhaps a bit too loud. 'Likely an American,' thought René. Seeing René, Gabe called him over to introduce him to the newest member of the group.

"René, this is Fred," Gabe said by way of introduction. "He's from the States, like me. He's a pastor of some church in Montana."

"Pleased to meet you," grinned Fred as he held out his hand. "So Gabe tells me you're a Canuck."

"Pleased to meet you as well," returned René, politely, as he grasped Fred's hand. The strength in Fred's hand surprised him. "And yes, I'm a Canadian."

"We were just talking about what we do or did for a living," interrupted Gabe sensing a bit of tension in René. "Fred was telling us about his work back home in the States and how it led to him making this spiritual journey. When Fred asked me what I did for a living, I realised that I didn't know what anyone in the group did. Somehow that question never got asked. Like I told Fred and the others, I am a writer, a story-teller of sorts retired from my position as a prof in an American university. But I think most everyone here has already figured that out," he laughed. "I have a hard time not telling stories, or not asking others to tell me their stories."

"Yeah, I kind of figured as much. For me, what people do or did for a living doesn't seem to matter much except for when I have to deal with issues that arise out of my clients' workplaces. I just take people as they are as I meet them," added René with just a hint of superiority directed at Fred for his "faux pas" of getting too personal, too soon.

"So what is it that you do?" asked Fred who caught René's tone. "You talk about clients. For me, what we choose to do to earn a living, has helped each one of us form who we are in the present. As my Pa always said, don't judge a man by what he says. Look at what he does for a living, what he has done if you want to know the truth of that man."

"Sounds like your Dad was a smart man," offered René with grace knowing that he had perhaps, judged the man too quickly and unfairly. "I am a psychotherapist, something that I have been doing for more than fifteen years. And, like Joseph, I am a writer."

With those words out of his mouth, Luca arched his eyes in surprise. "I am a doctor, a doctor of psychology," he pronounced with authority. "And like Gabe, I am a writer."

"Do you mean psychiatrist?" interjected Fred.

"No, no, not a psychiatrist!" retorted Luca with umbrage. "I am a doctor." Then turning to René, Luca continued on, "So, you are a psychotherapist? Could you tell me how you work with your patients, René?"

"Do you mean what are the therapy models I use?" questioned René in response to the question.

"Yes! Exactly!"

"Perhaps that is a discussion we could have later, good doctor," René gave as an answer. "I think we have yet to finish with this introduction of ourselves within the group."

"Yes, yes, you are right. Perhaps Asha would grace us with her story," added Luca with the typical politeness which René had come to expect of him.

"I'm a poetess," Asha said simply.

"Marvellous!" said Gabe exuberantly. "Perhaps we can hear one of your poems later, yes?"

"Of course, dear Gabe," smile Asha. "Later."

"And you, Sid?" quizzed Fred.

"I guess I am somewhat like Mark. My career, if it could be said that I have one, is simply to travel and share what I know about the human spirit. In a way, it is also similar to our good doctor Luca, and therapist René, as what I have to share is about our human nature, the human psyche. I guess you could say that in a way, I am also a teacher or guide."

"Hmm?" sounds kind of open-ended and mysterious to me," mused Fred. "So how do you earn money? After all, it takes money to do that."

"I depend on the good will of others for my material needs," smiled Sid. "It seems that when I find myself in real need, the human heart opens up and fills my need."

René looked at Sid curiously; the mystery of Sid was something he knew that he had to unravel before the end of the Camino.

"I guess that leaves you, Mark," added Gabe.

"I guess that you could say that I have been a guide for more years than I care to count, as well as a mediator," replied Mark with some thought. "It's been rewarding work, but I am looking forward to retirement whenever that comes about."

"Neat!" exclaimed Fred with all having taken part in this level of introductions. "It seems as though we are all teachers and guides somehow connected to the human spirit, the visible face of a universal spirit."

Freya and Miryam hadn't arrived at the hostel yet, so their stories weren't told.

"Now, added Fred turning to Asha, "would you be willing to recite one of your poems for us?"

Asha smiled as she stood up from her position at the picnic table. She began to glow as her voice began to emerge from deep within her very being. No words were formed, at least not words that could be recognized. As the notes ascended, it was as though her clothing simply vanished leaving her naked body radiating an ethereal light. She assumed a sitting pose as if meditating:

> "One body only I have, one only mind:
> With what mind, then, to meditate,
> And with what mind engage
> In the world's business, pray?
> Alas, alas, I'm utterly lost
> Between this world and the other world.

The words of the poem, sung by Asha, had weaved a spell that held everyone transfixed. The words continued to pour forth and one knew that they were in the presence of something holy and pure. If anything, it was a glimpse of paradise before humankind was expelled for deceit and shame.

The last strains of her voice disappeared into the air in which everyone present had fallen under the spell of her pure innocence. With the spell broken by silence, Asha then reappeared clothed as she had been only moments before. 'What sort of magic was this that came from Asha?' René wondered. 'Was I the only one to have this vision of a naked Asha?'

Gabe was the first to speak, "my god but that was beautiful, Asha. Did you say you wrote that poem?"

"Yes, Gabe," admitted Asha with a demure lowering of her head in modesty.

"But I have heard, or should I say, I have read those words before."

"It is quite possible, dearest Gabe, that you could have read the words."

Frowning, Gabe added, "Hmm? Now where did I see those words?"

René didn't want Asha to answer that question, or the unasked questions that remained. In an attempt to interrupt and change the subject, he spoke out to the group. "Well, now that deserves a celebration. How about we all head out for a pre-dinner glass of vino rojo or some cerveza? Perhaps Fred will tell us more about his work as a pastor in Montana."

The strategy worked as everyone sprang up as though the after-effects of a magical spell had finally released them from its grips. Asha looked René in the eyes with an unvoiced 'Thank you!' Through it all, Sid had maintained his ever-present smile. René doubted, somehow, that the spell had touched Sid. Sid seemed to know more than he would, or perhaps could, admit to knowing. With a breath of relief, René made his way back down the road with the group in search of some red wine. He felt increasing at odds with reality, it was as if everything in his life had just become an illusion. What was real and what was . . . what was the word? Oh yeah, Maya!

By the time all had returned to the hostel, all seemed to have returned to what could be called normal. Most became involved with cell phones, books, or their journals.

The day's sun had set before the group headed out for an evening meal. René didn't feel like joining the others, but he didn't want to have his new friends think he was anti-social. Besides, he really was hungry. Walking twenty-plus kilometres a day was a good way to build up an appetite.

As the group walked to find supper, René walked near the back of the group which had grown as Freya, Miryam, and another new guy called Jason, another American, had joined the group for the evening. In spite of being American, Jason seemed to be a decent guy who was not your typical American, loud and over-friendly. René relaxed as Jason walked beside him in relative silence. He was sure he would get to know Jason better in the weeks to come. There was no need to rush into friendships. Friendship was something that needed time to evolve.

The group found themselves gathering at the Café Camino, where the meal being served that night was fish, Trout to be more exact. It was a pleasant place. They enjoyed wine, beer and tapas, as well as a variety of appetizers, while waiting for their meal to be served. Naturally, the talk again turned to the

Camino as well as the conversations of earlier in the day. René sat back on his seat to listen and observe, rather than lean forward to participate in the conversation. Jason was seated on one side and Mark on the other. Before the fish arrived, René finally roused himself out of his introversion, and turned to speak to Jason.

"Jason, somehow I have this feeling that we may have met somewhere. Have you ever been to Canada?"

"I can't say that I recognize you, René. But to answer your question, yes I have been to Canada a number of times. I often get invited there to give presentations and lead one-day workshops," answered Jason.

"Perhaps I was at one of your workshops, or perhaps I saw a poster advertising such an event," René wondered aloud. "Usually I travel to Montreal and Toronto for psychology presentations, lectures and workshops. And of course, I also am a regular at presentations in my home city of Ottawa"

"Perhaps," agreed Jason. "However, unless you go to Jungian workshops, it is unlikely that you would have attended one of my events. I have presented in all three cities you have mentioned quite a few times, as well as similar events in Vancouver and Calgary. There are a number of very active groups in Canada that have hosted me and treated me well."

"That's it!" exclaimed René excitedly. "Now I know who you are! You're Jason Johnson. I have attended two of your Friday night lectures and Saturday workshops In Toronto, and once in Calgary."

"Well, there you have it," replied Jason. "I'm sorry that I don't remember seeing you or meeting you there."

"Perhaps if I told you that we have also communicated through various Jungian on-line groups where I'm known as Reg, and if I am not mistaken, you are Archie. I remember bringing that up the last time I went to a conference of yours in Toronto."

"Hmm, yes, of course I remember the on-line communications. If I remember right, the first time we chatted was back in the nineties when I was featured on a Jung-Books-Talk session. Well, well, well," added Jason with an appraising look at René. "So we meet again. Perhaps after this I will remember you more clearly."

"Ah!" interjected Mark who had been quietly listening to the exchange between René and Jason, as well as keeping some attention on the flow of conversation that was at the other end of the table. "It's time to eat ladies and gentlemen. Our food has arrived."

The meal was thoroughly enjoyed, though it was almost a repeat of the meal of the night before in Roncesvalles. Since it was getting late and there was another day of walking on the Camino to begin early the next morning, it wasn't long after the last bite that the group moved off to return to the hostel and a good night of sleep. With only twenty-six beds in their dormitory at the old school which had been turned into a hostel, the night was quieter that it had been in Roncesvalles where almost two hundred had shared the same room.

That night, once all the final tasks had been performed, René lay in his bunk with his journal and wrote:

> *A very strange day. Twice I got to hear Asha sing, and both times I thought I saw her unclothed as she sung. When the singing ended, she re-appeared looking almost normal wearing clothing. What is it that has me*

seeing so much nudity, imagining people naked around me? What's going on in this head of mine?

I am fortunate to renew an acquaintance with Jason Johnson. I'm looking forward to many discussions along the trail in the future with this man.

Chapter Eight – Meditation on the Path

René's quiet mood during the evening had made for a restless sleep. He couldn't blame the noise of the others as a reason for his tiredness with night drawing to a close, as was the case in Roncesvalles. What was really bothering him was something within him.

Like the day before, René was in a rush to take off. He needed to have some alone time on the path that would end in Pamplona that afternoon. He had avoided discussions of where the group would stay that evening in Pamplona so as to have some separation. With any luck, he would find himself alone with time to think and process what had happened during the first two days.

A few, Sid, Freya, Miryam, Mark and Asha, had talked of walking on to Cizur Menor, another five kilometres passed the albergues in Pamplona, with a promise to meet up again the following night in Puente la Reina.

René stole into the pre-dawn darkness having already studied his route out of Zubiri the previous afternoon. Setting a brisk pace, he soon covered the five kilometres to reach the Puente Larrasoaña, a medieval bridge that had so much character that René just had to stop and take some photos of it. Dawn had broken not long after he had left Zubiri, adding to the magic of the scene before him.

The early morning light added a certain dimension that encouraged René to take more photos than he needed of the bridge and the 13th century church called San Nicolás. Putting his camera back into his small lumbar pack, René continued to walk into Larrasoaña hoping that some place in the village would be open so that he could grab a quick coffee, as he had skipped out of breakfast and coffee in Zubiri.

The village of Larrasoaña had a population of only 200 and had one restaurant called Casa Sado that was open. René considered himself lucky as he ordered his first coffee for the day as well as a simple breakfast.

While sitting at a table, René took out his tablet and checked his eBook library. Yes, he had indeed loaded a few of Johnson's books onto the tablet. Having confirmed that fact, René put the tablet back into its spot in his backpack. He didn't want to read right now. All he wanted was coffee and some inner silence. The coffee came but the inner silence stayed away. Feeling frustrated, he didn't enjoy his breakfast as much as he usually did. He swallowed the food, not in the least aware of what the food tasted like.

Without staying long enough for a second cup of coffee, René returned to the medieval bridge so that he could rejoin the Camino path that lay on the south side of the Arga River. There was a steady, thin stream of pilgrims walking that Camino path; thankfully, most were focused on their feet and the pain after two days of hard hiking. For most, the physical pains had become their primary focus. Few of them seemed to even notice the medieval bridge they were crossing over.

René was fortunate. He had trained intensively since his return from a three-week winter sojourn in Mexico. Even in Mexico, he had walked every day, barefoot along a beach that seemed to never end. Yes, the climb of 1200 metres and then a 600 metre descent into Roncesvalles had left him hurting; however, it was a bearable hurt that had lessened during the walk from Roncesvalles to Zubiri, a walk in which he had a chance to consciously stretch his muscles.

René knew before he came, that he would suffer physical pain on the walk, but as long as he didn't fall or walk too far in one day, he felt confident that he could survive the long walk in spite of being in his early-fifties.

Back on the trail, René found himself pushing the pace. He soon found himself passing pilgrims and then pushing himself even harder as if he was in a race and needed to reach the finish line first.

"Whoa!" exclaimed Gabe as René passed him. "Are you some kind of rabbit? What's the rush?"

Registering the voice and then man, René immediately slowed down to let Gabe catch up to him. "I just got caught up in in my head, and the walking."

"So how did I get ahead of you?" laughed Gabe.

"It must have been when I stopped to take some photos of the bridge back at Larrasoaña, or when I stopped to have some breakfast."

"That explains it," grinned Gabe. "You walk faster than I do even when you aren't racing like you were just doing. Since you left before me, I thought that there was no way I going to see you until Pamplona. Talking of Pamplona, have you thought of where you're going to stay?"

"No," replied René, "I guess I just thought I would just find someplace once I got there."

"Same here," Gabe stated. "Maybe we'll end up at the same place?" he said with a bit of hope that René would take the hint.

"Sounds like a great idea, Gabe," René responded. "Thanks for waking me up just now. If you don't mind, I will keep your pace and be more aware of where I am," he added with a sheepish grin.

"I'd like that."

The morning passed pleasantly with a stop to change socks and then a few other stops to take more photos of the countryside and other bridges along the way. At Trinidad de Arre, there was a convent with a spectacular series of cascading water along the Ulzama River, a scene that had René again taking out his camera. The two new friends decided to stop for a mid-morning second breakfast and some much needed coffee at Villava, which was less than a kilometre further up the path from the convent.

They found what they were looking for when they came across the Paradise Café in Villava. It was a relief to finally take off his boots and socks, a habit that René had now passed on to Gabe. Gabe took out his copy of the pilgrim guide book and wondered if the hike up to Huarte might be worth considering. It would add four kilometres to their day's travel with half of that being all about retracing their steps right back to the spot they were now sitting in.

René suggested that they continue straight on into Pamplona, as there was a lot to see in the city. He was especially interested in seeing the Puente de la Magdalena, a twelfth century bridge. With the mention of the bridge, Gabe began talking of Mary Magdalene, a prostitute who became the closest of those who surrounded Jesus, likely becoming the wife of Jesus with whom she had a child, a son, if some translations of ancient papyrus were to be believed.

"Did you know that the feast day for Mary Magdalene is on July 22nd," added Gabe as a postscript to his narrative about what he had read about in reports of the ancient manuscript, The Ecclesiastical History of Zacharias Rhetor.

"No." replied René with some interest. "Interesting as that is also my birthday," he added.

"So you just turned fifty not too long ago?" deduced Gabe.

"Three years ago," René corrected.

"Okay," Gabe stated. "So we'll go on and see this bridge and skip out on a side-trip to Huarte. Sounds okay to me. Lead on."

Feeling refreshed and energized, the two men made their way forward and reached the bridge which was only just a bit more than two kilometres further down the road. The camera came out again as René took photos of the bridge from various positions. He was intent on seeing how the light would change the appearance of the bridge. He hoped that once back home in Canada, one of the many photos taken would evoke some of the mystery surrounding the saint for whom the bridge was named.

"Do you believe in the truth of the Bible?" asked Gabe while watching René take photos."

The question caught René by surprise. "Well, not literally," he said after a pause. "I mean, I don't believe in the Bible as most Christians do. I mean, I think the stories found in the Bible are more mythological truths than factual truths."

"That's an interesting choice of words, René – mythological truths not factual truths," mused Gabe upon hearing René's 'caught on the spot' response.

René added, "For example, Mary Magdalene was often identified as the Black Madonna, the Bride of Christ, something you referred to just a few moments ago. Mythologically speaking, at least as far as depth psychology is concerned, the Black Madonna signifies the union of masculine and feminine into a holy whole, or in other words, the source of consciousness arising from the unconscious." René realised that he had just got carried away with what Cécile used to call psycho-babble.

Gabe picked up the discussion where René had let it hang in the air, unfinished. "I agree with you about the Bible's stories being myths. Of course I don't mean that they are untrue in saying that they are myths. If anything, myths tell us more truth of our human story, our human past, than today's newspapers will tell the truth of our current human story."

"I can vouch for that fact," laughed René. "If you want to have even a sniff at what the truth is, the last place to look is in our newspapers or any other official media source."

"Don't be so quick to "diss" the media, René," counselled Gabe. "Wrapped up in all those often deliberate attempts to paint a false story of who we are as a human tribe in today's world, the truth seeps out through the cracks. No story that is false can hold itself together so tightly that the cracks don't show and point us to the truth about our times and our culture."

"That makes a lot of sense, Gabe," agreed René. "I guess no one could ever understand our world if they didn't have the words we proclaimed as our truth. I never thought of it that way."

René had finished taking photos of the bridge and showed them to Gabe. "You know, it's what these photos do as well if you think about it. The same bridge is in all of these photos, and in each photo a different story is told. No one photo tells the truth, but all of the photos together point closer to the truth of the bridge."

"That's some gift you have there, René. You're an artist with that camera."

"Thanks, Gabe," blushed René who then quickly added, "You have a great gift with your stories, Gabe."

The pair walked on through the outskirt streets of Pamplona into the heat of the city, with only an occasional stop for a. When they caught sight of the cathedral, Santa María la Real, René decided that he would come back in the later in the afternoon in order to capture its beauty. René had learned that in the golden light that paints the world just before sunset, there is a magic that lets us slip into an alter world.

René and Gabe had decided earlier to see if there was accommodation available at the 17th century Jesuit church, Jesús y María, which contained a hostel of over 100 beds. René didn't know it, but this was the albergue that a few of the others had decided upon as their stop in as well, a fact that Gabe knew.

Once they had registered, René learned that there was Internet service available for pilgrims to use. Dumping his backpack on his bunk, René took out his tablet and took the opportunity to write an e-mail to his family and friends and to upload the pictures he had taken since his last opportunity to post them to his Flickr account.

Since René's camera, had a feature that allowed him to transfer his photos to his tablet; the photos were soon transferred from the camera to his Flickr account. He had practiced the procedure a fair number of times back home so that he could do the transfers with relative ease. Putting the photos on his Flickr account freed up space on the tablet which had a very limited amount of storage space. René uploaded the last images and then sent a few of them to his Facebook account so that his children and grandchildren could see some of what he was seeing in Spain. While busy on his tablet, he set his camera to charging.

Finished with his e-mail and Facebook postings, René put his camera back into its holder and then went in search of Gabe and anyone else he knew that was around in the hostel. Gabe was in the courtyard talking with a few people that René didn't know. Gabe had an ability to be friendly and chat with just about anyone. René approached Gabe in order to let him know that he was about to head out to check out the heart of the old city and invite him to tag along. Gabe declined the invitation citing the pain in his feet and legs. He wanted to do a little walking as possible for a few hours. He also mentioned to René that he hoped they could have supper out together and with whoever else checked into the albergue later.

Going out for an evening meal wouldn't likely happen until somewhere around eight that evening, so René agreed to be back before eight so that he could join up with his new friends and whoever else decided to tag along with them. You never shut out any one who looked to be alone and in need of company, after a long and hard day's walk along the Camino.

For the next three hours, René wandered through the centre of Pamplona taking photos in the Plaza del Castillo, the Plaza Consitorial, and the Plaza San Francisco. Little cafés, old buildings, fountains and statues were caught in the lens of his camera. When he got to the western end of the old town where he photographed the church called San Lorenzo and a convent called Convento Recoletas, René turned to head back along the street down which he would walk out of Pamplona the next day.

He then walked to the eastern end of the old city in time to catch the light beginning to turn golden, the perfect time of day for photos of the cathedral. Finally, René decided it was time to rejoin Gabe and the others at the albergue.

"So Gabe tells me you are an artist with your camera," Fred remarked as René joined the group at the entrance to the albergue. It looked as they were just preparing to head out for some beverages and tapas which should tide them over until it was time to eat a proper meal.

"Some of my photos are okay, not too bad," shrugged René. "But, I wouldn't go so far as to say they are art," he quickly protested.

"Are you ready for a glass of vino, my friend," interjected Gabe. "Walking is thirsty work, believe me."

With Freya, Sid, Asha, Miryam, Mark and Luca not staying at the albergue, there were just four of them; René, Gabe, Jason and Fred, who were staying at the same place. Gabe somehow seemed to know the old quarter of Pamplona very well as he guided the small group to one of his "favourite" bars. He led the way to the Plaza del Castillo and to the Café Iruña.

"Now for us Americans, this should be a shrine, a pilgrimage destination of its own," chuckled Gabe. "This was Hemingway's favourite restaurant. Let's go in and have some tapas and vino rojo and check out all the photos of Hemingway that are here."

Gabe's enthusiasm was infectious, and the four men entered the pub with high energy. Fred pointed out the private bar area in the restaurant where there was a statue of the famous writer of <u>The Sun Also Rises</u>, a novel which had put Pamplona on the map for American tourists, especially during the festival called San Fermin, better known as the Running of the Bulls. They didn't get to sit within the private bar, but they were in close enough proximity that it didn't matter.

It was almost ten by the time they returned to the albergue, just before the doors were to be locked for the night. They never did leave the Café Iruña for their evening meal. There was enough to eat at the café and they didn't want to spoil the magic of the moment and place. Before turning off his small flashlight, René took a few moments to write in his journal:

> *Day three on the Camino took me to Pamplona. I began the day walking alone, but that changed as I met up with Gabe and then walked the last part of the trail with him. For a change, it was a normal day. I mean, there wasn't any surprises from Sid or Asha. They walked with a number of the others to stay at Cizur Menor, a longer walk than what I did today.*
>
> *I sent an e-mail to the kids and some friends. I have to admit that I miss them like crazy. It's been a good day.*

Chapter Nine – A Place of Spirits

René stayed for the pilgrim breakfast at the albergue in the morning, rather than rushing off to escape. The truth was that he had a headache, a hangover would probably be a better term to use. Not surprisingly, everyone was quieter than normal and not up to their usual, normal speed. When breakfast was done with three cups of coffee downed along with some orange juice, René decided it was time to head out at the prodding of the Jesuits, who were shooing out the lingering pilgrims so that they could get the place ready for a new set of pilgrims who would be arriving in the afternoon.

It was a long five kilometres before they reached Cizur Menor. Though they had travelled through parks and scenic locales, there weren't many photos taken. Gabe suggested that they stop and get their credentials stamped at the university as it gave them 'accreditation' with the university, for what that was worth. No one protested and all followed Gabe's lead before turning back to the path to Cizur Menor. Seeing the bridge over the Sadar River, René held back while the others trooped on, almost unaware that René was no longer with them. There was something about bridges that caught René's attention, and this particular bridge was beautiful.

With the photos taken, René began to walk on. He noticed that his headache was gone and that he now felt better and stronger. His steps soon allowed him to catch up to the group just as they entered Cizur Menor. Luca, Jason, and Gabe decided it was time for another cup of coffee or two. René had just begun to find his stride and said he would push on and meet up with them again in Puente la Reina. Fred asked him if he wouldn't mind having company as he wasn't ready for a coffee just yet. There was no doubt in René's mind that Fred was a fit man, so it was with only a little hesitation that he agreed to walk with Fred. René really wanted to be alone but it would be rude to not give Fred a chance to prove himself a good walking companion.

Leaving the others behind in Cizur Menor, they hiked along the path and entered a forested area which held the ruins of a castle called Guenduláin. Fred was patient as he waited for René to take a number of photos before they proceeded on to Zariquiegui which was only about two and a half kilometres further down the path. Finding out that there wasn't a bar in the village, they both began to regret not stopping in Cizur Menor with the others. Consulting the guide book, they realised that there wouldn't be a stop for coffee until Uterga, another six kilometres further along the trail.

Pushing on, their spirits revived knowing that it was only another two and a half kilometres to reach the Alto del Perdón, and the famous wrought iron silhouettes of ancient pilgrims struggling against the wind as they made their journeys to Santiago. Every book and every blog site that René had ever read about the Camino, mentioned the Alto del Perdón, the metal silhouettes of pilgrims, and the noise of the huge wind turbines.

It was a good place to stop and rest while looking out at the scenes before them. In the valley they had left behind them as they ascended the Alto, legend had it that the Devil engaged in a battle of will with a pilgrim who chose death rather than renounce God for some water. Of course the story went on to have the pilgrim saved and the Devil once again vanquished with the aid of Saint Joseph.

As well as providing a backdrop for medieval stories, the view showed them the way they had come from the Pyrenees and Pamplona to the east. Looking ahead, they caught a glimpse of places yet to be reached. It was a sobering moment to say the least. René took a few photos of the iron pilgrims bent against the wind as well as the long row of wind turbines. Another pilgrim offered to take a photo of Fred and René together with the iron pilgrims behind them, an offer they readily accepted.

All that remained to reach Uterga, was just over three kilometres. About a half hour later, they found themselves at a table at the Café del Perdón, which was attached to one of the albergues in the village. As usual, René lost no time in taking off his socks and boots in order to check out his feet and to let them air dry. Thankfully, all was well as far as his feet were concerned. Satisfied, René ordered lunch. Soon, a café con leche was nestled in his hands. René turned to his hiking partner and asked, "So tell me, Fred, you're not a Catholic, so why are you walking the Camino and visiting all of these Catholic churches and shrines?"

Fred paused for a few moments before responding, "Well, it's not really about Catholicism, is it? This pilgrimage pre-dates that split in Christianity that led to Protestantism. Besides, we all share the same Bible and the same religious roots."

"Yeah, I agree with what you are saying about roots and the Bible," conceded René. "But, why are you here with me in Uterga, on the Camino?"

"Like everyone else here, I am not really sure why I am here. It was an idea that squirmed its way into my head and then grew until it left me no choice," offered Fred as an answer. He continued on saying, "I should say that I did have a choice, we all have choices; but, the choice not to come was one that seemed to leave me retreating into a dark place and not going forward with my life. For me it became a choice of darkness versus light."

"I guess the same could be said for myself," added René. "Come to think about it, it sounds like we both heard what Joseph Campbell described as the "Call" in his book, <u>A Hero With A Thousand Faces</u>. Are you familiar with the work of Joseph Campbell?"

"Indeed I am. Indeed I am," chuckled Fred. "In my opinion, his work fits so well with the Bible."

"Really? You mean that the Bible is more mythology than it is the 'Word of God?'"

"Not at all!" corrected Fred, "The Bible is the Word of God. The problem is that we don't understand those words very well. Regardless whether one is Catholic or Protestant, we all have spent so much energy trying to make the words in the Bible 'fit' within our belief systems. Simply put, you can't understand what you don't already know."

With a burst of laughter, René proclaimed, "You sound like a psychotherapist or a Buddhist. Your words echo something I have frequently said to clients when they get stuck. However, I make sure to tell them that in time, an inner wisdom will rise up from the depths and allow them insight."

"But of course I am like a psychotherapist as well," grinned Fred in response. "You likely know that pastors do a lot of counselling of parishioners. It's not all about preparing sermons, weddings and baptisms."

"Point taken," acknowledged René. "Still, what you're saying is not very typical for a priest or pastor or whatever title one is given."

"That's another part of the reason I am walking the Camino," admitted Fred. "I get a lot of grief whenever I present what I come to understand about the scriptures."

"Such as?"

"Well," began Fred, "You see, I've got this website, or more correctly this blog site that I call *Spirit Distilled*."

"Really? You mean like in alchemy?"

"No, like in booze. The sub-title says that it is a *Getting Drunk With the Word of God*. There is a lot of foaming at the mouth on my part as I tell it as I know it. I talk about all sorts of non-traditional topics such as body-building, to sex, and other topics normally avoided."

"Body-building? I guess that explains why you are in such good physical shape for a pastor," noted René with a grin. "Surely that really isn't an issue for your parishioners. I imagine that most of the things you write about are kosher as far as church doctrine is concerned."

"Well, not exactly," mumbled Fred. "Aside from the usual safe topics such as Theology for Dummies, or an even safer topic, the Life of Christ, I somehow sort of found myself putting my foot in my mouth, with topics such as God and Sex, and God and Nudity."

"What! You mean you actually brought up those topics and you got to keep your job?" exclaimed René with more than a little bit of surprise. "How in hell did you manage that? As far as I understand, the only acceptable place for nudity and sex is when a man and a woman are attempting to conceive, and with the injunction that they aren't really supposed to enjoy it as far as Christian churches are concerned. As for nudity without sex, well, isn't that only acceptable when necessary such as when taking a shower? I've even heard that some churches are encouraging people to shower with a concealing robe on and with no mirror to tempt people to look at their own bodies."

Fred was laughing so much that he had spilled some of his cerveza, which he preferred to René's choice of coffee. "Talk about extremes," he laughed. "Right-wing fundamentalist thinking and belief systems don't quite make it onto my blog site."

"You're going to have to give me the URL of your blog site so that I can check it out," René requested before adding, "I will give you my blog site URL as well. I have been posting on it for a few years and now have almost 1500 blog post entries there."

"What do you write about?"

"I guess that you could say that I mostly write about depth psychology, of spirituality, and humans and the world in general. I typically choose a photo I have taken, then I use active imagination to see where that image takes me. I guess, in a way, you might say it is similar to stream-of-consciousness writing; or to be more precise, stream-of-unconsciousness writing," replied René. "Though I have to admit that I haven't been writing all that much in the past few months. I have been more focused on training for this Camino thing."

"Sure thing," agreed Fred. "We'll swap URLs later when we have Internet access. For now, I'd better make a pit stop before we head back out on the trail."

Just as René and Fred were paying their bill, Jason and Gabe arrived. They were talking about taking the Eunate detour, and then staying the night in hostel called Los Padres at the entrance to Puente la Reina. That was where the group had promised to meet Sid, Asha, Miryam, Luca, Mark and Freya. René and Fred agreed to the plan and said that they would likely wait for them at the Templar church in Eunate so they could walk the last four and a half kilometres together.

In addition to the Cathedral in Pamplona, René had marked the Templar church in Eunate as a must-see. The Iglesia de Santa María de Eunate, was rather unique with its octagonal shape and its reputed history in association with the Knights Templar. René had once thought he might want to spend the night at Eunate, but that idea was tossed out when he realised that he had a long way to walk and he didn't want to be away from home any longer than he needed to be in order to complete the Camino. Even the idea of rest days had been discarded for the most part in his planning. He did, however, promise his kids that he would stop walking and rest when, and if, necessary.

Walking down a beautiful boulevard in the flat countryside to the twelfth century church, with nothing to distract the eye from focusing on the church, René found himself constantly taking photos. When he and Fred got to the church, the doors were already open as if inviting them to enter. So many of the churches along the Camino to that point, had been locked and some of the churches had been abandoned. Seizing the opportunity, René didn't hesitate to enter. The church was all he had imagined it would be, and more. If asked to express his feelings, he would have been at a loss for words. His hope was that the photos he was taking would be able to better capture what was stirring within him.

René was still taking pictures when the rest of the group arrived. Gabe was the least impressed with the church as it was obvious to him that this was a poor attempt to replicate the church in Torres del Rio. "You know," had added to punctuate his disdain, "The Templars weren't even in this area, ever! This was the territory of the Knights Hospitallers, the Order of Saint John of Jerusalem."

"But don't you see then, that it all makes sense?" demanded Jason. "It even helps explain why this church isn't in a town like the church in Torres del Rio. The Templars were a secretive group and liked to hide their treasure in places where others least expected to find it."

"Bah, Jason" dismissed Gabe. "You are as bad as Dan Brown with your conspiracy theories."

In spite of their words, there were no signs of real conflict between Gabe and Jason. Their disagreements meant nothing other than that they trusted each other to plainly speak their minds. It wasn't much later when they all set off to make their way to Puenta la Reina and the Albergue.

The last few kilometres passed mainly on trails, with only a short stretch of pavement that took them passed two side roads that could take them to Obanos, if they had wanted to see that town. It was late in the afternoon when they finished their hike of twenty-five kilometres. As expected, they saw evidence that Mark and company had already claimed their bunks. Mark's unique wooden staff lay across his bunk, and Asha's bright pink backpack was hard to miss on a neighboring bunk.

The guys took turns showering and washing out their travel clothing. These tasks were now becoming routine for the pilgrims. There was no Internet service in the albergue and René didn't feel like wandering though the town in search of a free Wi-Fi signal. An e-mail for home would have to wait until the next day.

No one seemed in a rush to go out wandering through the village. Both Jason and Gabe were sitting on their bunks busy writing as usual. It seemed that if they weren't walking, they were busy writing. René decided, like them, that it was a good time to write something in his journal as well:

> *The fourth day on the Camino has been the hardest for me so far, something that surprises me considering that the first day was more than I had expected with the long climb up the Pyrenees. It wasn't so much that it was physically harder, but it sure was mentally tougher. I don't want to blame it on the few too many glasses of red wine, though that would account for some of my lack of energy. No, it had more to do with finding myself in a situation where what I had taken as certainties in life, have now been tossed out.*
>
> *I am finding myself questioning everything, as though scrambling to find a new truth. It's as if the sun has set on my old life and I am now entering into the dawn of a new life. But, I have to get passed the confusion and the darkness of the unknown first.*

Chapter Ten – Meditation Among the Ruins

There was no problem with falling asleep once the group arrived back at the hostel. The evening had been tamer than it had been in Pamplona. That wasn't to say that it was too quiet, as there were more than a few stories told, especially by Gabe and Jason who continued on with their ongoing banter. The route for the next day had been planned during the evening meal. They planned on following the traditional route rather than adding any extra kilometres by detouring to Zarapuz. Estella which was their next stop, and the trip for the day was long enough at almost twenty-two kilometres.

René decided to leave early while the others were slower to get moving in the early morning. He was joined by Fred, Sid and Asha who were more than able to match his pace. As he learned in previous days, Asha and Sid easily walked faster than almost everyone else. Freya also walked quickly, but she had decided to keep pace with Miryam. Fred was a good match for René as a walking partner when it came to pace. René was a bit nervous to find himself walking along with the two young East Indians. He hoped that there would be no naked surprises during the day from either of them.

As they left the hostel, René warned them about his intention to take photos at the Bogota Monastery ruins, and again at Mañeru, a village with Templar history. If they decided to walk on ahead, he would catch up with them at Cirauqui where they intended on having a breakfast break. With that plan in place, they quickly found their way through Puente la Reina, coming across another magnificent 12th century pilgrim bridge, and then onto the pilgrim path that went past the old ruins of the Bogota Monastery.

There wasn't much left at the site which they found at a slight distance off the path, but there was a special feel or aura as they wandered around the ruins. It was as if they had entered a sacred space that invited them to stop for a while.

Sunrise had broken just over the horizon a short while before they reached the ruins and the angle of the sun's rays touching the ruins evoked a sense of the spiritual. As he took several photos, René noticed that his friends had found a spot out of the view of the pilgrim path. The three of them had spontaneously decided to take a few moments for meditation. And to René's surprise, all three were naked. He debated whether to take a photo of them or to respect the sacredness of their meditation. He quickly rejected the idea of a photo. Putting his camera away, he felt himself drawn towards the three meditating. Next thing he knew, he too had removed his clothing and had joined them in their silent meditation.

A chime sounded as though telling René that it was time to get dressed again and rejoin the path. Upon opening his eyes, he saw Sid and Asha smiling at him, as well as Fred. It wasn't long before both Fred and René were furtively trying to put on their clothes without having anyone notice that they had been naked. Back on the pilgrim path, nothing was said about the nude meditation at the ruins.

The approach into Mañeru was downhill, which gave René another photo opportunity. Upon reaching the village, aside from a few photos, there was no desire to spend more time than necessary in the village. They hiked on to Cirauqui. They were surprised to see the friends they left behind in Puente la Reina already there at a café enjoying their breakfast.

"What happened to you guys?" asked Gabe, curious as to why they were behind them.

"We stopped for longer than we had planned at the monastery ruins," offered René. "I guess we lost track of time there, with taking photos and such."

"And such, what?" prodded Gabe.

"Well, we somehow found ourselves meditating behind the ruins," replied Fred.

"I guess the half-naked meditator had another one of his moments," teased Mark speaking of René who was now turning a slight shade of pink.

"No half-naked meditation happened," retorted René in defense.

"More like nude meditation," Fred blurted out. "It was weird. I mean there I was walking around the ruins and then I saw Sid and Asha meditating. It was as if I was being pulled by a magnet to join them. Next thing I know, the meditation was over and there we were, all sitting on the grass without our clothes on."

"Yeah, the same thing happened to me," admitted René expecting to have the others make fun of him or even worse.

"No sweat," said Mark. "I meditate nude all the time. It's the only way to meditate as far as I'm concerned. In my opinion a person gets closer to the Creator when one is nude. You know, making oneself vulnerable, not hiding behind the camouflage of clothing. You know, at one time, naked worship was the norm in the world, especially the pre-Christian and pre-Islamic world. Check out the Old Testament and older religions."

Gabe decided to add to the conversation with an observation, "You know, with the exception of our modern god, basically all of our gods and goddesses since the dawn of time have all been depicted as naked. It says something about our modern psyche, about our insecurities that has us covering up in front of each other and our god. We even make sure to have our god cloaked to hide any sense of his masculine sexuality so that he doesn't shame us, as well as ourselves."

"Whoa!" blurted René. "Enough talk about nakedness already. I'm trying to enjoy my food."

"Sounds like someone is a bit touchy about nudity," muttered Luca. "There's a complex there that needs to be confronted at some point in time, probably sooner rather than later."

The talk soon shifted to a safer topic as the Small Company of Pilgrims finished their meal. It was time to get back on the path and complete the walk to Estella. For a change, René walked at the back of the group. As they left the village of Cirauqui, they passed through an arch onto an old Roman road before crossing a highway onto a Roman bridge that was more than two thousand years old. René's camera again was busy with these ancient wonders. The group followed the road which passed by the ruins of Urbe, a village that was once prosperous and quite large. All that remained of the village are the ruins of its church. The path then followed along the Saldo River for a bit in order to reach another medieval bridge as they walked on to Lorca. The group decided to press on to Villatuerta, another five kilometres distant.

They stopped in Villatuerta for lunch with everyone ordering bocadillos, fries, and a beverage of choice. Predictably, as the boots and socks came off and backpacks were set to the side, conversation started to flow easily. Uncharacteristically, René wasn't drawn into the talk at the table. Rather, he had taken out his tablet in order to transfer the morning's photos from his camera to the tablet. That accomplished, he continued reading from Chogyam Trungpa's book, The Heart of the Buddha, where he had just begun reading from chapter seven, *Sacred Outlook*. As usual, he had his journal at hand in which he recorded those sentences that stood out for him. René had just started to write in his journal when Sid asked out of curiosity what he had found.

"Um, just a comment about egolessness," replied René as he lifted his head and saw Sid looking at him.

"Ah, a good topic," mused Sid with his ever-present smile. "So what does the author have to say about egolessness?"

"Chögyam basically says that in meditation that we learn to make friends with ourselves, and that we create our own confusion by ignoring our inner peacefulness. This is what he says is our first real sense of egolessness," explained René.

"Yes, that sounds about right," Sid said while nodding his head in that curious wobbly manner that René had noticed being used by other East Indians he had known as well. "What do you think about what he said about making friends with ourselves, René?"

"I think it's vital, Sid."

"Yet, this morning you weren't what I could exactly call friends with your body at all?"

"That's not fair," said René defensively. "I was naked for Christ's sake. How did you expect me to feel?"

"Well, as you just read, René, I expected you to feel comfortable in your body, a friend to your body. After all, your body is not your clothing, you are not your clothing, right?"

"But … but this is the modern world, Sid. People just don't go around naked, or haven't you noticed. We're lucky that we didn't get arrested and tossed into jail. Besides we could even have been given sex-offender status," spoke René with too much heat.

Sid just smiled and then remarked, "But when you were meditating nude this morning, you felt it, didn't you? You felt that moment of being a friend to yourself in spite of being nude, and that led you to experience egolessness. Perhaps it was the nakedness of your body that finally allowed you to open up to yourself more honestly than ever before? What do you think of that possibility?"

With an air of grudging acceptance, René replied, "Yeah, I have to admit that you might be right. For a while, it all just came together just like Trungpa described it."

"Good, just remember that feeling and how you got there," added Sid with his gentle manner and smile.

Lunch time was over. The group paid their bills and prepared to leave for the last three and a half kilometres to their next hostel, the Albergue San Miguel in Estella, a small city of 15,000 inhabitants.

As they walked along, Jason spoke up with a few thoughts that he wanted to share with the group, "You know, this walking on the Camino has become more than what it appears to be for me. I've been thinking about it, and I have to say that one way of looking at this journey, our journey of life, is to observe that we are presented with two questions, two very large questions."

Everyone had stopped their private bits of chatter to listen while Jason continued, "As I see it, one question is for the first half of our lives and the second question is for the second half of our lives. The question of the first half of life is essentially this: "What is the world asking of me?" The second question is directed at the second half of life is quite different: "What does the soul ask of me?" It seems to me that when we cling too long with the first question, we find ourselves in jeopardy, in violation of the soul and its summons. "

"That's pretty heavy stuff," Fred spoke to break the awkward silence that followed Jason' voiced thoughts.

"I am discovering a lot as we walk along," Jason replied. "My head is swirling with all kinds of thoughts and what we are sharing here, experiencing here is helping me distil those thoughts. I am in the process of writing a book, well not here, but back home. The manuscript is not much more than scattered notes on bits of paper at this point."

"Have you picked out a title for your book yet?" asked René who already owned most of the books that Jason had published.

"I hadn't thought of a title before coming to walk the Camino with all of you. But now, I think I will call it <u>A Call to the Soul's Journey</u>. It seems appropriate enough as we are truly engaged in a life-transforming journey here, as we walk together."

"Can you say more about the second half of life and the question and its answer?" prodded Fred.

"Well, it seems to me that in the second half of life, whether through choice or necessity, we become obliged to know the outer aspects of ourselves in order to understand our inner aspects."

"You lost me there, Jason," admitted Fred.

"It's like clothes, the outer aspect of who we are is disguised in the outer world, and the need to remove the clothing in order to become fully aware of our outer selves. It is vital to make the journey into the inner world to honour our souls. Essentially, we need to become psychological beings, or as Mark often says it, spiritual or soulful beings."

"Okay, I think I got it," said Fred. "Clinging to stuff, say like clothes, gets in the way of our getting at the heart and soul of who we are beneath our clothing. Cool!"

They had finally reached Estella. It didn't take long to find their hostel for the night and then go through the daily routines of taking care of washing themselves and their clothing. Rather than taking a siesta like a number of others, René decided to wander through the core of the city with his camera.

Estella was a small city. Yet, there was more than enough to be photographed, especially the bridge, Puente Carcel, another medieval bridge; and the churches of San Pedro, San Miguel and San Juan Bautista. There were also a few fountains that were worth capturing with his lens in the Plaza San Martin and Plaza de Santiago. René then returned to the hostel after a final round of photos using the late afternoon sunshine as a palette of colour.

Back at the hostel, he met the others who were just on their way out for beverages and tapas. While he had been out taking photos, René had purchased a few things with which to make his own evening meal in the kitchen that pilgrims were allowed to use. As a result, he begged off citing the need for some quiet time. When they left, he connected to the Wi-Fi and uploaded the photos. He found a few that were almost magical. He posted these to his Facebook account. Then, he wrote a longer-than-usual letter to his family and friends.

In spite of its length, René didn't mention anything about meditating nude. Rather, the letter was basically a mixture of travelogue and commentary about his new friends on the Camino. With the letter sent, René decided to make himself a cup of green tea. He had brought a few teabags from home for occasions such as this, melancholic moments.

With tea in hand, he chose a comfortable lounge chair and opened up his tablet to see what he could find that would match his mood. Nothing caught his mind and he found himself surfing the Internet before deciding to visit Fred's blog site. He laughed to himself when he saw that the front image was of a bar. He began to browse around the site checking out the various sections of what appeared to be a very comprehensive site. There wasn't any doubt about it, Fred was a prolific writer.

René's eyes soon found the section called God and Nudity and knew that this was what he had come looking for, answers that dealt with the issue of nudity, René's issue with nudity. The section was divided into three parts: Nudity, Modesty and Culture; The Bible and Nakedness; and finally, Naked Before God. It was this last section that particularly caught his attention. However, he decided that he had better check out The Bible and Nakedness before going any further.

'Wow!' muttered René. 'There are twenty-two posts on this topic. I guess I'd better start at the beginning.'

Of course, to start at the beginning as far as the Bible was concerned meant re-visiting the scene in the Garden of Eden, a scene where Adam and Eve lived naked without any shame. Fred had quoted from Genesis, "And the man and his wife were both naked and were not ashamed," as biblical evidence of the lack of shame at being nude. René read on.

> "Given the time we also need to remember that when God is done creating he calls all things 'very good' and this includes the fact that Adam and Eve were naked and not ashamed about it. Let's review: Good equals naked and unashamed."

"Good equals naked and unashamed." The words struck home for René. He saw that he had indeed equated nudity with shame, especially being nude in the presence of others. René knew that nudity wasn't bad, per se. But being good was a concept that he had a hard time with, especially nudity in public. He found himself pulled to read on. Fred went on to talk about "the fall" and the hiding in shame when God decided to visit them in the Garden again. Fred's commentary asks a troubling question: "It also makes me wonder something else – was the nakedness about their bodies or about their spirits?" René closed the webpage after having noted this last sentence in his journal just after the passage about nudity being good when one wasn't ashamed of being nude and that being ashamed of being naked equals bad.

Feeling hungry, René took his few groceries into the kitchen in order to prepare his evening meal. It was going to be a simple affair with pasta, some canned sauce and a generous helping of grated cheese as he had found a small wedge of Pecorino while wandering through the city taking photos. With his meal cooked, he saw four other pilgrims enter the kitchen in order to prepare a group meal. This was an idea he thought in which his group might take an interest. There wasn't any reason not to bring cerveza and vino to the hostel and enjoy a collective home-cooked meal.

With a final cup of tea, René turned to his journal, a habit he had been developing as the final pre-sleep time ritual.

It has been another strange day. I have to find out why there is some sort of magical energy coming from Sid and Asha. Again I saw both naked, the difference this time was that Fred and I also ended up naked while taking part in a group meditation. It was a good thing that we were out of the line of sight for passing pilgrims or else we may have had an incident to deal with and a lot of explaining to do, something that would be impossible as I can't explain it to myself, let alone explain it coherently in a second language. Yet, as discomforting as this was after the fact, while I was meditating, I found myself completely free. It was as though giving up control and allowing whatever was to happen, to unfold opened up a new door for me, one that promised more.

Later talks with the others showed that they accepted the event without any negative judgments. If anything, what was said was in support of that nude event. Even Jason Johnson seemed to feel that there was merit in nude meditation.

On another note, I have finally logged into see Fred's blog site and was blown away. This man is no lightweight when it comes to the world of spirituality and the issues of being human. And to think, that I had written him off as just another loud, know-it-all American. I sense and hope that we are becoming good friends, not just trail acquaintances.

Chapter Eleven – A Journey That Defies Common Sense

Before leaving the next morning, the group split into two, with one group taking the road less travelled from the Irache fountain stop, to the top of a sizable hill and then down again to rejoin the others at Cruce. The opposite group would have a stop at VillaMeyor de Monjardin for a mid-hike meal and beverages. René chose the road up the small mountain in spite of the fact that there would be no place along the way to buy coffee or a breakfast croissant.

René had three photographic opportunities that he didn't want to miss out on – the wooden bridge over a creek that would likely be dry at this time of year; the views from the summit of the hill which was a part of the higher mountain, Monte Jurra; and the views of Luquin with its Basilica, and the Church of Saint Martin. Travelling with him were just two others, Fred and Freya.

René still didn't know much about Freya other than she was the most beautiful woman he had ever seen. René was glad to have Fred walking with him as Freya's presence made him feel clumsy. When the plans were voiced the day before, René made sure that whoever was going to walk the route that passed Luquin, realised that they would need to buy provisions for the road as there would be nothing to buy en route, until they reached their final destination, Los Arcos.

The whole group travelled together for the first three and a half kilometres until the path separated. Just before the road-less-travelled junction appeared, they had reached the Fuente de Vino, a stop that allowed pilgrims to fill their water bottles and to help themselves to free wine. Two taps were set into the fountain which was operated by the monks of Irache. Knowing that they were going to make this a stop, all had brought an extra, empty water bottle which they would partially fill with wine at the fountain in order to toast each other and the pilgrimage, and anything or anyone else that deserved a toast. In reality, not much wine was drunk as the day was already warm and it was much too early in the day for wine.

Minutes later with the final toasts done, the pilgrims reached the junction and parted with loud wishes of "Buen Camino!" Mark's group set off downhill towards their mid-point destination of VillaMeyor de Monjardin while René's group began their ascent of the mountain slope. René was immediately impressed with Freya's pace. There was no question in his mind that she was the strongest walker in the group. She walked with an almost fierce determination.

René wondered what her story was, though he was hesitant to ask, as Freya had as of yet, shown no signs of being willing to talk about personal things. All he had heard from her were comments about the sights and the weather. Even with that, she rarely spoke much other than in private with Miryam, and it seemed that she was content to listen to and to watch the others.

Fred was walking behind Freya with his attention on his iPod, listening to music. René brought up the rear of the small group of three pilgrims. He divided his attention between the passing scenes, and with thoughts about how his world was shifting beneath him. In some foreboding way, he began to think that this pilgrimage had more surprises in store for him, uncomfortable surprises that would be testing him. He sensed that there was even a real element of danger up ahead somewhere. Having learned long ago to trust his instincts, René wondered what it was that was about to make his life difficult. Though caught up in his thoughts, his eyes constantly returned to focus on the figure of Freya who led the way forward.

The bridge was well worth taking the detour. There was no doubt that such a simple bridge evoked a simpler time. With a few photos taken, René soon caught up to Fred and Freya, both of whom were still in their own private worlds, still walking in silence. Freya had again, caught his attention, and with not-so-wholesome thoughts about her forming in his mind. She was, beyond question, the most perfect woman he had ever seen. Yes, Asha was also perfect, but in a saintly, innocent, and pure way, which left no room for worldly and carnal thoughts. Freya stirred an ancient fire within him. Banishing his tempting fantasies, René refocused on the path and the scenes passing by.

Soon they broke through the tree line and were able to see the valley below to the north and the distant peak of Monjardin. René broke the silence telling Fred and Freya that he was stopping for a change of socks and to munch on a hunk of baguette and cheese.

"Sure," agreed Freya. "I could use a break as well."

"Super idea," added Fred, his earbud headphones now dangling around his neck.

"Hey," exclaimed Fred as he noticed a gleaming necklace on Freya's neck which had been hidden by a loose silk scarf. "That's a beautiful necklace. It kind of looks Celtic with all that weaving and the star at the centre."

"It's not Celtic," clarified Freya. "It's much older."

"Older than Celtic?"

"Yes, think of the Norse gods and goddesses. This necklace is Norse, and is called Brisingamen."

"Neat!" admired Fred. Turning to René, Fred asked, "What do you think, René? Isn't it beautiful?"

"Yes, it is." René observed as he lifted his head to look at the necklace laying exposed on Freya's neck. René also noticed the swells of Freya's breasts and felt a peculiar discomfort, which became intensified as Freya caught his eyes looking at her breasts. Looking up and seeing her eyes appraising him, René felt the finger of an unnamed fear stab within his gut.

"I've heard of the necklace Brisingamen before," added Fred, unaware of the tension that seemed to have appeared in the air. "Wasn't that the name of the necklace worn by the Norse Goddess, Freyja? It's kind of cool that you pretty much have the same name as her."

Freya turned to look at Fred, "Yes, it's the same necklace."

"Where did you buy it? I think I'd like to get one like it for my wife," said Fred.

"I didn't buy it. It was given to me a long, long time ago."

Her short and terse response seemed to invite an end the conversation, and had precisely that effect. As usual, everyone's boots and socks came off while they took a rest on the side of the path along the treeline. They all took turns retreating behind the trees in order to answer the calls of nature.

René found a spot further off the path that was flat enough for laying back and closing his eyes thus getting the most out of this rest period. He didn't know why he felt so edgy and was still a bit ashamed at having been caught looking at her breasts. What the hell had come over him? This was way out of character for him. The problem was made worse for René as he believed that she wanted him to look, wanted him to...

Shaking his head, he quickly abandoned that line of thought. Temptation. Desire. Lust. Lifting himself to a sitting position he looked down at Fred and Freya. Fred was talking to her while she focused on René, again catching his eyes. "Shit," mumbled René silently to himself. René decided to cut his rest short and began putting on his socks and boots in order to again head up the trail.

"Whoa!" called out Fred. "What's the rush there pal?"

"I'm itchy to get moving, that's all," replied René. "You don't have to rush, I can meet up with you guys somewhere down the path."

Freya responded to René's statement with, "I'm ready to go now as well."

The three of them were again walking together up the small mountain slope to the peak. Oddly, René didn't stop to take any more photos, in spite of his original plans. Taking the lead, he just kept on going, pushing himself, and pushing the pace. Cresting the peak, the group began the long descent towards Los Arcos, a descent that would take them down, about 250 metres in elevation. René was flying covering distance, fleeing, as if in an attempt to escape himself.

"What the hell's the hurry?" complained Fred who walked at the rear.

Realising that he had been acting irrationally, René slowed down his pace with an apology, "I guess I just got caught up in my head."

"Any faster and we'd be running," huffed Fred as he caught up to René.

Freya had no comment to offer. Strangely she didn't seem the least bit stressed by the blistering pace. If anything, she appeared as normal and as collected as she always appeared.

"How about we stop again for a bit," complained Fred. "I'm starved and thirsty."

"We're almost at Luquin," suggested Freya. "We could stop there and have a trail snack. René could also take some photos."

"Okay," answered Fred, "But take it easy, remember the pilgrim motto, slow and steady wins the race."

"It's not a race," replied René who thought the saying was more about turtles and rabbits than it was about pilgrims.

"You could have fooled me with the pace you were setting," retorted Fred.

They reached Luquin, a typical hill village, a few minutes later. They found a place to sit in the village's small square near the Church of San Martin. As expected, the small café, San Isidro was closed, so they made do with the provisions they were carrying. It wasn't long before René excused himself to wander around the village with his camera, leaving his backpack with Freya and Fred. The church was quite square in shape and was closed thus limiting the number of photos René took. Returning to where Fred and Freya were sitting, René finally sat still long enough to break off a hunk of baguette and make himself a bocadillo of Chorizo sausage and cheese.

"I was just talking to Freya about nudity in Denmark and Norway," Fred mentioned when René had settled in to his seat causing René to almost choke on the bit of sandwich in his mouth. "You know, I am interested in how culture affects our relationship to our bodies," he added.

"Really, Fred?" René managed to sputter out after swallowing the piece of sandwich in his mouth. "You just don't talk about nudity to everyone. You've got nakedness on your brain. All people aren't as comfortable with the topic as you are."

Looking at René with a smile on her face, Freya added, "I'm not in the least uncomfortable talking about nudity, René. The truth is, as I was telling Fred, I am almost always naked when I am at home, as well as in many clothing-optional sites around my country and the rest of Europe. We Norse have a healthy attitude towards nudity, one that comes out of our earliest roots as a people. As you might, or might not know, our Norse gods and goddesses were usually portrayed nude," she added with a barely perceptible wink and smile directed at René.

"Umm," was all that René could say in response.

"We are born naked, and we die naked," Freya continued. "That's the truth of who and what we are. So, why not live naked when it is practical?"

Fred was quick to add his two cents worth into the discussion as Freya opened up, "That sounds just like Job. You see Job tears off his clothes and then sees that his nakedness is all okay in God's eyes," Fred summarized in support of what Freya had been saying. "And that isn't the only time that God has no issue with being naked in public either, he continued. "God commanded Isaiah to strip naked, including his shoes, and to stay naked for three years. God basically told Isaiah to be a nudist, a naked prophet, for three years."

"That was back thousands of years ago," sputtered René. "You'd end up in jail Fred, if you tried wandering around buck naked and preaching for three years. Take a look at Stephen Gough in the U.K., he tried walking around the countryside naked and he has spent a fair number of years in jail as a result."

"You're such a prude," laughed Freya. "Have you ever been naked in public, say at a beach or at a resort?"

"Never!" protested René. "Those places are all about sex, sex, sex. And believe me, even Fred's God doesn't approve of nude and lewd."

"Nude is not necessarily lewd," challenged Freya with more than a bit of heat. "Or, are you telling me that when you are nude, it's all about sex, sex, sex? It sure as hell isn't that way for me!"

"That's not what I said," René hastily apologised, "I simply said that being nude at resorts and nude beaches is not like being nudity as when one showers . . ."

"How do you know that?" demanded Freya. "As you've said, you've never been to either a nude beach or nude resort."

"She got you there, didn't she?" crowed Fred with pleasure. "And as far as being nude in public, well let's just say that I know you've been there and done that. Does naked meditation ring any bells?"

In frustration, René bent down to put on his socks and shoes, then slipped on his backpack, and left the two of them sitting there without saying another word. However, it wasn't long before he sensed that they were walking behind him. Every once in a while René heard them chatting though he refused to listen to what they might be saying. Eventually, the three of them reached the junction that took them back onto the main pilgrimage trail. There, they joined in as part of a larger flowing line of hikers who had not taken the high road, the road less taken.

The next two hours passed in a continued silence, as they walked along country lanes to Los Arcos. René again kept his camera in its holder around his waist as they passed by another set of ruins, another bridge over a dry riverbed, and then into the town of Los Arcos. When they finally arrived at Casa la Fuente, where the group had planned on staying, they found out that all the beds were filled. They then made their way further into town to try finding a place to sleep in a new hostel called Casa de la Abuela. They were in luck and soon installed themselves in one of the pleasant rooms. Anticipating the arrival of their friends, they reserved the rest of the remaining beds in the room. The hospedador, the host that was taking care of arrivals, informed them that if their friends didn't arrive by four-thirty, the beds would be freed and given to others who needed them as well. Since there were two and a half hours remaining, René felt that this would not be a problem. Fred offered to return to the Casa la Fuente to leave a note on the board there for the rest of the crew.

As soon as Fred had left, René busied himself with washing out his socks, top, and shorts. Freya followed his example and soon was washing her socks, undies and hiking clothes as well. Not noticing because his thoughts were elsewhere, Freya had removed all her clothes and proceeded to wash them while in her birthday suit. Suddenly, it registered on René that he was standing beside an incredibly fit and extremely beautiful, naked woman with long, blond hair, a woman who was tantalizingly desirable. Involuntarily, he felt his manhood responding, something that Freya noticed as well.

"Ah, so you still want to prove that nude is lewd?" she laughed embarrassing René even more. "Relax, René. I'm just washing my clothes and then taking a shower. Why get dressed to wash clothing and then get undressed a few minutes later to wash my body." She turned back to the rinsing of her hiking clothes and then hanging them up on a line to dry in their room. Then, she grabbed her shower bag and walked into the shower room. Before disappearing into the shower room, she asked, "Aren't you coming for a shower?"

Just as she disappeared into the shower, Fred had returned with the rest of their small company of pilgrims saving René from having to make a decision. Miryam was telling the others that she had a brother in Canada who was a Jungian analyst. Like her brother, and perhaps because of him, she had become fascinated with mythology, psychology and spirituality. As she was talking in depth to Jason, Gabe and Luca about this brother who lived in Calgary, Freya emerged from the shower, still totally naked.

René turned a bright shade of pink as the others saw her walk to her bed and take out something clean to wear. But much to his surprise, no one remarked about her nudity. All that is except for Fred who registered surprise with lifted eyebrows. It was as if it seeing someone nude was normal for the rest them, an idea that felt so foreign to René. Thankfully, Fred responded without gaping too much or commenting about her assets. But then, Fred hadn't made any such comments since René had met him. 'Is it just me?' wondered René.'

"Why are you blushing?" asked Luca quietly so that it was unlikely that anyone else in the room had heard him. "Ah, it's the sight of that fair damsel, isn't it? Well, you know what it says about your 'self' when you react with heat to a situation, don't you? You're a therapist."

"Yes, Luca," answered René, "It means that something within me was activated, a complex."

"Precisely! Why don't you and I go for a coffee or something stronger where we can talk about this, just the two of us?"

With a sigh of relief at having a way out of his present situation, René nodded agreement. The two of them set out to find a quiet corner in a nearby café. Luca ordered wine for both of them ignoring the protests of René who said he would prefer a coffee. When the glasses arrived with a carafe of local red wine and a plate of tapas, Luca raised his glass offering "Prost!" to which René replied with the Spanish equivalent of 'Cheers,' "Salud!"

"Now, shall we talk frankly?" began Luca in a tone that suggested that to do otherwise would not be considered as an option.

"I want to thank you, Luca, for taking the time for this conversation. God knows that I needed to talk to someone."

"So what is it that has got your libido so fired up?"

"It's all the talk about nudity, and now this exhibitionist and forward behaviour by Freya, her prancing around without a stitch on."

"Mm, so nudity bothers you?" asked Luca.

"Well, not normally. I mean before I came on the Camino, nudity wasn't a problem for me."

"What's the difference now?"

"It's the public nudity, and how it has seems to be coming at me from all directions. I mean, the first day it was Sid meditating on a rock totally naked. Then it was Asha walking and singing nude – twice. And then yesterday, I found myself pulled into a group meditation with Sid, Asha and Fred – a nude meditation. And then today, it was all the talk of the Bible and nakedness followed by Freya's more than obvious intent to stir me up in the hostel. I actually think she is trying to seduce me."

"Mm," Luca uttered sympathetically. "I want you to think about this last statement about Freya and her intention. Your reaction in the hostel, what I saw, told me that there was something in you that was the problem. As you know, people have a tendency to project onto others when the outer situation they find themselves in, activates an affect in response."

"Yes, Luca," admitted René. "I knew, I know. But I'll be damned if I can figure it out."

"Ha, ha, ha!" laughed Luca. "It isn't all that simple and you are very well aware of it. So, let me just think out loud here, then you tell me what you think? Is that okay with you?"

"Of course," said René feeling grateful for whatever it was that Luca would bring forward. After all, he was stuck and he knew it.

"You are on a journey that defies common sense, a heroic journey or a fool's journey. All of us walking here, whether we know it or not, are searching for something we have yet to define. All of us find ourselves longing for something, something missing. This is a universal longing that most of us answer with things, with ideologies. This is like the proverbial search for eternal youth, eternal beauty, and eternal life. But, it is really a desperate longing for consciousness."

"I don't really get how this helps explain my situation, Luca?"

"The hero, and here I mean you as well as all who are filled with longing for something missing, is first and foremost a self-representation of the longing of the unconscious, of its unquenched and unquenchable desire for the light of consciousness. But consciousness, continually in danger of being led astray by its own light and of becoming rootless, longs for the healing power of nature, for the deep wells of being and for unconscious communication with life in all its countless forms."

"Let's see if I can understand this in terms of what is going on within me," suggested René.

"But of course!"

"The whole idea of nakedness, of nudity is triggering a longing, or should I say, activating a longing that has been denied, hidden, within me."

"Precisely!"

"And it isn't really about nakedness, is it?" concluded René. "But if that's so, why is it nudity that gets me all steamed up?"

"Perhaps it's because nakedness is symbolic of letting go, giving up ego control," explained Luca. "There is a resistance to change, a refusal to let go, to move on."

"Yeah, that makes sense," admitted René. "It's also something I often find myself telling my clients. You'd think that I'd realise that for myself."

"Don't be so hard on yourself," counselled Luca. "Resistance is natural. Still, as you know, we have to let go of our certainties, our old truths, before we can cross the divide to a wider consciousness and new truths. It does get easier further down the road. That's the best I can tell you."

Both were silent for a while, sipping on the last of the wine. René broke the silence with, "Thanks, Luca. I guess we'd better get back to the others and then go out for another pilgrim menu dinner."

"Before we go, René, I noticed how you neatly sidestepped around the issue of Freya and your response to her which is a different story altogether," remarked Luca. "But, that is a subject for another time."

It was a surprise to René when Luca grasped his hand and drew him into a bear hug, then breaking that hug with a pat on René's shoulder.

Later that evening, when all were back at Casa de la Abuela, René returned to his nightly ritual of writing in his journal before sliding into another night of restless sleep.

> *Freya. She's driving me totally nuts. It's taking all of my resolve to keep my cool. I can't believe how perfect she is. I didn't think it was possible that any one would ever look as good to me as Cécile looked when we met and got married. Freya is impossibly beautiful and makes me think of the Greeks and their perfect goddesses. Did I mention that I saw her naked? Oh lord, I've got to rein myself in better as she knows she's captured my attention.*
>
> *There, that's what I mean. Too much Freya on the brain. Today's walk was good and I'm glad that I took the longer route. This afternoon, I got to talk with Luca as he noticed my agitated state when Freya walked*

naked into the dorm from the shower. He was spot on when he talked with me about a complex being activated. No answers of course, but the answers are there for me to discover along the way.

It's getting late and I'm tired. More tomorrow.

Chapter Twelve – Being One's Own Worst Enemy

René woke up from a restless sleep. For whatever reason, his dreams during the night continued to taunt him, just as the sight of Freya had taunted him the day before. Freya was in his dreams portrayed as a northern goddess wielding a sword and attempting to strike at him, as if to cut off his erect manhood. Then the dreams would change with Freya drawing him within her, possessing his body and his soul as the price for their union. Waking, he knew that he was desperately trying to blame everything in his life on cruel gods and goddesses only to find that blame pointing straight back at himself. René rushed with washing up and getting ready. Though there was no rush for the rest of the Little Company of Pilgrims. The group had decided to walk just nineteen kilometres to Viana rather than going all the way to Logroño which almost twenty-nine kilometres away. There weren't any hostels to be found between these two stops so it was an either-or decision.

René, however, decided he wanted to head out early and catch the sunrise and to take his time with planned photo stops in Torres del Rio, at the peak of Nuestra Señora del Poyo, and at the ruins beside the Rio Cornava. As well, he wanted some distance from the others, especially from Freya.

He told the group that he would likely meet up with them at Torres del Rio where he assumed he would stop for a meal and coffee. Miryam had phoned ahead to book beds for all of them in Viana, a bustling town of three and a half thousand people, at a place called the Palacio de Pujadas. Miryam didn't want to risk walking longer due to a lack of beds in Viana. Miryam knew she wouldn't be able to walk on to Logroño should all the hostels be filled by the time they arrived. She also doubted whether Jason, Luca, or Gabe would be able to handle that extra distance either. The others had seen the sense in her thinking and agreed in spite of the fact that they had always left lodgings all to chance thus far. Perhaps it was this fact that allowed René to leave early without someone else tagging along.

René had barely started walking when he spotted the chapel of Saint Blaise, an old way station along the Camino from the 12th century. Sighing because there wasn't enough light to get a decent photo of the Capilla San Blas, René walked on a dirt trail that took him across farmland. Seven kilometres down the trail, with the last two kilometres having him climb a hundred or so metres, he decided to stop for a café con leche at the entrance to Sansol. According to the guide book, it was only another kilometre to Torres del Rio, where he had originally thought he would stop. However, his feet were getting hot and there was a steep descent ahead followed by another uphill climb to reach Torres del Rio.

After ordering coffee and two servings of toast, René went through the ritual of taking off his boots and socks so that his toes could air and feel the freedom of being bare. 'Funny,' thought René as he looked at his feet, 'I don't seem to have a problem with my feet being bare in public, or my chest for that matter.' Rather than follow up on that thought, he looked around him and then at the overcast sky before mentioning to an unknown pilgrim at the next table. "It's a good day for hiking," René offered.

The stranger smiled and agreed. It wasn't long before the stranger joined René at his table, bringing his café con leche with him. "You headed to Logroño?"

René shook his head before answering, "No, the plan is to stop in Viana and call it a day."

"Seems like such a shame to waste this perfect hiking weather with a short walk. Why don't you join me and walk on to Logroño?"

"Well," apologized René, "I am travelling with a group, and reservations have been made for all of us in Viana."

"Where are your friends, behind us or ahead of us?" asked the stranger. "Oh, by the way, I'm David, like you, a Canadian."

"Pleased to meet you, David," replied René shaking David's proffered hand. "I'm René, and to answer your question, they are behind me. And, how did you know I'm Canadian?"

"It's the accent, along with the patch on your backpack, a dead giveaway. So, where in Canada are you from, René?" asked David. "I'm from Toronto, you know, the big T.O." he added with a grin.

"I'm from Ottawa," René countered with a grin.

"Ah, the city that rolls up its sidewalks by nine in the evening," laughed David. "I spent some time in the city and was bored to tears. Now, Hull, across the river, is a different story. Wine, women and song any day of the week and any hour of the day."

"Ottawa kind of grows on you," smiled René in response. "Besides, it's not really all that boring. You just have to know where the action is. Not all of the sidewalks are rolled up at night."

"You'd never convince me to live there," added David in jest before changing topics. "By the way, that sure is a nice looking camera," he said pointing to the camera René had sitting on the table beside his coffee.

"Thanks," smile René with more than a little pride. "Here hold it and look through the lens."

"Holy shit, is that ever light!" he exclaimed. "Mind if I take a photo with it?"

"No, go ahead," beamed René.

David looked through the 16-55 mm lens while panning around the restaurant until he settled on René when he then snapped a quick photo. Handing the camera back to René, he said "It sure beats mine."

"What kind of camera are you using?" asked René with interest.

"My smart phone camera," David replied showing him his cell phone. "It takes decent enough photos for my purposes."

"Both of my kids use smart phones as well for their cameras, even my daughter who has a real camera," commented René. "I don't have a smart phone so there's no temptation to depend on it as a camera."

David was surprised, "What? No cell phone?"

"No phone," admitted René. "Besides, who would I call while walking on the Camino?"

Ready to walk on, René asked David to join him, at least as far as Viana. The began the steep descent that took them to the San Pedro River and then crossed to enter Torres del Rio where René had decided to stop and take photos of another Templar Church, the Iglesia de Santo Sepularo. With photos of the church taken, as well as a few more of the town, the two then began the climb up to the peak of Nuestra Señora del Poyo, At Our Lady of Poyo, there was a hermitage that begged for a photograph to be taken. Stopping for more photos was also a relief after following the ascent of over a hundred metres in two and a half kilometres. With the photos taken, René bent down to tighten his laces. "It's a steep descent here," he said in explanation to David. "No point in getting a blister from my feet sliding inside of my boots."

Three and a half kilometres later, which they covered at a fast pace, they reached the next river, the Río Cornava where they saw the ruins of a medieval village. Viana was only five more kilometres away, about an hour's distance at the pace they were walking.

As they walked on, René began to think about going on to Logroño with David rather than stopping in Viana. He realised that if he went on, he wouldn't have to deal with Freya, or the incessant talk about nudity by Fred. It wasn't that he was trying to avoid his friends, he tried to convince himself. It was just that his newest friend was a very likeable person, a comfortable person to be around. Upon reaching the outskirts of Viana, René brought up the subject of going on with David.

"That'd be great!" he responded with pleasure. "But what about your friends who are supposed to meet you here?"

"We can meet up again at another stop."

"I have to warn you that I intend on walking thirty kilometres again tomorrow, all the way to Najera. I want to get to Burgos in three more days. I have to meet some of my buddies there," explained David.

"I was planning on a rest day in Burgos," René quickly invented as he hadn't planned on any rest days unless necessary. "I'll just meet up with them there. I've got a few of their e-mail addresses and I can let them know where I am when we get to Burgos."

"If you're sure, I'd love to have your company," said David with enthusiasm. Now, what do you say about stopping for lunch?"

They chose to eat at the Cafeteria El Porto just opposite the ruins of San Pedro. René wasn't worried about the others arriving before he left with David, to continue on to Logroño. There was no way they would have walked fast enough as a group. Besides, there wouldn't be any reason in their minds to hurry with their planned lunch in Torres. When René and David finished eating, they headed out of Viana.

Two and a half hours later, they arrived in Logroño. They found beds at the Albergue Santiago, which was beside the Iglesia Santiago. It was a small a small parish hostel that only had fifteen beds spread out over four rooms. Both David and René chose to eat a communal meal in the hostel rather than roam around the city. With a long walk set for the next day, they needed all the rest they could get.

Since they had arrived late in the afternoon, René didn't bother washing his socks or top – he had extras – as they wouldn't have a chance to dry before he went to sleep and he didn't want to spend extra time in the morning dealing with his laundry. When he sat down to write in his journal, he felt guilty, felt as if he had somehow betrayed not only his friends back in Viana, but himself as well. He knew he was running, running away. He just didn't know exactly what he was running from.

In the morning, René and David packed up in the pre-dawn darkness and slipped out of the hostel. By the time they reached Pantano, dawn had broken, though the cloud cover had denied a sunrise photo for the second day in a row, unlike the sunrise photos that René had captured on the previous days of the Camino. At Patano, they stopped for coffee and toast at a café, before walking on towards Navarette. They stopped briefly at the ruins of San Juan de Acre for a few photos, and then moved on to Navarette where they decided to have a second breakfast.

"Not bad," commented David. "We've covered twelve and a half kilometres in three hours including our stop in Pantano. We should be able to have an early lunch in Ventosa which is just seven more clicks down the road."

"Sounds good to me," René commented without a lot of enthusiasm. He wasn't tired, but he didn't seem to be enjoying the walk as much, as when he had been walking with the others.

"What's up?" asked David sensing René's mood. "Is the pace too much? We could slow down the pace if it is. We'll still get to Najera in good time."

"No, it's not the pace," confessed René. "The pace is okay, really."

"Missing your friends back in Viana?"

"No," he lied trying desperately to think of something to say to explain his mood. "I guess it is just some residue left from one of the discussions I had with them."

"Yeah? You wanna talk about it?" David asked hoping that René would open up. David had noticed René's withdrawal and had been looking for a way to break the silence that had marked most of the morning.

"Well, I guess I could," offered René. "But not now. I need to think a bit more and see how it sorts out. Otherwise, I would simply be reacting. Thanks for offering, though. Later, okay?"

The seven kilometres left to reach Ventosa passed with few scenes that caught René's photo-seeking eyes. Lunch was a quiet and rushed affair, which had René only drinking one cup of coffee. All that remained was just over ten kilometres to reach Najera, ten relatively easy kilometres.

At the seven kilometre mark where they met a pilgrim footbridge over the Yalda River, they took advantage of a picnic table to stop and give their feet a well-deserved rest as well as a final change of socks. The overcast skies had kept the temperatures more moderate, but those same clouds began to suggest that rain was not far off. There remained about three and a half kilometres until they would be in the old part of Najera where there would be a number of hostel options to choose from. David surmised that they would likely reach their destination before two-thirty.

David was right, they found themselves placing their backpacks on their bunks in the municipal hostel only a few minutes before two. It had taken the two of them seven and a half hours to walk thirty kilometres, including the stops for photos, sock changes, and meals during the day. René was glad to lay back on his bunk and not do anything for a while. Even taking a shower would have to wait in his opinion. Two hours later, René woke up still dressed in his hiking clothes. With a groan, he forced himself to move from the bed. He desperately needed a shower and some clean clothes if he intended to go out for supper.

Looking around the room, he saw others similarly suffering from too long of a walk. 'What the hell was I thinking? I'm over fifty years old,' René muttered to himself. 'This is dumb.'

He found out from one of the hostel staff that there was a laundromat close by. So he decided to take his dirty clothes there for washing and drying, as he needed clean clothes for the next day, especially clean socks. When he had finished showering and was dressed in his cleaner town clothes, René went in search of the laundromat. David wasn't in the hostel. René assumed that he was already eating nearby. For René, eating would have to wait until he finished his chores.

Supper was fast food which René had found near the laundromat, a couple of burgers and a large order of fries. He decided to make efficient use of his time as he wanted to get back to the hostel as soon as possible so that he could get as much sleep time as he could before they had to head out again the next morning.

When his laundry was done and folded, René wasted little time in returning to the hostel. If anyone was to ask him about Najera, he wouldn't be able to tell them a thing about the place other than the burgers were mediocre, the fries okay, and that there was a laundromat a block and a half from the hostel.

Back at the hostel, teeth brushed and laying in his bunk, René took out his journal.

> *I think I made a poor decision in fleeing from my friends. I thought I was making a wise decision to stay out of temptations way by not being around Freya. I didn't trust myself and so I fled like some thief in the middle of the night. I blamed Fred for his honest, wondering about the natural human body, rather than*

see how he was wrestling with the contradictions between his Bible and his Church. I blamed him for my own struggles that have surfaced. I had even been critical of Sid and Asha who are the purest souls I have ever met in my life. They gave me a taste of bliss and I dismissed it. While I was at the Laundromat, I read something that struck me as important.

"The demands of the unconscious act at first like a paralyzing poison on a man's energy and resourcefulness, so that it may well be compared to the bite of a snake. Apparently it is a hostile demon who robs him of energy, but in actual fact it is his own unconscious whose alien tendencies are beginning to check the forward striving of the conscious mind."

I guess that says it all, doesn't it? Projection, blaming others when it is my own stuff that is the poison. I sure hope that I can rejoin the others. I hope they will want me back in their group.

Chapter Thirteen – On Someone Else's Path

Morning came much too soon for René. He was stiff and sore all over. The plan for the day was to walk another twenty-eight kilometres, all the way to Grañon. René knew he was going to be walking slower so there was no point in delaying. He heard David already getting ready in the bunk beside him. With a quick trip to the bathroom, René returned, put on fresh, clean socks and hiking clothes before lifting his backpack onto his back. Soon both of them were quietly slipping out of the hostel trying to avoid waking those who were still sleeping.

Walking through the dark of early morning, David and René maintained a silence until they had reached the edge of Najera where they found themselves back in the countryside.

"You are quiet this morning, René. Did you have a good sleep? You were sleeping when I left to check my e-mail and still sleeping when I came back to see if you wanted to go out for supper."

"Yes, I guess I needed it," answered René. "These long walks are telling me that I'm not a spring chicken anymore," he added with a hint of humour in his voice.

"How does breakfast in Azofra sound to you? It's about six "K" from here, about an hour and a half, give or take."

"Sounds perfect."

As they began to climb steeply up a hill, walking on a dirt track through a treed park, the faint light of dawn was muted. It was a tough start but the short down-hill that followed allowed them to stretch their legs out making the rest of their walk to Azofra quite pleasant. René finally managed to get a few great photos of the sunrise as it crested the hill they had left behind. Only a few clouds remained in the sky from the previous day's overcast conditions, and they had put on a display of mauves and pinks which René had hoped had been captured by the camera. The colours lifted René's spirit and a smile formed from a place deep within him. For René, photography had this magic of finding something beyond the outward appearances, something breathtakingly spiritual.

They stopped for coffee and toast at the Café Centro.

"I see a much more content René this morning," noticed David as they removed their boots and socks. René's socks weren't damp yet, but it was a ritual that was becoming automatic.

"Yeah," admitted René. "Wasn't that some sunrise?"

"Here, let's see how your photos turned out?" asked David as he reached for René's camera.

René turned on the camera and set it to reviewing taken photos and then handed the camera to David.

"I took some of the same photos, but I never got them to look this good," whistled David in awe of the images that had been captured. "You're going to have to send me the link to your Flickr account. I'm assuming that you have one."

"I do have one. Well actually I have two Flickr accounts," René answered. "One is for my archives and the second one is for specially selected photos, more like my personal art studio. I will send you both URLs. Of course that means I'll need your e-mail address."

While they ate their breakfast, the two men continued with chatting about inconsequential things, small talk that was serving to repair the initial bond between them, a bond that had been stretched thin to almost the breaking point by René's withdrawal. Their next stop was planned for Cirueña, almost ten kilometres distant from Azofra. By then, they anticipated a second breakfast. With the plan in place, the two then continued on their way.

"So?" wondered René. "Tell me a little more about yourself. Are you married? Any kids?"

"Okay," replied David. "Yes, I am married. Or at least I should say I was married. Her name was Beth. Beth wasn't my first wife, but she was the love of my life. When I first saw her, I knew that she was the woman that I wanted to spend the rest of my life with. The problem was that we were both married at the time. Things somehow seemed to work out and we married and had four kids together. Beth died this past spring of cancer."

"I'm sorry to hear that," offered René.

"Thanks. As for my children, all boys with Beth, I have other children from my previous wives – don't ask – Sam is the oldest, Bob is next, then Nathan and last is Sol."

René could tell that Sol was the son that David favoured most. "I have two kids: a girl and a boy – Elise, and Jérôme who is our eldest. You already know that my ex-wife's name is Cécile. She was the love of my life, but I screwed up and have been alone since."

"So you've never got involved in another relationship?"

"No, I mean that it wasn't as if I had fallen out of love with Cécile. I guess that in spite of the fact that she remarried, I haven't really moved on." Wanting a change in topics, René asked, "So, is this Camino about trying to move on following

Beth's death?" asked René with as much gentleness as he could voice.

"Yeah. I've been having a hard time coping with her death. It's not just her death that has me walking here though. I screwed up big time in each of my earlier marriages and it caused my children a lot of pain. I left a big mess behind me. I didn't want anything to do with the wives and the children I left behind, well except pay child support which I did. The mess had nothing to do with the kids growing up poor. Still, the kids have made bad choices along the way. I wasn't there for them when they needed me. What hurts me the most, is not being there for my daughter, Tammy. She was raped as a teenager."

"Ouch!" winced René. "You don't have to tell me more if it causes too much pain. Let's focus on the positive. Tell me about how you met Beth."

"One afternoon I was hosting a pool party at our private estate just north of the city, with my workmates and their significant others – wives, girlfriends, boyfriends – as well as these guests, a few trusted friends were also in attendance. I am a consultant in Toronto for a firm that is worth billions. Actually, I am the CEO of that company and hold the majority shares which kind of makes me the owner," added David as if that information was somehow important to his story.

"Anyways, most of us guys were drinking on the deck as usual while the women were hanging out at the pool skinny dipping. It wasn't a sex party, don't get me wrong. Well, there was this one woman standing at the side of the pool talking to my wife, who was in the water. When I saw this woman, I was undone. She was the most beautiful woman I had ever seen. Of course, being married at the time, I kept my distance as she was the wife of one of my field managers.

Later that evening, the party moved inside and everyone was in their birthday suits. I encouraged this level of openness as the boundaries of authority vanish and everyone becomes equal when everyone is naked. Well, as a host, I took turns dancing with all the wives of the executive board members and managers of my company. I saved for the second last dance for Beth, the goddess I had fallen in love with, as my wife was to be my last dance partner, and I felt something I had never felt before. It was as if I had been punched in the gut and left gasping for breath."

David stopped his story and looked at René. "I don't know why I am telling you this story? I've never told anyone about it."

René shrugged his shoulders with a slight shake of his head, "It happens to me all the time. I guess my training as a psychotherapist has made me a good listener, a listener who accepts what is said without criticism or moral judgments." René knew what David had felt like as it seemed to be exactly what he felt in response to Freya, especially a naked Freya.

"Well," resumed David, "As I was saying, I fell head over heels in love with Beth that night. Being her husband's boss, I misused my power and sent him off on a half-year assignment to Britain. With him out of the picture, it didn't take long for me to learn that Beth had fallen in love with me as well. Well, one thing led to another and she became pregnant with Sam. As soon as we found out about the pregnancy, I knew I either had to convince her husband to return immediately so that he would think he was the father of the new life in his wife's womb, or he needed to have an accident take him out of the picture."

René looked at David with shock, "You didn't?"

"Yes. He refused to return as there were still negotiations that he felt still needed his presence. He wanted at least another month to wrap up those negotiations before returning back to Toronto, which would still be two months earlier than had been originally planned. You see, I felt I had no choice. He died in a car accident. I then divorced my third wife and wasted no time in marrying the young widow. It's not a pretty story at all."

"So how long did you stay married to Beth," René asked.

"We were married 25 years when she passed away. As I said, she was my soulmate."

David went silent after telling his story. The last few kilometres were walked under a depressive mood that seemed impossible to dispel. Upon reaching Cirueña, they stopped for a mid-morning meal at Café Jacobeo having covered fifteen kilometres in juar over three and a half hours. The talk during their stop for coffee, toast and a few pastries, was kept light and non-personal.

From Cirueña, there remained six kilometres left to walk to reach Santo Domingo de Calzada. Most of the way to Santo Domingo was flat so they covered the distance in less than an hour and a half which meant that they weren't ready for another meal, so they pressed on to Grañon which lay just another seven kilometres away. They estimated it would take them about two hours more to make it to Grañon where they planned to call it a day. As they passed through Santo Domingo, René made sure to take a few photos of the colourful older section of the city, especially the Parador Hotel and the Cathedral, which were found along the Plaza del Santo.

René entered into the Cathedral towing David behind him as he was intent on getting photos of Saint Dominic who had been the man behind building the pilgrimage trail to Santiago. Once inside the church, he caught sight of a side chapel dedicated to Mary Magdalene. The chapel reminded René of a conversation he had with Fred several days ago. Taking a few final photos, the two men left the cathedral and the village of Santo Domingo.

The seven kilometre walk took two hours. René was hurting. He knew he had gone too far, too fast during these past three days. He also knew he wouldn't be walking the next day. However, he kept that decision to himself with the intention of letting David know later, likely when they were having their evening meal. They found themselves a bed with no problem, at the hostel attached to the Church of San Juan de Bautiste. They spotted a bar-café, a little tienda, which was like a small confectionary story, and a pharmacy near the hostel.

Booking into the parish hostel, and then freshening up with a shower and clean clothes, they decided that supper would likely be what they made for themselves in the communal kitchen. With that decision made, they headed over to the café for something to drink before heading to the grocery store to buy something to prepare for their meal, René was hoping that they could find the fixings for some spaghetti. While David was enjoying a glass of beer, René had his favourite, café con leche. It was as if he was addicted to this type of coffee. Sitting back with his coffee in hand, René began to let David know that he needed a day off from walking.

"I'm sorry, David. I am completely worn out. There's no way that I could walk sixteen kilometres to Belorado, let alone another twenty-eight to reach Villafranca Montes de Oca," René apologised. "I truly am sorry, but this old man has gone too far, too fast. I hope you understand."

"Yeah," David sighed with an air of disappointment. "I was wondering how you were holding up, especially since Santo Domingo."

"I assume you will have to go on, what with your needing to be in Burgos early in two days' time."

"Yeah, it has to do with business," explained David. "It was one of the conditions I set for myself when I left Toronto; that I would make time for meetings in Burgos and Leon. I have a tight schedule and millions of dollars are riding on the results of these meetings."

"Let's just enjoy this evening," suggested René. "Who knows, I just might show up in Burgos while you're still there. What do you say?"

"Sounds great. Now let's go get some stuff for supper. We need to buy a bottle of wine too. Can't say goodbye without sharing a few good toasts to honour our respective journeys."

When they returned to the community kitchen at the parish hostel, they were invited to add their meal to a general potluck meal with the others who were staying that night at the hostel. While René prepared the spaghetti sauce, David ground up a hunk of hard white cheese while the rotini was cooking in the pot. They had bought rotini noodles as the tienda had run out of spaghetti. Someone had managed to find a grocery store in the town and had purchased fresh veggies to make a large salad. One woman had bought a selection of fruit from a vendor who had a table set up a table in the square and had created a fruit salad. While the smells of the evening meal were wafting about in the kitchen, someone opened a few bottles of cheap local wine to make the pleasant task even merrier. When it was time to sit down at the communal table to begin the meal, the parish priest joined them at the table and offered a prayer of thanks for the food and for the path that had led them to gather together on the Camino.

René managed to find a quiet moment to hug David and wish him well with the rest of his journey. It finally dawned on René that he had spent the last few days on someone else's journey, not his own. It was time for him to carve his own path again on the Camino regardless of what lay in store for him.

> *Well, that decision to "run" was a mistake. Trying to walk someone else's path for the Camino rather than my own, no matter how uncomfortable my path was, was a serious and complete failure. I really didn't escape from the complex surrounding nudity was concerned as David's story had more than enough nudity in it, and it was the wrong kind of nudity.*
>
> *If anything, these past few days have taught me that there is a difference, something that Freya, Asha, and Sid were trying to tell me when I refused to listen. Maybe this episode was actually worth it? Maybe fate was conspiring to have me face my complex? Makes me think of what Jung once said:* "When an inner situation is not made conscious, it appears outside as fate."
>
> *It's time for me to contact and then rejoin my Camino family, our Little Company of Pilgrims.*

Chapter Fourteen – Our Ladies of the Way

Out of habit, René woke up when the others began stirring. He could have slept in, but he realised that going back to sleep would be impossible. In spite of the ache in his lower back and the pain in his feet and legs, the urge to walk was too strong to resist.

"I thought you were going to rest here for a day?" whispered David who was putting his sleeping bag liner into his backpack.

"I have decided to walk to the next town, Redecilla del Camino. After spending some quiet time in the church there, I will figure out what I am doing. All I know, David, is that I have to trust myself with the rest of this Camino, something I have avoiding like the plague."

"I understand," sympathised David. "What do you say? Wanna walk together to Redecilla? It's your call."

"I'd love too."

Not long after leaving the village of Grañon, they passed a sign telling them that they were entering into the province of Castilla y Leon. The walking soon became easier as the route was almost flat as they covered the four kilometres to the village. Once there, they embraced and with promises to keep in contact, and with wishes of "Buen Camino!" David walked on to continue his pilgrimage of penitence.

It was a quiet, almost silent village. The church Nuestra Señora de la Calle, was closed at this early hour, however, the hostel, Hospederia, was open and had a bench next to a drink vending machine. Two pilgrims were just leaving the hostel complaining about the hostel and the village. From the scowls on their faces, René somehow doubted that they found anything on their journey worthy of their high standards. Some people are just never satisfied. 'There I go again,' René muttered to himself, 'being judgmental when I have no idea of their story!'

René walked into the hostel only to be told that he couldn't get a bed until eleven later that morning. René asked if there was a café nearby where he could have some desayuno, some breakfast. The woman gave him directions to the café-bar in the village. With a grateful "Muchos gracias, señora!" René turned to exit the hostel and get his backpack which he had left on the bench. He heard her respond, "Vaya con Dios y Buen Camino, señor!"

René found the café without any problem in the tiny village of a hundred and fifty souls. Ordering his coffee and breakfast, he took out his guidebook to come up with a plan for the rest of the day. He noticed that the next villages were even smaller. However, there remained only thirteen kilometres to the town of Belorado where he had planned to stop for the day. The idea of slowing down and smelling the roses along the way, elicited a smile from him, a welcome feeling. He had the time to slow down and see more clearly, to capture what his eyes might see, those images hidden behind the façade of outward appearances. He resolved to begin with the church he had passed in the village. Thanking the owner, René returned to explore the Iglesia Nuestra Señora de la Calle, Our Lady of the Street – Our Lady of the Way.

In spite of taking his time, René arrived in Belorado early, perhaps too early to check into a hostel where he could leave his backpack while discovering what Belorado had to offer him. Much of the walking to reach the town was on a senda, a gravelled path that paralleled the highway. Regardless of the time of check-in, René made his way to the albergue. Much to his surprise, the hostel had a restaurant where he could have lunch and free Wi-Fi. It had been a few days since his last e-mail to those back home in Canada. As a bonus, the hostel had just opened up receive pilgrims. All the signs told René that he had found a place where he was supposed to be for his own Camino. When he had chosen his bed, the first one to do so as it was so early in the day, and had sorted out the tasks that needed to be taken care of, René returned to the restaurant carrying his tablet and his journal. As always, his camera was in its bag on his hips. He ordered a bocadillo and a huge plate of papas fritas, French fries, to go along with his café con leche as he was suddenly feeling hungrier than he had for some time.

Finally, with his appetite satiated, he leaned back in his seat to enjoy another cup of coffee as he connected to the Internet in order to download his messages and then upload his photos from the morning's walk from Grañon. He was surprised to see an e-mail from Fred among the many others, too many others. He definitely needed to unsubscribe from most of the mail-outs from companies and interest groups. Of course, his priority was to read the three e-mails from his kids and his ex-wife Cécile, and then reply to them before doing anything else.

Cécile and the kids had been worried about his silence of the past few days. Was he alright? Where was he? Feeling guilty, he checked to see if any of them were on-line so that he could chat with whoever he could connect with, even try a Skype video call. He checked and saw that no one was on-line before realising that it wasn't even six in the morning yet, back home in Ottawa. He'd try again later when it would be more likely to find one of them on-line. René took his time to write lengthy responses to these e-mails, making sure to let them know that he would Skype them later. As he wrote, a few tears began to course down his cheeks.

When another pilgrim in the restaurant, one who had stopped to eat, but not to stay, saw his tears, she asked him, "¿Esta bien?", René answered the concern expressed with a smile that he was definitely okay. His tears were good tears about missing home and his family. Satisfied, the woman turned back to talking with two other ladies who were obviously her walking companions.

René then returned to Fred's e-mail. He also wondered if René was okay. He was worried that maybe René had given up on the Camino. The group was still walking together, well that is with the exception of Freya and Miryam who had simply disappeared the same day as René had left. They had talked of walking faster and further without saying why. He hoped that René would write him soon and let them know where he was and how he was doing.

René wasted no time in replying to the email:

Hi Fred,

Sorry for disappearing like I did. As I write this, I'm in a small town called Belorado. I had met up with another Canadian who walking hard and fast, I guess like Freya and Miryam. It was only yesterday when I realised that I was running, not from Freya or the whole business of nudity, but from myself, something that I didn't want to surface and have to deal with. I sent the other Canadian, David, on ahead as I am too tired to keep running. I am now walking at a snail's pace, just doing seventeen kilometres today. I hope that somehow, we can meet up again on the Camino. Let me know where you guys are at, and we can figure out where and when we can meet up.

Cheers, René

Next, René upload his photos to his Flickr account, choosing a few for posting to his Facebook account for family and friends. René made sure to include the fact that he had already hiked 250 kilometres leaving just 550 left to reach Santiago. When he finished all of these tasks, he took his tablet and journal back to his bunk as he wasn't ready to write in the journal anymore. The hostel had a luxury that he just couldn't pass up, a swimming pool. Though he was the only one in the pool, he chose to swim in his extra pair of hiking shorts just in case someone decided to also go swimming.

Refreshed by the water in the swimming pool, René lay in his bunk to try connecting with his kids or with Cécile. There were messages that told him they would be home for a call later, asking him how long he would stay up. He returned the messages saying he would try again just before he went to sleep. With extra time now on his hands, he decided to go out to explore the town. He didn't have to worry about where he would eat that evening as he intended in enjoying the pilgrim menu at the hostel's restaurant.

He walked to the town square, Plaza Mayor, as that seemed to be the best place to start as it was just a block away. At the centre of the square was a treed area within a circular walkway. The town hall made for a good photo as well. He also saw a long covered walkway along one side of the square that was held up by pillars giving the whole thing the appearance of wealth and privilege which was to be expected as the houses were former homes of nobility in Belorado. René then walked away from the square in order to get photos of the town's numerous churches and whatever else he could discover. He stopped for a late afternoon coffee at one of the many small cafés that could be found on the narrow winding streets. He was tired, more than physically tired. He began to think that this would be a better place and time for a rest day than in Burgos.

After a good rest at the café, René made his way back to the hostel and checked for messages thinking that Fred might have replied. To his pleasure and surprise, there was an e-mail waiting for him.

> *Hi there, René,*
>
> *Great to hear from you. We are about a day behind you. I talked with the others and they think we could be in Belorado by late tomorrow afternoon. Could you reserve beds for us? Let me know as soon as you can.*
>
> *Cheers, Fred*

René quickly headed to the registration area to see if he could indeed reserve beds for his friends as well as to find out if he could stay a second night. Getting affirmative responses to both questions, he returned to answer the e-mail.

> *Just a quick note, Fred. The beds have been booked. Looking forward to seeing all of you tomorrow.*

Sending it off, he decided to take advantage of the time until the evening meal to do some reading and listening to some relaxing songs stored on his tablet.

René found himself at a table with pilgrims who were only walking as far as Burgos. Each year they had been walking during their vacations all the way from Le Puy en Velay, in France. They had two more years of hiking planned to reach Santiago. Since René was fluent in French they were able to chat with him in their native tongue. It wasn't often that René got to speak French on the Camino. The evening passed quickly and pleasurably for all with many toasts of good cheer and lots of laughter. When the meal finally ended, everyone made their way into their respective rooms to get ready for sleep and another day's walking.

René woke up early as usual, as the pilgrims around him prepared to leave for the day's hike. The morning had been spent reading and doing laundry with occasional breaks for coffee. The weather had been cooler with an occasional shower thrown in. As noon approached, Freya and Miryam wandered into the hostel for lunch. When René appeared a short while later for his own lunch, he was surprised to find the two women there.

"Ah, there you are," stated Freya as though she had expected to see René. "I thought we would catch up to you today. You gave us quite a chase."

"You mean you were walking ahead of the others just to catch up with me?" asked René in surprise. "What if I had kept on going and not stayed an extra night?"

"Well," stated Freya with obviousness, "I knew that you would have to slow down sooner or later. At some point running would break you and then we would catch up to you."

René was stunned and speechless.

"Now, let's order some lunch," Miryam suggested

The two women talked about their walk since leaving the others behind then in pursuit of René, while he continued to pick at his food. When they had finished their meal, Freya and Miryam checked in to the hostel. They then took their packs into the same room where René had spent the night.

"God, I need a shower," said Freya as she stripped down to get ready. Miryam soon followed suit and both paraded naked past René on their way to the shower. Again René felt his face flush with heat, however, he refrained as best he could from letting them see his embarrassment.

"No need to be embarrassed, René. After all, you've seen more than one woman's nude body in your lifetime. We're all the same, with the same bits in the same places," lectured Freya with a hint of humour in her voice. Turning back, she gave her butt a little wiggle knowing it would only embarrass René further.

The women emerged from the shower towelling themselves off using their micro-fiber towels that most pilgrims used in an effort to keep their pack weight down. Since it was raining again, they decided to check out the indoor swimming pool. They wrapped their towels around themselves and padded barefoot down the hallway to the pool to see if it was busy. Finding it empty, Freya told Miryam that she would be right back as she was going to get René to join them.

"Okay, out of those clothes right now," she instructed René. "You're coming swimming with us."

"I don't think we're allowed to swim in the pool without bathing suits," protested René."

"We're in Europe, not North America, for crying out loud. Get over it. Now get your butt out of those clothes or I'll take them off for you."

René was certain that Freya would follow up on her threat if he didn't strip down. Seeing as it was just swimming, he slipped off his shorts revealing that he wasn't wearing briefs of boxers beneath the shorts. "Well?" she asked as if he was a slow learner, "get your towel and let's go swimming."

René slipped into the water dropping his towel at the last minute when they got to the pool. Seeing that they were the only ones in the pool, he gave a sigh of relief as the water enveloped him.

"Not so bad now, is it?" called out Miryam. "Do you know how to swim?"

His answer was to swim the length of the pool underwater to the deep end. When he surfaced, the two women were swimming leisurely towards him.

"Doesn't that feel good?" asked Freya. "It sure beats swimming with a swim suit on. I love how the water feels on my body as it flows over me. I mean it feels delicious. Don't you agree?"

René hesitated for a moment as though he had to consider his answer. To his surprise, he had to agree, "Yeah! It does feel good, better than swimming in my shorts like last night." Then stealing a quick glance to the door, he asked, "But what if someone comes in and sees us? Doesn't that bother you?"

Both women looked at him as if he had said something ludicrous. "Why should it bother us?" answered Miryam. "They won't see anything they shouldn't see. A man is a man, and a woman is a woman."

"Besides," added Freya, "No one will come in."

Freya came closer to René and touched his arm. An electric shock from her touch surprised him.

"Um," he protested weakly, "I'm married and faithful to my wife."

Freya looked at him with a hint of surprise and even anger "You're not married. You used to be married. And as for being faithful, I would say it was more about cowardice than about faithfulness. Anyways, what the hell has that to do with swimming in a swimming pool with two women?" she demanded. "Don't get the wrong idea there buddy. This isn't about sex because you sure as hell are not getting any from us! Men," she sneered, "That's all they think about, sticking their pathetic little spears into women. God, you're all so pathetic."

Confused, René looked at the two women and asked, "Then what has this been all about?"

"It's simple. We're naturists and we love being nude whenever we have the opportunity. Whatever gave you the impression that it was anything more than that?" quizzed Miryam.

"Uh ... well ... you said you were deliberately wanting to catch up with me ... and . . uh . . . I mean you practically forced me to be here swimming nude with you. What was I supposed to think?" pleaded René.

"What? So we said we knew we would catch up with you. We sure as hell didn't say that we were trying to seduce you; which by the way, whether you know it or not, we could do successfully if that was our intention. After all, you're a man and, men are not all that much in control of themselves, their bodies, as you might think. Your body gives you away, René. No, I'm not, we're not trying to get you into bed with us."

"So why?" he asked even more confused than ever.

"Why what?" demanded Freya.

"Why all of this? This inviting me to take a nude shower with you, to swim nude with you? All of that!"

"The shower room was for several people and I don't know anyone who showers any other way than nude. As for swimming nude, I already told you. Swimming is always better when one doesn't have to wear a bathing suit. Even you said if feels good."

The two women swam off leaving René alone in the deep end. When they got to the ladder, they climbed out, dried themselves off as best they could, then they left closing the door behind them. René swam over to the ladder and climbed out then tried to dry himself off quickly so that he could wrap the towel around his waist. Then, he sat down on a bench alongside the pool and tried to figure out what had just happened.

When he returned to his dorm room, he quickly slipped on his shorts and a top. Both of the women were gone and René suspected that they had gone sightseeing in the town. Looking at his watch, he figured he might as well go back to the hostel's restaurant and grab a cup of coffee and try to sort through all of it. Out of habit, he put his camera pack around his waist and grabbed his tablet and journal. He intended to stay at the restaurant until Fred and the others arrived.

It was a soggy crew that arrived late that afternoon. In spite of the dreary day, they were glad to have finally rejoined René, Freya and Miryam. Mark was especially pleased to see Miryam again. After they had showered and changed, laundry was done with the dryer being a welcome feature at the hostel, as it was unlikely that their clothing would have dried out otherwise in time for the next day's hike.

"Man it's good to see you again," exclaimed Fred as he slapped René on the back. "I was afraid that I would have to listen to Gabe's stories without ever getting a word in edgewise for the rest of the Camino," he grinned.

"It's good to see you as well," admitted René wearing a smile of appreciation as well as relief. "Freya and Miryam got here four hours ago. From your email, I would've thought they had been ahead of me, not behind me.

"So, where shall we go for something to warm the innards, a nice cerveza or two would really help right now."

"Well, there is a good place along the town square, not too far," replied René. "However, the restaurant here has it all as well. No need to get wet again if you don't have to."

The whole crew celebrated being back together for the rest of the evening. There was a heated discussion about whether or not to make the fifty kilometres to Burgos a two-day or a three-day trek. In the end, with the reality of having a rough stretch of hills along the way to Burgos, caution won out. The next day would be a short day of twelve kilometres to Villa Franca Montes de Oca. The following day they planned on an eighteen kilometre hike, with the remaining twenty kilometres to Burgos on the third day.

Looking around at his friends, René felt that he had made the right choice in spending a rest day in Belorado. Sid caught his eye and called him over to the end of the table where he sat.

"I have missed you, my friend. How has your meditation been?"

René thought for a second before replying, "The truth is Sid, I didn't meditate at all since my last meditation with you, Fred and Asha."

"Ah, tomorrow, perhaps we can meditate together again," suggested Sid. "Asha and I have talked about large-group meditation. It now seems to me that with shorter hikes for the next three days, this would be an excellent opportunity for all of us to try this. What do you think?"

"I like that idea," admitted René who realised that part of his moodiness of the past three days could also be attributed to not meditating. "It would help bring us together, almost as if we were a sangha. I have to admit that I miss taking part in group meditation. So how do we go about making that happen?"

"I will take care of that. As long as you follow my lead, all will work out well."

"Great! I'm looking forward to it," admitted René with a smile.

Then it was time to turn in. Once the night routines were done, René took some time to write in his journal. All was well in his world again.

> *Good intentions to accept nudity as natural, I again ended up making a fool out of myself with Freya and with Miryam. They quickly put me in my place for assuming that nudity, their nudity, was an invitation for sex.*
>
> *It was good to be all together again. We are going to slow down the pace a bit for the next few days, something that Sid suggested might be a good time to have the whole group join in on meditation.*
>
> *I finally got to connect with the kids – we did a group call. They have been enjoying the photos and the e-mails whenever I have managed to connect with the Internet. I warned them that there would be more silent periods as getting connected wasn't always possible. I think that they will handle my silences a lot easier*

knowing that. I also asked them to call Cécile and let her know that I was okay.

Now, it's time for some sleep.

Chapter Fifteen – A Bump On The Road

The walk to Tosantos, only five kilometres away, had taken the group almost an hour and a half. They had left Belorado after eating breakfast. The skies were clear and fresh after the rain the day before. Luca had decided that we could all use some coffee in the tiny village that was supposed to be home to eighty people. Over coffee, a decision was made to make a small detour that would add less than two kilometres to their short hike for the day, to see the hermitage of Our Lady of the Rock, Ermita de la Virgen de la Peña, a twelfth century structure built into the face of a cliff. Since the group hadn't had the time to visit the cliff-face ruins in Belorado, as well as René's curiosity, René was in favour of the project.

As expected, the hermitage was locked, the mysteries of the Virgin Mary and her Christ Child locked within it. As they turned to head back to Tosantos, Sid nodded to René who understood that this is where Sid was going to lead them in group meditation. Picking up his cue, René remarked to the group that this seemed a good place to stop for a little while for meditation.

"What do you think, Sid?" he then asked turning back to look at his accomplice.

To his surprise, Sid had already taken a Lotus pose on one of the rocks, as had Asha who sat on a rock slightly lower than Sid. Both were now naked. René wondered how this had all happened so fast without his even noticing. The group responded in silence as they found their own rock, or patch of grass, to sit on in various poses and positions. Their clothing lay in small, folded heaps beside them. All turned to face Sid. Realising that he would the last to take his seat, René hurried to find his own place on the grass, in a spot left free, next to Asha.

In a moment he was sitting like all the rest, clad only in the early morning sunshine. Sid led them in meditation surrounded by nature.

An hour later, they returned towards Tosantos and continued on with their journey. Their next stop was planned for Espinosa del Camino where another bar-café would be found. It wasn't that they needed to stop for another rest; it simply was that they didn't want to rush into Villafranca. Somehow there was an unspoken need to make the moment last a bit longer before they got busy with ordinary life in another hostel.

While sitting peacefully relaxed a little while later in Espinosa, René turned to Sid and asked about something that had stuck in his mind. "Sid, you said something about illusions, about how everything is our thoughts. It reminded me of what various Buddhist writers and teachers have also said. Are you a Buddhist? It is hard to imagine any of the Buddhists I know, meditating nude. Well, that is with exception, perhaps, of the New-Agey kind of Buddhists."

"No, I am not a Buddhist, I am simply Sid. Though if you check closer, you will find that there are a group of Buddhists who do live skyclad. They are, as a group, embracing Tantra and all that Tantra comprises. Vajrayana, is often depicted with the image of Yab Yum, a version of the Hindu Shiva-Shakti union of male and female. In psychology, if I am not mistaken, you call this the union of consciousness and unconsciousness."

"Yes," replied an enthused René. "Jung called this the Holy Marriage, a state where the parts of the self are made whole. So, I am guessing that you are Hindu, or maybe even Jain if you're not a Buddhist?"

"When I was a child, I was raised as Hindu. However, I left the confines of that religion, and have been looking for something that felt more authentic. I am still on that journey of discovery," he explained to René and the others who were now listening to their conversation. "I didn't find what I was looking for in the outer world, just the realisation that the answers weren't likely to be found out there."

"I understand, I think," responded René. "But, if there aren't answers to be found, why are we all searching for the answers?"

Sid considered the question for a moment as if searching for the best way to answer the question. "It isn't that there aren't answers; it's that we have all been looking for them in all the wrong places. I don't know if I can explain it all that well. I've tried going deep within, through meditation, fasting and so on; I've tried every outer world experience as well only to end up frustrated. Then, it hit me. What if the answer is in the middle? With that idea, I finally found some peace of mind. I call it the middle way."

Standing up, Sid put on his backpack, "Well, enough about me. Let's go find our beds for tonight."

René looked curiously at Sid as he began walking down the trail. 'The Middle Way. That is the concise definition of Buddhism,' he thought. 'Who is this Sid anyway?'

The village of Villafranca de Montes de Oca was small, however they had no problem finding beds for the night in the hostel section of the San Anton Abad Hotel which meant they would have free Wi-Fi, a bar and a restaurant within. Since no one had worked up much of a sweat, laundry was ignored with the exception of socks and underwear. After a quick shower, René headed down with the others to the restaurant to see what was on the menu for lunch. As usual, René couldn't resist a bocadillowith papas fritas, along with yet another coffee.

When lunch was over, several of his friends walked with him to take photos of the village's church and other sites that were waiting to be discovered. It didn't take long for them to find themselves at the western end of the town. The guide book talked of another hermitage about three kilometres down a side road. Feeling well rested, René wanted to check it out, and perhaps find the reservoir that was near the hermitage. Fred, Freya and Miryam decided that they, too, wanted to do a bit of exploring.

For some strange reason as they walked down the quiet paved road, the place made René think of the Canadian prairies with the rolling hills, grain fields which had recently been swathed, and large, square bales of straw. René was soon busy taking photos of farming in Spain. Earlier on the Camino he had taken photos of vineyards, which weren't part of the typical Canadian farming culture with a few notable exceptions in British Columbia and the Golden Triangle area of Ontario. After what seemed like an hour and with still no reservoir or hermitage in sight, René called a halt.

"I think we're on the wrong road."

"What? God, what a typical man," complained Freya. "And I suppose you didn't ask for directions back in Villafranca, did you?"

"I was following the guide book," he protested.

"Good excuse," Freya muttered. Turning to Miryam she said, "Let's head back. I'm ready for a good glass of wine. With that, both women began walking back down the road towards Villafranca.

"I guess we'd better join them," remarked Fred. "We're definitely on the wrong road. But, no sweat man," he added. "You've seen one hermitage, you've seen them all."

They arrived back at the town and stopped for a drink at the El Pajaro Bar. By then, Freya had cooled down and was back on speaking terms with the men.

"So tell me, Fred," she began, "Do you have as many hang-ups about nudity as René does?"

"I don't think I do," Fred answered a bit cautiously, "Not that I'd say that René has hang-ups about nudity either. You've both seen him meditate nude."

"You don't know the half of it," Freya continued. "I mean, what do you think when you see a woman or two naked? Do you, like, get embarrassed, get horny, or what?"

"Ah," remarked Fred, "I'd have to say it is all about context."

"See," said Freya as she turned to René, "He's got it. Just because we're naked doesn't mean we want to jump in the sack with you!"

Fred turned to René with a look of confusion on his face, "What was that all about?"

"Trust me," sighed René, "You don't want to know the half of it. Let's head back to the hostel and see what the others are doing. The women will come when they're ready."

It was just a few blocks back to the hostel from the bar which was just close enough to avoid having Freya continue her challenge of René and his issues with nakedness, especially of women being naked.

Back at the hostel, René retreated to his bunk and logged into the Wi-Fi network. When he saw that Cécile was online, he smiled realising that unless she was talking with one of their kids, she would finally be able to talk with him. The call went well. He could hear the two young children she had conceived with her second husband as they stood beside their mother. They called him Uncle Ray and as always, it made him smile inside and out. When the call was done, René had no desire to join the others for the evening meal, with his feelings of homesickness.

"Let's go to dinner," stated Freya as she came into the dorm in search of the absent, René. Seeing the hint of tears that remained at the fringes of his eyes, Freya responded with concern rather than her usual combativeness, "What's the matter?"

"Nothing's the matter," said René defensively.

"Bullshit! Now, what the hell has got you upset?"

"I just skyped my ex-wife," he admitted. "She was upset at my long silence, worried for our kids as well as the two from her second marriage. Though we're divorced, there are still strong feelings that connect us. I feel as if I am being selfish and inconsiderate of others, people I love, with spending almost six weeks in Spain, just walking. The sad thing is that I don't even know why I decided that the Camino was something I had to do in the first place."

"So what are you going to do, quit? Go running back to mama with your tail between your legs? She doesn't need you, René. She's married. Why can't you let her go?"

"But I don't even know why I am doing this anymore anyway," René said as he buried his head between his arms.

"Did she ask, beg you to come home? Is that it? Is she still controlling you? I don't think so. I think you are feeling guilty and sorry for yourself."

"No. She didn't ask me to come home. She wouldn't do that," admitted René.

"Exactly!" pronounced René. "God, men are so pathetic sometimes," she muttered to herself. "Do you think that she will be happy to find out that her tears brought your pilgrimage to a crashing halt? Do you think that was her intention?"

"I ... I don't know ... maybe not ... "

"Listen. Look at me, dammit. And listen."

René lifted his head with tears streaming down his face, a man torn with indecision and guilt.

"Of course she was upset. You went silent in a foreign country. If you ran back home without finishing this, you wouldn't fix anything – there's nothing to fix. All that would happen is that she would then feel guilty for sabotaging your pilgrimage. And, she would be angry with you for that. Now, wipe the tears off your face and let's go eat."

Reluctantly, René followed Freya to the hostel's restaurant where the others were already busy chatting and enjoying tapas while waiting for their meal. He offered a weak smile as he took a seat at the table between Freya and Luca. Almost as soon as he was seated, the first course of that night's pilgrim menu was served. He ate mechanically, not really paying attention to what he was eating, or what others were saying. René was thankful that Freya had decided not to make a fuss over his quietness, or to embarrass him in front of the others.

When supper was done, René was the first to leave the table, saying to the others that he was going to write in his journal. Wishes of "Buenas noches! Good Night! and Gute Nacht!" rang out as most of them decided to follow René's example. Only Fred and Jason remained behind to finish their beer and try to get the last word in their discussion.

> *I got lost today when I was leading a few of the others on a side trip to a hermitage. That wasn't the only place where I was lost. When I finally talked with Cécile on the computer, I got lost again. I didn't know why I was making this pilgrimage anymore [I still don't have that answer] and I got lost in guilt feelings ready to throw away the pilgrimage. Freya got mad when I suggested that I should return home. She was saying that I would just be making Cécile feel guilty for showing her feelings. In her anger Freya reminded me that I wasn't married anymore.*
>
> *For the first time, I have to be thankful for Freya's presence. Though I haven't admitted it to her, she has helped me get a better understanding of what has happened. This pilgrimage is harder than I had anticipated, harder on the head and the heart. I have until Burgos to think this through thoroughly before making a final decision about staying on the Camino or leaving.*

Chapter Sixteen – Changes On The Journey

The first three and a half kilometres, the next morning, were straight uphill, climbing two hundred metres in that short distance to reach the peak of Mojapán. A monument and picnic table gave the small company of pilgrims a place to sit for a short respite before they tackled a very steep descent to the Peroja River. They crossed the river on a footbridge before immediately beginning another ascent to yet another peak. At the top, they began the descent into a valley which offered the group another option to see another hermitage. At the crossroads where they sat to change their socks and give their feet a rest, René agreed with Sid that the hermitage would be a good place for them to do another group meditation. Looking at the hill that had yet to be climbed, the others agreed. After all, the total distance for the day wasn't so much that it would put any extra pressure on them to walk faster as a result.

The three hundred and fifty metres down the side trail was the Ermita de Valdefuentes, was close to a river in what could only be described as a wilderness area. The hermitage was a small square building that had been repaired two hundred years earlier. The hermitage was all that was left of an old Camino hospital. There were open areas in the forest of oak and evergreen trees which provided an excellent place for the group to meditate without having to worry about passersby. Sid chose his spot on a slight rise that allowed the rest of the pilgrims to sit in the open sunshine, just slightly downhill from him. Besides time for meditation, Sid had something he wanted to say, what could best be described as a teaching. Soon all in the group were settled into various meditation positions with their clothing left to the side.

After about twenty minutes of silence, Sid began to speak:

"The essence of life is that it's challenging. Sometimes life is sweet, and sometimes it is bitter. Sometimes your body tenses, and sometimes it relaxes or opens. Sometimes you have a headache, and sometimes you feel a hundred percent healthy. From an awakened perspective, trying to tie up all the loose ends and finally get it together is death, because it involves rejecting a lot of your basic experience. There is something aggressive about that approach to life, trying to flatten out all the rough spots and imperfections into a nice smooth ride."

"To be fully alive, fully human, and completely awake is to be continually thrown out of the safety of a nest. To live fully is to be always in a no-man's-land, to experience each moment as completely new and fresh. To live is to be willing to die over and over again."

Fred was confused with what he heard, "What does that mean, Sid?"

"Simply, probably it can be said that to be fully alive, we should risk, we should allow ourselves to be vulnerable – be here now, not looking forward or backward, or trying to control the moments, events, and people of our present, or from our past."

"I think I got it," Fred spoke with caution.

"Maybe you have," chuckled Sid. "But don't hold on to that thought too tightly."

Following another twenty minutes of silent meditation after Sid's teaching, everyone got back into their hiking clothes and continued walking the last four kilometres to San Juan de Ortega, where they had planned on having lunch. Once they regained the main pilgrim trail, they hiked up to a peak, which had a wayside cross, and then began a gentle three and a half kilometre descent into San Juan. They found the bar, a place called Marcela's on the plaza with a restored church dating back to 1150, only a few steps away.

The group didn't rush through their meal. They had only six more kilometres yet to go until their planned stop at Atapuerca. As they sat around their adjoining tables, Jason addressed Sid, "Your words earlier remind me of Buddhism. In fact the whole thing, well with the exception of being naked while meditating, seemed Buddhist, the practice of the middle way."

"I like that idea of the middle way," remarked Sid. "But I have to tell you that I am not a Buddhist. I'm not even sure what or who a Buddhist is supposed to be."

"Well, I just wanted to add that in my book which I recently wrote, In The Middle, I talked about some similar ideas. Perhaps you'd be interested in what I had to say about these ideas?"

"But of course," Sid returned with a gesture of his hands to include the others. "I think we would all like to hear your thoughts."

"Well, your talk reminded me of how our lives are tragic, in the sense that we often die psychologically, before we die physically. In the book, I said, if I remember correctly, 'We live tragic lives when we live unconsciously.' Of course, I was paraphrasing Carl Jung's words when I wrote that."

"Interesting. Of course, I agree with you that to remain unconscious is a tragedy."

"You also spoke of death and dying. For me, as I understand it, death not an end but a passage. I believe that it is necessary to go through the Middle Path to more nearly achieve one's potential and to earn the vitality and wisdom of mature aging. It's sort of like answering the call to the Camino, you know, a summons from within to move from the false self that is attempting trying to control life, to living provisionally, to risk authentic living."

"Excellent! I like how you referred to it as a call from living provisionally to risking authentic living."

The exchange ignited a broader dialogue amongst most of the group with the exception of René and Freya. René noticed Freya's silence and sensed that he would be hearing from her later on the topic. That foreboding retreated as he listened to the ebbs and flows of the conversation until it was time to put socks and boots back on and enjoy the barely perceptible downhill walk through Agés and into Atapuerca.

The group checked into the hostel, La Hutte, which was just below the 15th century church of San Martin. Next came the regular rituals of washing clothing and showering before relaxing for a few moments on beds. After a short rest, Mark roused the group with a call to go and have a brew. They found a small bar-café close by and sat beneath table umbrellas while enjoying their preferred beverages, and some convivial chat. After a day of hiking up and down mountains, there wasn't much interest in exploring the village for most of the group. So, René found himself alone as he left to wander with his camera.

The day had been a good one for René. Before they had gone to the bar for a drink, he had managed to send Cécile and the kids' e-mails about the day and about the plans to be in Burgos the next day keeping the e-mail focused on these small things.

René returned to the hostel about ninety minutes later, satisfied with the images he had captured. As he neared the hostel he saw a few of his friends, Fred, Gabe, Freya and Miryam, sitting at a table enjoying a few snack foods and the sunshine. Rather than return to the tight quarters of the hostel, he decided to join them. Fred was explaining his blog site to Gabe. Like most pastors, Fred spent a lot of his writing time explaining traditional topics which gave Fred a lot to talk about.

Freya was listening to Miryam talk about life back in Israel. Her home was in a small fishing village called Magdala. René decided to listen to Miryam's story of her home by the sea where generations of her family had fished; and about religion and the politics of life in her village. Miryam had lost her husband who had been charged with treason and executed. She had been a widow and a single mother ever since. Their son had grown up and now had his own family. Her family had roots going back several hundred years and perhaps even thousands of years in Israel. As she finished, she turned to René. "What about you, René?" asked Miryam. "Tell me about your home."

René explained as best he could living in Canada's capital city in eastern Canada. Like her, he had roots going back hundreds of years in Canada, European roots. However he also had aboriginal roots, which went back thousands of years, though there was no way to track that part of his heritage. When he finished telling his tale, and answering Miryam's questions, it was time to head back and gather the others and head out to their evening meal.

The next morning, the small company of pilgrims found themselves on the trail early. At first light, they left Atapuerca. They soon found themselves again climbing up a hill that turned from a gentle climb into a much steeper climb up a rocky path. At the top of the hill, the view back to Atapuerca and the surrounding countryside was too much for René to resist. As the others began their long descent, he photographed the scenes in front of him, including the trail of pilgrims going forward, which included his friends. Tucking his camera back into his pack, he hustled down the trail to catch up with the others. By the time they reached Orbaneja Riopico, they had covered eight kilometres. It was time for coffee and a second breakfast, time to give their strained legs a rest from the workout, especially the descent, which was hard work on the dirt and stone trails that were poorly marked.

However, because of their nearness to Burgos, the rest stop wasn't as long as their usual pause en route. At Castañares they stopped at the crossroads. They had to decide whether to follow the path along the highway, or to take the path along the river which would add about a half kilometre to their distance. Not surprisingly, there was no consensus, so the group split in two with Jason, Gabe, Luca, Mark, and Miryam taking the main trail into Burgos. René, Fred, Freya, Sid and Asha opted for the optional route along the river. The plan was for them all to meet at the Cathedral in Burgos where they then could make a decision on where to stay for the night.

When René's group became unsure of their path, he asked for directions to the Puente de Santa Maria, which was the entrance into the old, central part of the city. From that bridge, they would then go on to the cathedral. Though they had walked four hundred extra metres and had stopped to enquire about directions twice, they arrived at the cathedral before any of the others. However, it wasn't long before Fred spotted the others as they entered the plaza. Just under twenty kilometres in five and a half hours; it was early enough in the afternoon, so registration at a hostel wasn't going to be a problem. The only problem was which one to choose? René thought that they should stay at the Albergue Divina Pastora as it was very small with only room for eighteen pilgrims. However, the majority were in favour of the Albergue La Casa del Cubo. Since both places were relatively close to the cathedral, René had no problem with the group's choice.

Soon, they were checked in, getting bunks on the fourth level, in the quietest part of the hostel. Their post-walk routines kicked in and before long everyone was ready to head out for lunch and then a bit of sightseeing. For lunch, they decided to return to the Church Plaza where they had seen a restaurant that would be the best place from which to start their tour of the Cathedral before branching out. Since they were likely to wander, the plan was to meet again at the hostel by seven that evening so they could go out to a pilgrim meal together.

Following lunch, René let his camera and instincts guide him as he wandered. He was fortunate in that he had a built in sense of direction, which allowed him to easily landmark his walking path in most cities. With a city tourism map as backup, which he had picked up at the hostel's desk, he made stops at the San Martin and San Esteban churches before heading on to the Plaza Alonso Martinez. From there, he decided to walk down the pilgrim path to the Arco San Juan and the Plaza Santa Lesmes. Following a strange trail of streets that seemed to disregard all sense of order and planning, he finally arrived at Plaza Mayor where he got photos of City Hall. As he was heading back to the cathedral square, he saw a group of his friends sitting outside a tiny bar enjoying tapas, beer and a few other bits of strange-looking finger food.

"Ah, speak of the devil," called out, Mark. "We were wondering when you'd get enough photos. Here, pull up a stool and have a cool one."

René grinned as he joined the group. For whatever reason, he had come to see Mark as a quiet and trusted friend in the group. Looking around he saw that Luca and Jason were also present. It seemed as though the women were off shopping. As for Sid, Gabe and Fred, they didn't have any idea where they had disappeared to in the slightest. In front of the guys, sat a few empty plates and several empty glasses which told René that they had spent most of their time at the bar.

"So," remarked Mark, "Do you think you got enough photos?"

"Enough for now," laughed René. "I want to get some more of the cathedral before sunset, and then again after sunset when it is lit with floodlights."

"What the hell, excuse my French, are you going to do with all these photos?" Mark cajoled. "I'd hate to be your family or neighbours being forced to sit through a photo presentation of your Camino. Why you must have thousands of photos already?"

Chuckling, René asked Mark if he wanted to see all of them that evening. The good-natured ribbing continued, while they passed a congenial half-hour sipping their drinks before René decided that he wanted to get a few pre-sunset photos. René said he'd meet the guys back at the hostel before too long.

On his way back to the hostel, René decided to take a different street, as the map indicated that a grocery store was nearby. He wanted to add a few items to his backpack for the next day's walk, especially a few pieces of fruit, and perhaps a couple of carrots to go with some cheese, chorizo and of course, a baguette. His backpack would be a little heavier in the morning, but the taste of fresh fruit on the trail would make carrying the extra weight more than worthwhile.

During the night Mark, Jason and Luca began to experience severe stomach pains and vomiting. Miryam was the first one to wake upon hearing their moans and groans. She roused René and sent him to find medical help as it looked to her like the men had food poisoning. Less than a half hour later, the men had been taken to the local hospital with Miryam, Freya and René trailing behind them to find out what they could from the doctors. Everyone else tried to go back to sleep with little success, with the exception of Sid and Asha. Miryam, Freya, and René returned to the hostel just before dawn as the first of the pilgrims staying in the hostel began leaving.

"Well," began René sounding exhausted, "It seems that Mark, Luca and Jason won't be walking for a few days. The doctor wants them to stay put for at least two days in the hospital, and possibly another day after that in Burgos. He wants them close by, just to make sure they are well enough to resume their Camino."

Miryam spoke up, "The guys are adamant that the group continues on walking without them. I will be staying here in Burgos with them until they are well enough to go on."

Everyone knew that Miryam had a special connection with Mark, so no one protested her decision to stay. They had known each other for a few years, and it wasn't an accident that had Miryam joined the group. Freya protested saying that she should also stay with Miryam, but to no avail as Miryam wanted them all to go on. It was with a heavy heart that they prepared to leave. With promises to keep in contact via email, goodbyes were said, with more than a few tears shed.

The walk from Burgos was a long and quiet twenty-one kilometres, with everyone feeling the loss of four of their friends. The high clouds obscuring the sun, added to the sense of gloom felt by each of them. The land itself appeared bleak, as they crossed the flat terrain of the Meseta. Lunch was eaten in Tardajos, following a meditation near the Río Arlanzón.

The last ten kilometres into Hornillos del Camino were a bit easier, as the Little Company of Pilgrims began to adjust to the absence of four companions. They found their lodgings for the night in the Albergue Municipal near the Gothic Church of San Román.

That night found René writing in his journal in Hornillos del Camino:

> *It's been a hard day, our first day on the Meseta. We stopped for meditation by a river before the town of Tardajos which helped us deal with our sense of loss with Mark, Miryam, Jason and Luca left behind in Burgos. Strange how life goes on in spite of everything. It seems that the world simply reshapes itself to make room for the changes around us and within us.*

Chapter Seventeen – Taking Risks And Being Vulnerable

In spite of the sense of loss, or maybe because of it, the six hikers stayed closer to each other. Following a night in Hornillos, the next night was spent in Castrojeriz where they began to adjust to the changes. In Castrojeriz, as René took photos of the sites they saw, he began to show the others how he saw the world through the lens of a camera, how the camera had taught him how to see beyond the prosaic, three-dimensional world into a more numinous world of untold stories of the past, and of times yet to come. For René, it was something that he hoped would bring him closer to the others, and them to him. And so it was, with improved spirits that they began their third day as a Little Company of Six Pilgrims.

Knowing that there wasn't going to be a café until Itero de la Vega, they all had taken a few pieces of fruit or other snacks, to be eaten along the way. There was no chance of walking the ten kilometre distance to Itero without a rest stop as no one wanted to risk blisters on the Meseta. They arrived in Itero de la Vega ready for coffee and toast. Their stay in Itero was brief. Soon they returned to the path with the plan for a small lunch in Boadilla del Camino.

By mid-afternoon, they arrived in Frómista, their destination, and checked into the municipal hostel. They found themselves in a dorm room with only eight beds with no other pilgrims booked into the two remaining beds. Once their clothes washing and shower routines were done, Sid asked if the group could do their meditation for the day in the room before heading out for a late lunch. Meeting with agreement they prepared themselves for meditation. With the door to their dorm closed, they risked doing meditation free of clothing. Should someone open the door and see them, they were certain that seeing the meditation activity, whoever would have opened the door would close it quietly and wait for their meditation to be ended.

"Ah," Freya remarked once meditation was finished and everyone had put their clothing back on, "That felt good."

"Yeah," echoed the others. "We definitely needed that."

"Okay, let's go eat. I'm starving," suggested Fred, which was received with a few cheers and smiles.

While they ate, Freya checked her smartphone for messages. "Listen to this!" she exclaimed. "It's a note from Miryam that she sent this morning. They are planning on leaving Burgos tomorrow morning and go as far as either Tarjados or Rabé de las Calzados, depending on how the guys feel!"

"Whoo hoo! Bravo! Yay!" erupted from the others.

Freya continued reading and a frown creased her forehead. "What is it?" asked René.

"Another message sent just a short while ago, it seems that Jason is returning to his home. He has given up the Camino," she announced in a quiet voice.

This news put a damper on their celebrations for a short while. However, hearing that Miryam, Luca and Mark were still intent on going through with their Camino, soon brought smiles back to their faces. The evening meal finished with a toast to their absent friends.

The next morning, they began to hike before sunrise following the senda that paralleled the highway for four kilometres before turning off to head towards Villovieco, where they thought would be a good place to have breakfast. After a hearty breakfast, their first of the day, they followed along the river which was treed. With an eye for spotting a perfect meditation location, Sid found a semi-secluded space off the path for their mediation. As always, the meditation lightened whatever extra weight their spirits were carrying.

Following meditation, they stopped for a few photos at the Puente Ermita de Virgen del Río. A half hour later, they arrived in Villalcázar de Sirga where they stopped for coffee and a small snack. René was telling the group about how the Templars had been active around Villalcázar in the 12th century. He noted that the Santa Maria la Virgen Blanca church, was a Templar church from that era. As the church was open, he persuaded the others to visit it with him.

Later, back on the road, they returned to walking on the gravelled senda which would take them the remaining five and a half kilometres into Carrión de los Condes, their planned stop for the day. An hour and a half later, they registered at the Albergue Santa Maria. Seeing that the room was big and already occupied by several other pilgrims, they were glad to have taken time to meditate near the river, earlier. When they had finished their chores, it was time for a drink and tapas.

"So, Freya, tell us about your home, growing up," asked Fred.

As soon as he heard Fred's request, René winced. He knew how much Freya hated talking about herself and how she rebuffed even innocent inquiries that René had made, since they had met each other. To his surprise, Freya began to answer Fred rather than scowl.

"As you know, I come from the northern part of Europe, a Nordic country. My family was, and still is, rich; and so I grew up with everything I could possibly want. Well, that is with the exception of parental love. My father was in shipping and it seemed everything he touched turned into gold. Everyone treated him as if he was a god. You know, even gods don't have time for children. As for my mother, well, I never did know who she was. I grew up with my brother, Fredrick, under the care of constantly changing stream of nannies and tutors, and whatever live-in woman my father had at the moment. Dad never stuck with any woman long enough for us to have a mother, or even a step-mother. My father was a bitter man, as the one woman he did want, didn't want him in spite of all of his money and power. I don't think he liked women all that much once he had been rejected by her; he sure as hell didn't respect the women we saw in his life."

"When I was barely old enough, my father married me off to a man who was even more powerful. We fought all the time, my husband Orin and I. The only good thing I can say about Orin, is that he gave me space, enough space to be my own person."

"You know, I don't hold any grudges against my Dad, as he made me become an independent person, someone who could handle a man like Orin. I can outshoot him, but my greatest weapon of leverage with Orin is the fact that I am a witch," concluded Freya.

Fred sat back, startled with what Freya had just said – she was a witch. "Umm, is that why you like to be naked?"

Freya looked at him and laughed, "No, I like being naked simply because it feels good. I basically grew up naked like any normal kid in my country. I only wore clothes when the weather conditions demanded it; and of course when I am around others who tend to freak out when seeing naked people," she added, looking directly at René as she added the last part.

Gabe was curious and asked, "Would you say that you were a white or black witch, Freya?"

"Am a witch, not "was" a witch," clarified Freya. "There is no difference. Like everything else, there is no split. It's like Sid keeps reminding us, non-duality, remember? Sometimes I find myself on the light side; and sometimes, thankfully not that often, I find myself on the dark side. You can't have one without the other."

"Yes, I guess that makes sense," affirmed Gabe.

"Freya?" interjected Sid. "Do you mind if I say something here to help explain what you mean about being both a white witch and a black witch?"

"Not at all, Sid."

Sid folded his hands together as though carefully composing his words before speaking. "In my father's house, he's a Brahmin, we have quite a few statues representing various deities in the Hindu faith. There are two female deities, Shakti and Kali that share a space on the same shelf as Shiva and Yama. Both the dark side and the light side are held together as one just as a man and a women who are joined together become one. It took me many years to understand that the statues were my culture's attempt to show that we humans also have a light side and a dark side, with the light side represented with consciousness and the dark side represented by the unconscious."

"Okay, that's something I understand," admitted Fred. "It's like saying every human is both saint and sinner. It's all there within oneself."

"Precisely!" nodded Sid approvingly. "As you were saying?" said Sid turning back to Freya.

"I've said all that I want to say for now," concluded Freya, "Other than to say, we should get ready for dinner."

As he relaxed in his bunk before lights out that night, René turned to his journal:

> *Freya says that she is a witch. I don't believe in witches, but there is no question that she has bewitched me. As I heard her tell her story, I began to understand why she is so tough, so hard-edged. It's amazing how finally knowing another person's story lets one become more understanding of that person.*
>
> *The talk of dark sides and light sides buried within each of us made me think again about complexes and shadows. I am finding more and more similarities between Buddhism and depth psychology. I think that there is a book here for me to research and write, comparing the two when I go back home.*

Chapter Eighteen – Losses Along the Way

The Little Company of Pilgrims rose early again the next morning and off just as the sky was beginning to lighten. René loved this time of morning when the first kilometres were passed in silence. The sky was partly cloudy, which promised a beautiful sunrise. Sid and Asha were walking at the front with Fred and Gabe close behind them. As usual, the two were talking about the Bible and various myths of the ancient world that were eerily similar in comparison. And, as had become the norm since leaving the others in Burgos, Freya walked beside René on the path. When he stopped for photos, she would slow her pace without stopping, knowing that he would eventually catch up to her. They walked, for the most part, in a comfortable silence for those first hours of the day.

When the skies began to turn colour, they all turned to look back the way they had come so as to see the colours highlight the few clouds in the sky, and to watch the golden globe of the sun peek over the distant horizon. The Meseta was big sky country, reminding René of the Canadian prairies. The moment the sun cleared the horizon, they all turned to continue walking. They had a longer walk than normal that day in order to reach Terradillos de Templarios. With no stops for a coffee for seventeen kilometres, they had made sure to bring enough water and snacks to ensure that they would stay hydrated and had enough energy to keep a decent pace while walking. The trail was straight, an old Roman road that crossed open fields and bogs.

As they walked, the sky began to cloud over to the point where it brought welcome relief from the sun. The light breeze with which the day had begun had become stronger, though not to the point where it became a foe. When they reached the Fuente del Hospitalejo, at the seven and a half kilometre mark, they decided to stop for a change of socks and to munch on some fruit and bread. Most had bought juice boxes for this first stop. Sid studied the land, and in spite of the few poplar trees found by the Fuente, he agreed that this was too open for their group meditation. So, once they were ready, they resumed their walking until Calzadilla de la Cueza. Four hours after they had begun their walk, they reached Calzadilla ready for a real break, for coffee and something more substantial to eat.

"I wonder if it's going to rain?" worried Gabe.

Looking again at the sky, René said that it was unlikely. The clouds were too high and the briskness of the breeze said that if there was any moisture at all, it would only be a brief shower. But even that was unlikely. Regardless of René's assessment of the weather, no time was wasted in Calzadilla. There would be time enough for a second cup of coffee in Ledigos just another six kilometres up the road.

About one kilometre past Calzadilla, they arrived at a junction which gave them the option to continue straight on the senda, or to take a path through woodland. Sid mentioned that the woodland trail would likely offer them a chance to meditate in spite adding three hundred metres to their journey for the day. Sid's recommendation was accepted. Walking on the senda felt boring, and they were willing to walk extra distance simply to escape the senda. So, they headed for the treed rise to the south. As Sid had predicted, they did find a good spot for their skyclad meditation, far enough off of the path for a sense of privacy. Including the time taken for meditation, the remaining six and a half kilometre walk to Ledigos took them just over two hours.

It was lunch time. Although there was only about three and a half kilometres left until their final destination for the day, the appearance of the bar-café was all it took to persuade them to stop. Being so close to Terradillos de Templarios along with the peace that had returned following meditation, had effectively cleansed them of the pressing need to hurry. For René, the thought of a hot cup of café con leche was more than enough reason to take a break at the café.

"It's hard to imagine that when we stop later, we'll have made it half way from Saint Jean Pied de Port to Santiago," remarked Fred. "When I began, I was so worried that I would crash and burn and then have to go back home without finishing."

"I can't say that I was worried about being able to make it to Santiago," admitted Gabe. "I have all the time in the world and I just assumed I would have walked slower with rest days along the way. Speaking of rest days, we still haven't had one, René excluded," he added with a wink.

"I could use a rest day as well", admitted Freya.

"Really?" questioned Gabe with surprise. "You don't look the least bit physically tired. If anything, I'd say that you're in the best shape of all of us."

"Sometimes rest days are not about the body," she remarked.

"I agree, Freya," added René. "I think we should probably plan an extra night in either Sahagún or León."

Asha and Sid said that they would find any choice the group made acceptable. As a group, they agreed to look seriously at their options later that day in Terradillos de Templarios.

An hour later, they had checked into the Albergue Jacques de Molay. On the side of the hostel was a large red Templar cross which was in keeping with the name of the hostel, named after the last Grand Master of the Templars. They couldn't get a room that was just big enough for the six of them as they were a little too late. All they had choices of were a room for two and a room for five. Fred and Gabe agreed to share the room for two in order to spare the others their habit of snoring at night. The other room was still empty with the fifth bed not filled at this point, though it would likely be filled later in the day.

With the guarantee of privacy, there was no rush to change into clean clothing while going through the routine of showers and the washing of the day's hiking clothes. René remarked to himself on how he was changing, remembering how he had reacted seeing Asha, then Freya and Miryam naked. He had reacted with shame and guilt. Now, seeing anyone nude brought little reaction; well, that was excepting Freya. He even began to find his own nudity to be more comfortable, at least within the confines of this group with whom he had meditated nude so often.

When the last of their chores were done, they were laying on their beds to rest, read or write. Freya was busy sending text messages back and forth to Miryam in order to find out how the others were doing and where they were for that night. Sid and Asha, had retreated into their separateness, while René wrote in his journal.

> *Cloudy day today. We found a quiet place in a rare forested area here on the Meseta, to meditate. However, because of the need to hurry in order to ensure enough beds for us in Terradillos de Templarios, we cut our meditation short. Later this evening we will be planning a rest stop. I am amazed at how peaceful I am beginning to feel as I walk the Camino. It seems that the pangs of guilt for not being at*

home in Canada, where I could be available if needed, has receded. I'll check later to see if there is Wi-Fi here so that I can get my e-mail and upload photos. More later.

Finished with his entry, he got up and put on a clean tee shirt so that he could join Gabe and Fred in the dining area of the hostel.

"I have just found out from Miryam that both Jason and Luca have now left the Camino."

Freya's statement was received with more than a bit of shock.

René asked, "Did she say what the matter?"

"Yes. It seems that Luca pushed himself too hard after the food poisoning in Burgos. A doctor told him that he needed a minimum of seven to ten days rest before he could again try walking the Camino."

"Jeez!" exclaimed Gabe in frustration. "What a shitty way to end a pilgrimage!"

"There is some good news though," added Freya who had wisely told the others the bad news first. "Miryam and Mark will catch a bus to meet us either in Sahagún or León. We just have to let them know where we will be stopping for our rest day."

"Excellent news, Freya," said René with relief that it wasn't all bad news. "I guess we'd better decide where we are going to take our rest day. What do you say, Freya? Any preferences?"

"I'd rather do it sooner than later. We'd get to Sahagún tomorrow morning; however, it would be three full days before we'd get to León. I think Miryam is hoping to join us sooner than later."

"That sounds about right," reasoned Fred. "I think we are all in agreement with that idea. Right?"

There were nods of agreement from everyone. Freya took out her smartphone and texted Miryam with their decision. It was just a few moments later that a responding text was received. They would meet tomorrow in Sahagún. Miryam would text them the information about their arrival time later that night, when she found out the bus departure times for Sahagún. René noticed an immediate improvement in Freya's mood. She was obviously happier knowing that a reunion with her European friend, was close at hand.

> *Freya is now smiling again. Seeing her smile is like seeing the sunrise. Miryam and Mark will be rejoining us tomorrow in Sahagún.*

Chapter Nineteen – Challenges, Temptations and Trust

They arrived in Sahagún at ten-thirty the next morning. Miryam had sent a text message telling them that the bus would be just before one, during the noon hour. This gave René and the others enough time to get their backpacks stored in their rooms, as well as time to find their way to the bus depot. They had decided to skip staying in an albergue, deciding it would be best to stay in one place for both nights. A bonus as far as Freya, Asha and Miryam were concerned, as they would be finally being able to take baths rather than showers. The women had settled on the Pacho Inn which had free breakfasts and free Wi-Fi included in the price for the rooms. Myriam had booked four rooms for the eight of them. The group would sort out sleeping arrangements later. Miryam had made reservations at the Pacho Inn the evening before.

"Let's head out for a second breakfast," suggested Fred. The fact that they only had to go downstairs to the café-bar made the idea sound even better. Asha and Sid decided to pass on lunch in the café, saying they were going in search of a grocery store for some fruit and a few vegetables instead. Since the bus depot was within easy walking distance along the main street where the Pacho Inn was located, there was no need to rush. As for heading out as a tourists, or to take photographs; that would have to wait, likely until late that afternoon.

As they sat inside the café, the first discussion was about room assignments. "Okay, as I see it," began Fred, Gabe and I should take one room, René and Mark could share a room, Freya and Miryam in the third room with Sid and Asha in the fourth room."

"It's not going to work as much as I would like that," said Freya. "Miryam tells me that she and Mark have become even closer. They have been staying in hotel rooms together since we left them in Burgos."

"Oh." René said startled with the news. "Does that mean we should be booking single rooms for you and me?"

"What? Are you telling me that you would rather be alone than share a room with me?"

"No, I just thought that you would prefer that; you know, privacy and all that."

"That's the problem, you're always trying to think for everyone else. I do know how to think for myself and make my own decisions," fumed Freya. "Men."

Gabe looked at Fred and winked. "I saw that, Gabe," challenged Freya. "You're no better. Don't think that just because I have to share a room with René that he is going to be getting any benefits." Then turning back to René she said, "Unless you want to have privacy."

Sighing, René caved in, acknowledging that it would be pointless after more than two weeks of living together as a group in tight spaces. "And no," he added talking to Gabe and Fred, "There won't be any hanky-panky." René shook his head wondering how this had happened. This definitely wasn't going to be mentioned in his next set of e-mails or status updates on Facebook.

Before it was time to head to the bus depot, Sid and Asha returned carrying a couple of bags of fruit and vegetables. As a result, the six of them were able to meet Marie and Mark as a whole group. As the two missing pilgrims exited from the bus depot, there were cheers from all their friends. Miryam quickly rushed to Freya to embrace her. Soon both were crying while the men were giving Mark hugs and slaps on the back. Everyone seemed to be talking at the same time. Fred was carrying Miryam's backpack as they walked back to the Inn.

"Are you hungry?" Asked Fred, "We waited for you. There's a decent restaurant at the Inn. Or do you want to rest up first after your travel."

"Do I look like an old man to you? Don't answer that," laughed Mark. "We've been resting for a few days already. Let's just put our backpacks in our room and then we will go and have lunch."

When lunch was over, René said that he wanted to wander with his camera to discover what Sahagún had to offer, and asked if anyone wanted to wander with him. Mark, Gabe and Fred took him up on the offer leaving René to wonder what Sid and Asha would do while the women caught up with each other. Sid and Asha had become slightly withdrawn over the past few days other than when it was time for meditation. With a shrug of his shoulders, René joined the guys as they headed into town to see what they could see.

According to his map, the Iglesia de la Trinidad and the Iglesia San Juan were only a few minutes away on Calle Arco. The Trinity Church, both a tourism office and an albergue, was just across the street from the Church of Saint John. Neither building held much interest, so they continued on down Calle Arco to reach the Iglesia San Lorenzo which was massive in comparison to the diminutive Iglesia San Juan. René had to use his wide-angle lens in order to fit the whole church into the frame. The group agreed that it would be worth returning with Miryam and Freya in order to explore the interior of the church the next day.

They walked just a bit further and reached the main square filled with cafés and neat little shops as well as the Sahagún city hall building. They then followed the Avenida de la Constitucion to the Iglesia San Tirso and the ruins which they would pass as they left the city when they resumed their pilgrimage two days later. The pilgrims' path went by the church, then through an old stone arch in order to leave Sahagún. More photos were taken and then they returned to their hotel via Calle Nicolas, which passed by Plaza Santiago. They had made a large circle of the centre of Sahagún.

Back in time to take a quick shower before heading out with the women for cerveza, vino rojo and tapas, René decided to upload his photos to his Flickr account and send a quick e-mail addressed to his kids and to Cécile.

They

Small Company of Pilgrims had decided to eat their evening meal a block away from the hostel, at a medieval restaurant. Everyone had enjoyed their meal of baby lamb, in the rustic atmosphere of the restaurant. Not surprisingly, the restaurant was attached to a hostel-hotel which they would likely have chosen to stay in, had they known about it. The Camino was good for business, especially restaurants, bars and hotels. In Sahagún, the Camino route from Madrid joined the Camino Francés which meant there would be even more pilgrims to feed and house, and more pilgrims on the trail.

During dinner, plans for the next day were proposed with the visiting of the museum, people watching at a café or two, and then investigating the interiors of several of the churches. Gabe had agreed to go with Fred, Miryam and Mark to attend a church service. However, René, Freya, Sid and Asha had declined going to mass without stating their reasons for doing so.

Back at the Pacho Inn, the group stopped for a nightcap at the bar. Sid and Asha excused themselves and retreated to their room for the night. After a single glass of wine, René decided he needed some alone time. Back in the room he was sharing with Freya, he found a suitable spot for meditation, something he had missed with the excitement of the day. He placed his pillow on a hotel towel for his meditation cushion and took his seat and entered into meditation, following the in-breath and out-breath to catch that moment of emptiness that existed before another in-breath returned him to his body.

Only a few minutes after he had begun meditating, he heard the door opening and sensed Freya's presence. She closed the door quietly so as to not disturb his meditation. He heard her movements in the room, not as a distraction, but as natural elements that belonged there. He had learned long ago to be mindful and not dwell on, or deny sounds, smells, and other distractions while in a meditative state. He knew that Freya had also taken her seat to meditate with him noticing her breathing and then letting that awareness go as well, as he sank deeper into his own meditative state.

When he opened his eyes, he saw her eyes looking into his eyes and felt her sense of peacefulness. Nothing needed to be said as they both began going through the rituals of preparation for sleep. As René removed his sleeping bag liner and spread it on his side of the bed, Freya went to the bathroom to brush her teeth.

René waited until she exited the bathroom and then went in to brush his teeth as well. He had just begun brushing when she returned with a small bag and began to run the bath. He saw her in the mirror as she climbed into the tub and gave a sigh of satisfaction as the water touched her skin.

"God, I've missed having a bath," she murmured with her eyes closed. René tried in vain not to continue watching her in the mirror. He quickly finished brushing his teeth and left the bathroom. He slipped into the sleeping bag liner and propped himself up to write his final entry for the day into his journal. As he wrote, his mind focused on the words being written so he didn't notice the sound of the bathtub draining, so it was with a start that he saw her towelling dry beside the bed.

"You don't need a frigging sleeping bag liner. The bed has fresh sheets and blankets."

"Um, I thought ..."

Freya cut him off before he could say anymore, "That's the problem. You're thinking again. When are you ever going to learn to just be, to take life as it is, instead of trying to think your way through everything, trying to control everything?"

"But I don't have any pyjamas for sleeping in."

"That makes two of us. Now get that stinky thing off my clean bed," she ordered.

René quickly slipped out of the liner, conscious of his nudity and hers as well. As he put the liner on top of his backpack he felt his body begin to be aroused. Anxious that she would notice, he tried to slip quickly under the sheets without letting her see his aroused state.

"Don't even think about it! Don't make me regret trusting you to share a room with me!"

For the next few minutes, René lay at the edge of the bed, tensed while focusing on his breathing. It was only after Freya muttered a "Good night, René," that he began to release the tightness in his body. "Good night, Freya."

~

The rest day in Sahagún had gone well. The Little Company of Pilgrims gathered together in one room for a group meditation in the evening to mark the end of their stay in Sahagún.

"I want to talk about openness," began Sid. "Openness demands a deep appreciation of what is not the self. For example, when we fall in love, our whole attitude is open toward that person. We get an abstract flash of our lover, a flash that comes into our mind at first, a flash that is primal. Anyone who becomes immersed in that love has the kind of openness that brings about these primal flashes. It is an almost magical sensation, flashes without a name, or concept, or idea. As we open ourselves to these flashes and then let them go. We don't struggle to possess them; awareness then comes very slowly and settles into the reality of just being there, just being here, just being now."

With the sound of his words fading into silence, everyone slipped into meditation with a focus on openness without trying to control or own what would emerge. Thirty minutes later, a collective sigh of contentment brought the meditation to a close.

Returning to their room, Freya and René slipped into what was becoming a growing sense of comfort around each other. René was not yet sure, but he had begun to suspect that their comfort together was dependent upon his risking to be open, to trust fully, and to dare giving up control as Sid had talked about during meditation. It seemed to him that Freya responded to his changing state of being in ways that matched him. When he became tense, she tensed. When he relaxed, she relaxed. It was as if they were joined in a way that he had never felt joined before with Cécile. In the past, both he and Cécile struggled with giving up control. He was sure that it was fear based, a fear that dated back to both of their childhoods where control was vital, at least the control within their minds, and the control of their minds.

Carrying the sense of openness from meditation with him into their room, risking vulnerability, Freya responded with a reciprocal openness. Little needed to be said as they went through the rituals of preparing for bed. As René waited for Freya to join him in the bed, he wrote:

> *It's getting better. I'm getting better. The Camino is working a magic upon me, a good magic. However, if I shut down, close the doors to possibility, that magic would turn black. I am ready to go on, ready to commit to doing the whole Camino. I had thought I was running from Freya, running back to what had been lost with my divorce, hoping somehow that it could all be undone. But, I was really running away from myself, from being honest and open with myself and all that is around me. Now, I can breathe freely as though a weight has been lifted off my chest.*

As Freya slipped beneath the covering sheet, René turned out the light beside the bed and folded Freya into his open arms, holding her back against his chest, breathing without expectation knowing that this was as it should be.

"Good night, Freya."

"Good night, René."

Chapter Twenty – Illusions of Control

They had reached the Puente Canto, an old Roman bridge that had been last repaired in the sixteenth century, about a half hour after leaving the hotel. Back on the Camino, everyone felt well rested and cheerful as they walked on towards Santiago. They had waited until after a local pilgrim mass in the morning to leave the hotel, and after making sure that they all had eaten a good breakfast. The light was perfect, as far as René was concerned as he stopped to take photos of the bridge from various angles, attempting to capture the play of morning light on the old stone.

Just over an hour later, the reached Calzada del Coto where they found themselves again on the Via Romana, the old Roman road that would take them to Calzada de los Hermanillos. Three and a half hours later, they stopped for a cup coffee and some food at the Via Trajana in Calzada de los Hermanillos.

They had already walked fourteen kilometres, all that they were going to do as it was too far to hike to reach the next albergue in Reliegos, a hike of another eighteen kilometres. They were early enough in the day to have their pick of the village's albergues, so they chose the Casa El Cura which was at the end of the village.

Mark added his voice to the ongoing discussion about good and evil. "In my opinion, you can't have it an either-or scenario."

"Why is that?" challenged Fred. "I think that we can choose between the two on both a personal and a collective level."

"So," continued Mark, "You are saying that with the right effort, humans can consciously control their lives through continually choosing good over evil?"

"Yes, that's right."

"Then," added Mark, "You must be saying that the human species basically, and intentionally, chooses evil over good. Take a look around you, Fred. The world is going to hell in a hand basket and taking the planet along with it. That's a damning statement if we truly control our choices."

"But we can choose, Mark," protested Fred. "Once we have been shown the light, so to speak, we can choose to follow that light and become a light to the rest of the world."

"I'm assuming that you are referring to light here as God as Father, and God as Jesus."

"Of course."

"But that begs the question, doesn't it? If it is dependent upon something external, a god or goddess, then the self has no ultimate control. Control ultimately rests with the god or goddess."

"Ultimately," agreed Fred, "It does come down to the Grace of God and his son, Jesus Christ."

"Ergo, it is then God who makes the choices for good and evil. Nice way to pass the puck. Blame God for the mess that we're in."

René decided to join in the debate, "If one does good unintentionally, do we credit that person with doing good? If a person does evil, unintentionally, do we then charge that person with doing evil? An example to perhaps illustrate the questions; consider that a thief with a dark heart and dark intentions, accidentally kills a bystander while robbing a bank. Unknown to the thief, that bystander was a serial killer that had for a number of years, evaded detection as he raped and murdered young women. And a second example, a good father and community citizen came across a young, homeless man who appeared to be dying in a ditch. He offered food and shelter to that man allowing the young man to regain his health. Unknown to him, this young man would go on to rape and murder young women for years to come. This young man, and the accidentally killed man, are one and the same person. This is what makes good and evil so impossible to separate," added René. "I keep coming back in my head to the oneness that embraces both. You can't have a shadow without a light is a saying we have in the field of psychotherapy. No one is either saint or sinner. Like Sid has been telling us, non-duality, all is one."

Sid, grinned at René as he said, "I wondered when you were finally going to challenge that old coot, Mark and the American Pastor, Fred."

René returned his grin adding, "Honestly, I had no intention of saying anything. The words just popped out of my mouth."

Paying their bills at the café, the group went to the hostel to book their beds which turned out to be bunk beds.

A short while later, Miryam came into the room being shared between Freya, Sid, Asha and René. She was laughing as she spoke of the intense debate still going on in her room with the three other men. Sid and Asha were out, likely searching for some fresh fruit and vegetables. "You sure stirred up a shit storm in there, René."

"Sorry about that," René offered as an insincere apology and a grin.

"No you're not," she retorted as she gave him a punch on the shoulder. "It's Fred and Mark arguing one side while Gabe is trying to hold his own against the two of them."

"No surprise there, and Gabe can hold his own. You'd be surprised."

Miryam then turned to Freya and asked her to go for a walk with her, to get some fresh air. "Of course, you are welcome to come along for the walk too," she added to include René.

"It's okay, go on. I've got something else to do," replied René.

"Yeah, we know," laughed both women who looked at the camera pack that René was quickly fitting around his waist.

"You know," added Freya, "it's as if you are having an affair with your camera. I swear you're addicted to taking photos; maybe it's just a way to avoid becoming involved in deep relationships with people. Just saying," she concluded as she turned to walk out the door with Miryam.

Later in the evening with the day rushing to a close, René once again found himself writing in his journal:

> *It's just about time for bed and I've been reading Pema Chödrön's book again. As I read, I was struck by how her words echoed what Freya had mentioned earlier. Pema talked about addictions as being attempts to escape. I've been noticing that when I wander off from the others, or more honestly, wander off from inner voices that are trying to wake me up – wander off with my camera – I get caught up in that addiction of trying to capture scenes as if what is vital and real is out there waiting for my camera. Pema says we use our*

addictions to soften the discomforts and truths that we don't have the courage to face

What are those truths that I am fleeing from? Obviously they have something to do with nudity, well not really nudity, but what nudity implies in terms of vulnerability and honesty.

Chapter Twenty-One – Tired, Dusty and Falling Apart

The next morning, they were out the door before sunrise, back on the Via Romana. The only site of green trees in an otherwise barren landscape was found as they crossed the Río Valdelcasa, a struggling group of pines. It was there that the group left the track, walking to the end of the thin forest to find a place for their meditation. They had walked almost seven kilometres without pause since leaving Hermanillos.

Refreshed and wearing clean socks following meditation, they walked on another ten kilometres to reach Reliegos where they stopped for lunch. Though tired, they returned to the Roman road rather than walk on the senda that followed the highway into Mansilla de las Mulas. Tired and sweaty and covered in trail dust, after a long twenty-five kilometres, they checked into the Albergue Municipal. They were soon installed into one dormitory as a group much to their relief. It wasn't long before the round of showers and clothes washing began. Fortunately, there was a washing machine and clothes dryer available for use which allowed them to wash all the clothing at the same time, a task volunteered for, by Asha. An hour later, they all gathered around the hostel's restaurant for something to drink and to munch on. René was thankful that neither Fred nor Mark was interested in renewing their ongoing debates. There was something positive to be said for being bone-tired.

René was tired as well, not really interested in returning to the Santa Maria church for more photos. When they left the restaurant, it was only to sit in the hostel's garden area to read, check e-mails, or to make journal entries. Everyone was soon wrapped up in their own private worlds and silence, a silence that no one had the energy or the will to break. When the day's light began to shift to the gold of late afternoon, heralding the approach of sunset, René decided to take his camera out for a stroll, and to get a few photos of the village. The light was too inviting to deny the impulse, in spite of his tiredness.

As the light shifted from gold to more sombre shades, René spied a small grove of trees by one of the irrigation canals that framed the village. He noticed that he was close enough to the lights of the village to risk a quiet and private meditation. Without thinking about it, he folded his clothes to serve as a seat on the dry grass between two small bushes, and took his seat. And with practiced skill, he turned inward to focus on his breath.

> *I found myself meditating for the second time today, somehow hoping that it would help me get through a tiredness that I never did find a reason for. I was heavily weighed down with a tiredness that was not physical, but which stole even my normal enthusiasm for taking photos.*
>
> *As I meditated, alone, I wrestled with thoughts that began to surface – strange how I forget how this typically happens when I meditate. I heard the voices of Sid and my Buddhist guide back in Ottawa telling me to look at what arises without trying to do something about what appears, without trying to grasp them or banish them – just notice what arises and then let the thoughts drift off.*
>
> *Back in the dorm, I read more of Chödrön's book, <u>When Things Fall Apart</u>, and was struck by what she had to say about meditation. She talked about how in meditation we get to see what's really going on in our lives, how we avoid denying and shutting down, thus allowing awareness to illuminate the darkness of*

ignorance. Her words, "We're able to see how we run and hide and keep ourselves busy so that we never have to let our hearts be penetrated."

Ouch! Chödrön sure touched the sore spot, the soft spot within me that I have been trying so hard to deny exists.

I am afraid of opening up my heart, afraid that it will again be broken.

Chapter Twenty-Two – It Comes Down To Trust

Excitement was the first thing that René noticed when he woke up the next morning. Everyone in the hostel, including the other pilgrims he didn't know, were up in the pre-dawn darkness anxious to get started on the next leg of their pilgrimage. León was now only about nineteen kilometres away. Usually the early morning rush was about getting to the next destination early enough to secure a decent bed for the night. However, this wasn't the motivation for this particular morning. There were more than enough beds to be found in León, which was regarded as the two-thirds done destination, a significant milestone on the Camino. As well, León was a Mecca of sights that would require more than a few days to take in and digest, more time than a pilgrim had to spare.

Though there was no intention of spending more than one night in León, René and his friends wanted as many hours as possible to savour the essence of the fabled city, which owed its roots the Roman Legionnaires who had established a military garrison there, the same Romans who had built the Via Romana they had been walking on for the past two days. An early breakfast was hurriedly eaten, and the Small Company of Pilgrims soon found themselves walking just as the sky began to lighten just before sunrise. With any luck, they had presumed they would be in León before noon. They did plan for a coffee stop in Arcahueja at the ten kilometre mark.

René managed to get a few sunrise photos. while looking back as the sun rose over Mansilla de las Mulas and the distant barren landscape. He then turned and took a few photos of the backs of his companions, backs that had grown strong carrying backpacks for more than four hundred and seventy kilometres. Then, putting his camera away and picking up his pace, he walked alongside these people who had become his pilgrim family.

The stop in Archahueja was brief, just long enough to change socks and swallow the obligatory cups of coffee. As a result, it was about eleven-thirty when they arrived in León. Not wanting to spend the night in another albergue that would limit their evening time with its curfews, a decision to spend the extra money on a hostel-hotel was made. Miryam had phoned ahead from Archahueja, and booked everyone into the Hostal San Martin, right in the heart of the city.

They made their way down the pilgrim's route, the Boulevard El Cid without stopping for photos until they reached the hotel-hostel. Freya went with Miryam to straighten out the rooms with the staff at the front desk, checking them in using the same pairings that were used in Sahagún. Everyone went to their assigned room in order to freshen up and drop off their backpacks. The plan was to gather in the hotel's lobby as soon as they could, in order to sort out where they would go first as a group before separating until late afternoon. When they stopped for lunch, they would plan the rest of the day.

Once in the room, René noticed that as in Sahagún, Freya would be sharing a double bed with him. He had been expecting this and secretly hoping for it as well. He put his backpack on the floor propped next to Freya's, against the wall between the bed and the bathroom. He washed his face and changed his clothing and declared himself ready only to have Freya tell him to comb his hair. Ready, the two of them walked down the stairs to the hotel lobby to meet with the others.

A few minutes later, when all had gathered, they all set off down the street and found the Cafeteria Calle Ancha just around the corner on Calle Ancha. Ordering sandwiches and beverages, they studied the brochures Gabe had picked up at the hostel's front desk, as well as consulting the map in the guide book. They decided that they would all return to the Cafeteria Calle Ancha by seven that evening in order to compare notes and choose a dining spot for the evening. They had learned early in their travels along the Camino that the evening meal usually didn't get served until sometime between nine and ten in the evening.

Just as everyone began to disperse, Freya lightly tugged at René's tee shirt and mouthed the word, 'wait.' René was surprised that she wasn't going off with Miryam and Mark. He had assumed that as usual, he would wander the streets searching for the heart and soul of León through the lens of his camera. With the last of their friends gone, she simply said, "Miryam and Mark are going back to the hotel for some private alone time. I don't want to spend the afternoon alone. I hope you don't mind if I tag along, do you?"

René realised that Freya was asking, not assuming as she spoke. This was a side of her he had not seen before, a softness that showed her vulnerability. Of course there was no way he would leave her on her own. To be honest, the idea of exploring the city with her was more than he could have wished for. With a smile, he said, "Of course not. I hope you don't mind if I sometimes get lost in my head while taking photos. Sometimes I become oblivious of others when I'm taking photos."

Freya laughed with amusement, "And you think no one has noticed this before now? Lead on, Mr. Photographer. Don't worry about me. I will keep an eye on you in case you wander off. We wouldn't want you to get lost now, would we?"

They made their way to the Catedral Pulchra Leónina, the León Cathedral of Saint Mary, also known as the House of Light, where they were both entranced with the towering twin spires with a giant rose window on the wall of the main façade of the cathedral.

Both entered the cathedral and wandered in silent awe of the light pouring in, and the magnificence on display. They left the cathedral almost exhausted, and breathed a collective sigh of relief at finding themselves outdoors and walking down the street. As they walked south along the avenue, they passed through two gates, la Puerta Obsipo and la Puerta del Sol. They walked on to the Plaza Mayor and then on to Plaza San Martin which was near a church called Santa Maria del Camino. At that point René said he had had enough of churches and so they went in search of street life, living evidence of León's vitality in the modern world.

René asked Freya what she would like to see before they began the slow walk back to the rendezvous destination. She mentioned the San Francisco Gardens, which were close by and a shopping plaza that was across the street from the gardens. Once inside the green space of the gardens, they found some shade on the grass where they could sit and relax,

"Thank you, René, for sharing this afternoon with me."

"I should be thanking you for asking and then not running off screaming while I took so many photos," he responded feeling slightly uncomfortable with her appreciation.

"Do you think we could meditate here in the park?" she asked. "I think it would do me a world of good after that explosion of culture we just experienced. I need to slow down. I feel like I am racing inside."

"Of course," he replied, before adding with a smile, "But we'll have to keep our clothes on. I'm not so keen on finding out what the inside of a Spanish jail is like."

With practiced ease, they soon slipped into a deep meditative state, and just as easily emerged into the outer world twenty minutes later.

"I don't think I can do without meditation in the future," Freya acknowledged. "I'm glad that I discovered it here. I never meditated before the Camino. I was always on the go, always looking for dragons to slay and wars to win back home. Have you been meditating long? It looks as if you were born meditating."

"I began meditating about thirty years ago, when I was at university. Like you, I doubt that I would do well without it. If anything, it is now becoming more and more important in my life."

"Well, it's time to check out the plaza across the street," Freya said as she took his hand to pull him up. "There's money to be spent."

In the plaza they found a place selling ice cream and fruit smoothies. They decided to buy smoothies. They carried their drinks with them as they wandered around the plaza before beginning to walk on to their next planned destination, City Hall in the Plaza San Marcelo. In spite of his earlier protestations about not photographing another church, René took several photos of the Iglesia San Marcelo before they continued down Rua El Cid toward the Pantheon and the Basilica San Isidoro. René realised that Freya looked tired from the constant walking. Since they were only a block or so from their hotel, he suggested that they return and relax for a while before heading back out to meet the others.

Back at the hotel, Freya wasted no time in running a full bath then laying back to let the water wash away the accumulation of muscle fatigue. René sat on the bed, leaning against the wall as he checked his email. He was partway through answering a letter from his son when Freya called out, "you want the water?"

"Sure! I'll be there in a minute."

"It's now or I pull the plug," she warned good-naturedly.

René knew that she would indeed pull the plug, so he set his tablet aside and stripped off his shorts and top to go into the tub. She was towelling off as he let the water enter into all of his pores.

"Don't forget to wash your hair, wild man," she teased as she hung up the towel and left the bathroom. A few moments later she added, "And don't forget to shave. There's no need to look like a medieval pilgrim."

René laughed to himself. She sounded like a wife talking to her husband. He was sure that she was missing her home as much as he was missing his. He wondered if she was substituting him for her family back home. Regardless, it felt good to be needed and trusted. He winced at the thought of Freya as his wife, winced because it was a thought that could only torture him more than he could bear, because he knew that she only saw him as a Camino friend. Taking a breath, he secured his feelings behind safe, prison walls.

When he finally left the bathroom, Freya was asleep on the bed, laying on her side with her back to him. She hadn't put on any clothes and looked so innocent and vulnerable lying there. He did his best to quietly retrieve his tablet which had a corner under her. She stirred and said "Lie beside me for a while. Just hold me until I fall asleep, okay?"

Trust. It had to come down to trust. Yes, he was a man, and she was a woman; and yes, he desired to make love to this perfect woman. But here, they were not lovers. They were pilgrims, lonely and dependent on trust and increasingly, dependent upon each other. And so, he lay beside her as she spooned into his body, pulling his arm across her belly, holding his hand, as they both went to sleep.

An hour later they both woke up and realised they'd have to hurry in order to meet the others on time at the Cafeteria Calle Ancha.

"So, how many photos did you take today, René?" teased Fred.

"At last count, about four hundred and seventy, give or take a hundred or two," he laughed in response.

Gabe spoke up, "How about we eat at the Albany restaurant tonight? It's at the corner by the Cathedral. That way René can get a few night photos to complete his set for today. The menu looked okay when we walked by there."

No one had a better idea, so they all agreed to head to that restaurant early so as to get an outside table with a good view of the square and the cathedral. They hadn't ordered anything yet, so they decided to make their way to the Albany where they could enjoy a few glasses of wine, do some people watching, and then have a great meal to celebrate simply being alive on the Camino.

~

It was after eleven in the evening when they happily straggled into their hotel, all of them having had more than one glass of vino too many in the course of the evening. There were going to be sore heads in the morning when they returned to walking the Camino. René was no exception as he was a bit wobbly on his way back to the room. However, he had enough awareness to wash up and brush his teeth before slipping into bed, pulling the covers over him. Freya was slower in coming to bed. When she got there, René was already asleep. She slipped in beside him, wrapping her arm around him and resting her hand on his abdomen, fingers just lightly touching the base of his shaft, and then she fell asleep.

Chapter Twenty-Three – Between Heaven and Earth

They left the hotel after swallowing as much coffee and orange juice as they could swallow and making sure that their water bottles were filled. It wasn't because they were heading into dry, desert country where water would be scarce, but because they knew hydration would allow them to avoid suffering too much from hangovers. They walked almost eight kilometres through the city of León to finally reach the country side. They had stopped at Fresno del Camino for coffee, toast and a change of socks before turning continuing on to a quiet path that took them through a small village called Ocina.

Seven and a half kilometres after Fresno del Camino, they stopped for lunch at a café called Chozas. When lunch was over, they picked up their backpacks to walk the last four and a half kilometres into Villar de Mazarife where they were to spend the night.

They found beds at the Albergue San Antonio de Padua in Villar de Mazarife. The village was small and offered little to draw the pilgrims out of the hostel other than to sit in lawn chairs out front. They were glad that the hostel had meal options as they wanted to waste as little energy as possible. They simply wanted the day to be over.

> *I didn't write last night – too much wine. We're now at an albergue where I find myself alone in my bunk thinking about Freya, about the feel of her against me. I wonder if she is thinking about me.*

~

The next morning, there wasn't the usual rush to get out the door for René and his companions. Unlike most of the other pilgrims in the albergue, they had decided against walking thirty-two kilometres to reach Astorga. The village of Villares de Órbigo at seventeen kilometres had become their next destination to end the day of hiking that lay before them. They left Mazarife in full daylight with clear heads, grateful that the headaches of the day before were finally banished.

The walk to Orbigo was pleasant, in a quiet kind of way. As they crossed an irrigation canal, they noticed that the open farming country had become treed parkland when they had walked just over six kilometres from Villar de Mazarife, It was an inviting place for another private outdoor meditation. A half hour later, following meditation, they returned to the path and continued on to Villavante where they stopped for coffee, their last stop before eventually reaching Villares de Órbigo. Once checked into their hostel, they gathered for a meal at a local café-bar.

"It's a shame that everyone can't enjoy nude meditation," commented Fred. "I have written about it on my blog site, but in truth, I hadn't ever experienced nude meditation like I have here in our group. It's one thing to meditate nude in a private place in your private home; and it's something vastly different to meditate with others while nude, in the outdoors, surrounded by nature. I wonder why the Good Lord didn't talk to us about this in his preaching."

Ah, but he did!" confirmed Mark. "Well, not so much talking about it, but in doing it. You have to remember that he took his work to the poor, the dispossessed, and the slaves who were often as not, working and living without clothes. The disciples of Jesus worked, for the most part, nude as well, especially those working as fishermen."

"That isn't in the Bible," argued Fred.

"It doesn't have to be in the Bible, Fred. You have to put the stories of the Bible in context. Historical evidence is clear on that subject," Mark reiterated. "Why would, or should, the Bible contain information that is widely understood?"

"But!"

"No buts, Fred. Besides the historical evidence, look at what is said in the Old Testament. You know the stories of Isaiah, of David, and others who praised God while nude. God commanded nudity as part of celebrating faith more than a few times."

"I guess you're right. I never thought that meditation was the same thing as praising the Lord."

"Beyond question. Mediation is prayer, meditation is bowing to the greatness of God."

"Okay," grinned Fred. "I get it. Still it would have been nice if He had made a commandment or at least a teaching to help us in the future accept the holiness of the natural human body."

Gabe decided to weigh in on the topic upon hearing the word commandment. "I think that maybe God did," he suggested.

"Care to explain what you mean by that?" encouraged Mark.

"Well, when God gave us the Ten Commandments, He was telling us what not to do, telling us which behaviours needed to be proscribed, prohibited, which behaviours were forbidden? Right?"

"Of course," Fred was quick to insert before Mark could interject.

"Well, since humans at that time in history, as Mark has already pointed out, were often were naked, either at work, or in their religious duties, it only stands to reason that God approved of nudity, and that being nude wasn't considered to be unnatural and immoral."

"Well said, Gabe!" proclaimed Mark. "You've got it spot on. Now if only today's religions could understand something so obvious. Nudity was natural, is natural. Nudity wasn't a sin so it didn't have to be proscribed. For too many people in today's world, nudity is viewed as something almost evil, perhaps even more evil that what the Commandments told us not to do."

In an effort to avoid the ongoing discussion, René decided to go for a walk into the countryside. He needed to be alone, and he needed time to think. Making sure he had his camera bag and journal with him, he slipped off, ostensibly to take some photos of the non-descript village. It wasn't long before he found himself in the country side looking for a quiet space, out of view of passersby. As he walked the side of the village, there didn't appear to be any spots near enough to meet his needs, so he returned to the hostel. He would have to find his space within himself, something he had long practiced back home in a busy world.

That night, he turned to his journal:

> *Sometimes, I can actually feel myself changing. It's as though weight is being lifted off my shoulders allowing me to stand tall. Between the conversations of my Camino family and the practice of nude group meditation, as well as trusting myself to be nude with Freya, it's as though a darkness is lifting.*

I now own my body and accept it as a gift, rather than feel a need to deny it or hide it. Well, that is most of the time I can sense this. And then there are moments when I find myself back in the shadows, afraid.

Chapter Twenty-Four – A Pile Of Rocks On The Way

Eleven kilometres into their walk the following morning, the group stopped in San Justo de la Vega for coffee. Then, with the break done, they continued on to Astorga, a thriving large town which had its own cathedral. Aside from their plans for an early lunch in Astorga and a few photos, they had decided to walk on another ten kilometres to Santa Catalina making for a respectable twenty-five kilometres of walking. The Small Company of Pilgrims was intent upon reaching Pontferrada in another two days, a task that required hikes of twenty-two kilometres each day in order to reach that destination.

René had long thought that a rest day in Pontferrada would be a good idea. His desire to explore that city, which was home to a Templar castle, was his real motivation for staying an extra night in the city. He told the others of his idea. Gabe was as enthusiastic as René was. He also wanted the opportunity to visit the castle and especially explore the library within it. It didn't take much persuasion on René's part for the others to agree to stopping for an extra day in Pontferrada.

When the group of pilgrims reached Santa Catalina, they booked into the Albergue El Caminate, a small private hostel that only provided for sixteen pilgrims in two rooms. The hostel did have its own café-bar and patio which meant they wouldn't have to wander in search of food.

Meditation, which had been skipped during their hike during the morning, was done within the small dorm which afforded all the privacy that they needed. Dinner and conversation was quiet with everyone retreating into their private spaces before it was time for the lights to be turned out. René turned to his journal for his final entry for the day.

> *It was a long, even boring walk today, and everyone is tired. I didn't take many photos and had little passion for doing so. I could tell that all of us now need another opportunity to recharge ourselves, something that I hope we will be able to do in Pontferrada.*
>
> *Though we haven't said anything much to each other during the day, I still managed to feel connected to Freya. I think it is because of the body language I see in her eyes and that unique smile that she has.*

~

They woke to an overcast sky that hinted at showers the next morning and soon found themselves walking at a quicker pace, climbing up to reach Rabanal del Camino. Half an hour before Rabanal, a gentle rain began to fall. There was no talk of meditating outside in nature. Finding shelter from the rain in a café, they decided that they might as well eat a hot meal while waiting for the rain to ease up. An hour later, the rain retreated leaving the air wet with a fine mist. Leaving the café, the group continued to wear their rain gear as the sky promised more rain before the day was to be done. It wasn't long before their early brisk pace began to falter as they tackled the long hike up to the famed Cruz de Ferro.

"Did you bring a rock from home?" Fred asked René as they stood at the base of the mound of stones that surrounded the cross.

"I brought five stones," he answered. "One for Cécile, a second one for our children, the third stone is for my brothers and sisters, the fourth is for my parents, and the last stone is for myself. However, I'm saving my stone for Finisterre though, not here."

The eight pilgrims took their turns placing their stones with silent prayers and meditations, taking their offerings to wherever it was that such heart-felt offerings went. When all the stones had been placed, they couldn't help but hug each other before leaving the cross and hill of stones in silence. For the last two kilometres into Manjarin, they continued to walk in silence. Manjarin wasn't a village as they had expected, but a ruin of where a village had once stood. All that seemed to remain was a gaily flagged shop that served as an emergency hostel for those not able or willing to walk further.

Manjarin offered the most basic of services. Rather than beds, there were mattresses on raised loose boards; and, the toilet was an outhouse. Though they knew in advance what they were getting into when choosing this stop, the reality of its starkness began to sink in. It was only the smell of the coffee and the haunting taped music played by the owner, which convinced them to stay the night rather than walk further in hopes of finding someplace better to sleep. They were the only ones who had arrived by mid-afternoon. It appeared doubtful that anyone else would be stopping unless later in the day.

Once they had settled in, each claiming their personal spaces, and while waiting for Tomas to cook them a communal meal, René wandered off to explore the surrounding area as the sun had broken through the clouds, and had warmed the air. René hoped that he could find a place for meditation outdoors in order to take advantage of the sunshine. It wasn't long before he found a sheltered small space that was perfect. Stripping off his clothes, making sure that they were placed on top of his camera bag so as to not become too damp, he settled into a comfortable half-lotus position. The ground wasn't smooth, but it didn't take too much effort to make it comfortable enough without needing to use his clothing as a buffer between himself and the ground.

Closing his eyes, his senses became heightened allowing him to feel the earth beneath his bare skin, as well as the freshness of the air and the rays of sunshine that fell upon his as though a blessing from whatever it was that filled him with peace. This was his heaven. He began to turn his attention to his breath in search of that gap between out-breath and in-breath, an empty space that had all the answers to questions he would never ask.

When he opened his eyes a half hour later, he looked out at the scene before him. It was time to take some photos. That night he wrote:

> *I'm writing by the light of my flashlight so as to not disturb the others. Freya is sleeping in her sleeping bag liner just inches away from me. I often wonder what she thinks about as we walk the Camino. We are never very far from each other on the trail. I also wonder what she dreams about.*
>
> *I think I'm falling in love with her.*

Chapter Twenty-Five – Trust And Intimacy

René and his companions arrived in Ponterrada at one-thirty the next afternoon. The walk down the mountains, a descent of almost a full kilometre, with two very steep downhill sections making the walk more difficult than they had forecast. They had stopped in Acebo for coffee and again in Molinaseca for an early lunch. Miryam had pre-booked the Hostal Rabal, which was within easy walking distance of the castle and the centre of the city on Avenida del Castillo. By two-thirty, they were all in their rooms in the hostel-hotel. The group had agreed to meet later in the hotel bar, at five that afternoon, for tapas and beverages. Until then, most had intended on staying in their rooms for quiet time, reading, and for writing in their respective journals.

Freya ran the tub in their small hotel room while René gathered their hiking clothing for washing later. Just as René was settling himself on the bed to check his messages, Freya called out to him asking for him to bring her shower bag which she had left on the small dresser. He got up and found the bag and brought it to her.

"Sit down and talk with me, René."

"Sure. What's on your mind, Freya?"

"I think you need a haircut. I saw a unisex barbershop just a short distance from the hostel. I could also get my hair done. It's a rat's nest. Would you come with me? We can do it later while our clothes are being washed."

"Sounds like a good idea to me," he agreed with an indulgent smile.

"Are you going to shave now, or after your bath?

"After my bath. Why?"

"I was hoping you'd let me use your razor, your older one, so I could shave my legs."

"Not a problem, Freya. I'll go and get it for you." He got up and looked into his kit bag and took the used razor out of it. There was still one more razor left of the three disposable razors he had brought from home. "Here," he said as he gave the razor to her.

As she reached for it, he turned as though to leave the bathroom. "Don't leave. Sit here with me. I don't want to be alone right now. Talk to me about anything at all, okay?"

So he stayed sitting on the toilet seat while she shaved her legs in the tub. He talked about his life at home in Canada, his three young grandchildren, and their passions for books, Lego and puzzles. While he talked, she continued to use his razor to shave her mons pubis, gently stretching the skin so as to not cut the delicate surface. He found it increasingly hard to maintain his train of thought as he talked, as his eyes couldn't turn away from her vulva which glistened with thin threads of water. His body reacted as well, swelling with long repressed needs, primal needs.

"Here," she said as she handed back his razor. Looking down she saw his erection as he had to stand up and move closer to get the razor. As he took the razor from her hand, she bent over and kissed it, then looked up at him saying, "Your turn in the tub."

The shock of having his manhood kissed left him speechless.

"Oh, I hope you to shave off that scraggly mess as well," she said as she touched his genitals. "I don't want to be pulling hairs out of my teeth later."

It was as if he had been struck dumb. Her words barely penetrated as he found himself getting into the tub. He sat there still speechless, staring at her as she briskly towelled herself off. Hanging up the towel, she reached for the razor he had left on the ledge of the tub. "Here let me do it."

When René and Freya joined the others at the hotel's bar later that afternoon, Fred and Gabe remarked on René's haircut.

"It's amazing what a good woman can do with a scruffy old man," laughed Gabe. "Who would have guessed that you could actually look somewhat presentable in public? Still, you don't hold a candle standing beside Freya. Beautiful haircut, Freya!"

"You're looking pretty good for an old fart," chortled Fred. "However, I think I will stick to my pilgrim beard and moustache until I get home. I'll see how the wife likes it," he added. "You do look different without the moustache by the way, somehow almost younger."

Mark, ignored René as he took in the glow in Freya's face which accented her trimmed hair. He didn't think for a moment that the glow was due to a visit to a barbershop. He nudged Miryam and whispered, "Finally!"

"Okay," Miryam spoke loudly in order to get everyone's attention. "There's a nice little café, the Café de Arles not too far from here. How about we go there for something decent to eat. It's still a long time until dinner tonight."

In agreement, all followed her and Mark. The two of them had been scouting out restaurants earlier when they found the café.

Next door to the café was a grocery store, which necessitated a stop as well. René carried a small silk grocery bag in his camera waist pack, which he proceeded to fill with an assortment of fruits and veggies, along with some crackers and several juice containers. He knew that he would likely eat all of it the next day, while he and the others went walking to discover the treasures of Pontferrada. Freya had managed to sneak in a few granola and chocolate bars into his bag as well knowing she was going to be with him for the day.

While the others were chatting over tapas and wine, René pulled Fred to the side and said, "We have to talk." René then told the others that he wanted to get a few sunset photos and that he would be back in an hour, which then prompted Fred to announce that he was going to go with René. René had his camera in hand as they walked down the street.

"What's up?"

"I'm in deep shit," René confessed. "Freya and I have crossed the line from friends into something much more intimate."

Fred looked at his friend, surprised with his admission, not surprised at the content of his confession. "You know that just being 'friends with benefits' is dangerous and destructive for both parties, don't you?"

"This isn't just 'friends with benefits,' Fred. Believe me. That's why I said I'm in deep shit. It's a hell of a lot more than that."

Fred considered how he was going to approach René's concern. "You know, sex is a powerful force, René. You know that the Bible distinguished ordinary sexual activity from sex, which results in 'knowing' the other in a way that would never be possible without sexual union. For example, from personal experience I can tell you that you that there are things I know about my wife's spirit, emotions, mind and body that no one else knows, because I have had sex with her and, her with me. This is what I mean about 'knowing' the other."

"But, Fred, I'm worried that she might just have been feeling sorry for me, or that she was simply satisfying her physical needs, that she really isn't in love with me."

"I don't understand why you would think that, René. But from a spiritual point of view, I can't see that a sin has been committed. When sin is committed, it usually involves not respecting this union and spiritual and mental/emotional side of it as well."

"I know that I have to be ready for it to end, but somehow it seems as if I'd be cutting off a large piece of myself in the process," complained René with evident stress. "I mean, at the end of the Camino, she'll be heading home and I will be left behind, broken. We're not married, there is no real commitment, and no promise of commitment."

"Regardless if there is a marriage covenant or not, sexual intercourse makes two people one in the spirit, as well as the flesh. That is, when sexual intercourse activates the heart and soul. So," Fred continued, "in essence, you would be cutting yourself into two parts in abandoning the union of two into one. Don't assume that it will be over when the Camino is over."

"If Freya leaves me when the Camino is done, I'll lose my heart. I don't think I could take having my heart broken again."

"That is between you and Freya and the future. Sorry, René, I know that this doesn't solve anything, but at least you don't have to add the element of having sinned into the equation.

Now, let's get some of those photos before we are gone too long."

Back in their hotel room, René was still suffering as though tortured, regardless that he was the one torturing himself. He knew now that there a deep connection between himself and Freya, a union that seemed to be magical and almost holy. With his ex-wife, Cécile he had thought he had found the woman who completed him as a man, a woman with whom he conceived two children out of love. But, that had all come crashing down as she left him for another man, a stable man who also loved her. Since then, he had kept his distance from love, and to be honest, distant from all women. But now with Freya, it was as if he had twinned himself into mystery and magic, becoming a god to her goddess, something not of this earth.

He lay beside her as she slept in peace, her foot lying atop his; and sleep evaded him.

Chapter Twenty-Six – A Picture Worth a Thousand Words

Two days later, they left Pontferrada bound for Villafranca del Bierzo. René had decided that he would deal with the issue of Freya in his life later, likely when the last step on the Camino was taken and it was time to head home. The return home to Canada, alone in all probability. He believed that Freya would simply vanish back into her world when the time came to leave the Camino. Yet, for now, he wanted as much of Freya as she would give him. All he had, all he would ever have, was now, so he threw himself fully into this union with Freya, for what time was left to them.

The Small Company of Pilgrims stopped in Camponaraya for coffee and a sock change, in spite of the fact that during the seven kilometres, they hadn't really worked up a sweat. Three kilometres after that stop, they entered a wooded area. They had found their meditation retreat for the day. Another three and a half kilometres later, they stopped for lunch in Valtuille de Arriba rather than walk the final five kilometres to Villafranca.

René had been taking photos during the walk, as normal, and had just put his camera back into his waist pack before settling in to eat his bocadilla, fries, and his café con leche while the others were chatting, animated after their extra day spent in Pontferrada. Miryam had assumed maternal control of the group during their evenings out to make sure that spirits stayed uplifted, and that drinks were imbibed in moderation so that no one would suffer from painful hangovers.

"René," called Sid in an attempt to engage his attention. "I've noticed that you rarely seem to look at your photos once you've taken them, unlike everyone else here with their smartphone cameras. Why is that?"

"Likely it's because I take too many photos," he laughed in response. "But seriously, it goes back to when I first studied photography back in the days of single-lens reflex cameras, before digital photography showed up. I learned to take photos with care, especially when I went on photography field trips with my university classmates. Back then there was basically no chance of retaking a photo if an image turned out bad."

"That sort of makes sense, in a way," admitted Sid. "But if you checked the result immediately after taking the photo, wouldn't you still have an opportunity to retake the photo? I mean, before continuing on, don't you agree?"

"Hmm," responded René, "Well there is something else at work here. Part of my rationale lies in Buddhist thought where I've learned how important it is to be in the moment. I found early on, when I first got a digital camera, that I left the immediate present to return, even if only going back a few seconds, to the past. I learned to trust that I had gotten the right photo somewhere among the excessive number of photos that I had taken.

I trusted that I would find what I needed from the images after enough time had passed, time which added perspective to making decisions about the worth of a photo, just like I did when I worked in a darkroom with negatives and contact prints."

Mark jumped in to the conversation as well. "Unlike these other jokers, I don't have a smartphone or a camera. But, I have also noticed that you rarely take photos of people. What's that about?"

"I guess I feel it's intrusive. Pictures of people are powerful things; and besides, most people don't really appreciate a passing stranger taking their photo, especially if that stranger is an older man. I guess I try to respect those things as much as possible."

"But, we're not strangers. I don't remember you taking any pictures of us."

"Ha ha ha," laughed René, "Well most of the time you guys are either naked, or eating, or drinking. Now we wouldn't want to immortalise those scenes, would we?"

"It didn't seem to stop some of the others with their cell phones," Mark grinned. "You should see some of the photos they have taken. Besides, there is nothing shameful about us being nude. The nude self is beautiful and should be celebrated, not hidden. And, if I am not mistaken, the art world agrees with me."

"Well," admitted René. "I have taken a few photos of you guys along the way, usually as you were walking along the path and I was able to capture the panorama that was unfolding in front of us."

"But those could be photos of anyone, couldn't they?" challenged Mark. "I mean, wouldn't you just see our backs?"

"And shadows," added René. "But you're right. I haven't really taken many photos of us together. But now that you mention it, I'll make a point of taking more from now on. But if I do, they still will end up being stored until the future when I've had a chance to evaluate the results, after the Camino of course for most of them. There are a few that I check on in the evening with a view to posting them on Facebook for my kids and others back home. I promise I'll e-mail all of you the ones that are worth sharing."

"Sounds good to me," stated Mark, a sentiment that was echoed by everyone else. "Miryam, give me your phone, but first put it on picture display mode. I want to show René the photos you took at the café de Arles two days ago in Pontferrada."

René looked at the photos and remembered the joy he experienced with his friends. Mark then brought up a photo of René and Freya while they were talking to the others. "Now what I like about this photo," remarked Mark, is this," he said pointing to Freya's hand resting on René's lap. "As they say," Mark continued, "every picture tells a story of a thousand words. That picture tells a story that would rival Doctor Zhivago."

Embarrassed, René turned bright red. "Oh God, I'm screwed."

"Don't worry, we won't be posting it to our Facebook accounts and telling tales of the love life of one René Beauchemin on the Camino. The point is simply that perhaps you haven't been taking our photos is because of what they might say about you, not necessarily about what they would say about us? Photos expose and make vulnerable. And, I'm not being judgmental about what's going on between the two of you – it's beautiful – I'm just saying that you, too, have to risk being fully honest to yourself and with others. And amongst us, some of that naked honesty involves natural scenes of our life here while nude."

René thought long and hard about what Mark had said as they walked into Villafranca del Bierzo. He somehow couldn't deny the depths of his feelings for Freya and understood that by not taking her photo, he had in fact created a false record of his journey to this point. Of course, the same could be said about avoiding taking photos of the others. Was he intentionally, subconsciously creating a record that was intended to deny the importance of all of his companions on this pilgrimage, deny perhaps their very presence? The psychotherapist in René then asked, 'What is behind this resistance, René?'

Before they had left Pontferrada, Miryam had called ahead to book rooms at the Ultreia Hostal which would allow privacy for her and Mark, as well for René and Freya. The hostel had its own bar-café but not a restaurant which meant that the group would have to go out for the evening meal. Once the Little Company of Pilgrims had been assigned their rooms, they retreated into them to wash their hiking clothes and take showers before gathering, as usual, in mid-afternoon at the hostel's café. René and Freya took advantage of their privacy for reconnecting intimately. Contrary to his habits, René forgot about checking his e-mail and sending responses or uploading his photos taken earlier that day.

"Enough," said Freya as she pulled away from René's embrace with a smile of satisfaction that had her glowing. "Go check your e-mail. Don't forget to send your kids an e-mail so they don't worry about you. If you forget, you'll just feel guilty."

"I already feel guilty," admitted René as his palm lightly passed over the skin on her hip as she faced him.

"Go take a cold shower and then write the letter, René," she commanded as she turned away to rise out of the bed.

Freya didn't bother putting on any clothes. Freya only wore clothing when she was out in public, a public that would take offense at her exposed skin. She was never ashamed of being naked with people she trusted. Rather than feeling vulnerable, being nude gave her a regal strength, reminding René of the images he had seen of goddesses in mythology.

Returning from his shower, he grabbed his tablet and opened it to access the Internet and download his e-mail. He looked up to see Freya coming back from the bathroom to get her shower bag when he decided to take a photo of her as she smiled at him, a photo that would automatically upload to his Flickr account along with those from his camera. It was the first intimate photo he had taken of her, but now was not the time to study it. There were messages waiting for him.

> *Mark taught me a valuable lesson today, a lesson about honesty. Unconsciously, I had been avoiding taking photos of my companions here on the Camino. Why? What story was I trying to create, and what truths was I trying to avoid being exposed?*
>
> *As I thought about it, I found that I seemed to be creating a story that would leave my companions invisible, as if they were spirits and not people at all. I thought I might have even been trying to protect myself when at the end we all would end up going our separate ways.*
>
> *Investing in people does set the scene for separations to be more about painful loss than a simple, "Adieu." With Mark's acute awareness, I realise that I have to be honest with myself and with my camera.*
>
> *The first effort came earlier, a single shot with the built-in camera on the tablet. I haven't shown it to her or even to myself yet. Perhaps tomorrow when the time is ripe.*

~

The small company of pilgrims left Villafranca at first light, headed towards La Faba, which lay twenty-five kilometres away. La Faba was on the mountain slope leading to O'Cebreiro. They had chosen to follow the main pilgrimage route rather than take the optional, longer and hillier route, as they had to save energy for the ascent to O'Cebreiro and their destination for the following day, Tricastela.

The views were worthy of many photos, as they walked into Trabadelo for a second breakfast. With less than two hundred kilometres left to reach Santiago, their energy levels had begun to surge in anticipation. Less than thirty minutes later they left the café and were again on the trail, not stopping until they entered the village of Herrerias for lunch. Herrerias was perched on the first rise of the mountain, three kilometres before their stop for the night at La Faba. Herrerias was two hundred metres lower in altitude than La Faba which was three kilometres straight uphill.

The hostel in La Faba was communal which meant that the separation into separate rooms wouldn't be possible, something that curiously gave René a sense of relief, which then turned into guilt. What was he afraid of? Why was he feeling guilty? Once they had washed their clothing and had taken showers, they decided to go out to the local café to see if it was a better option than cooking in the communal kitchen. Before the café there was a small grocery store which they checked out to figure out what was possible should they decide to go back and cook their dinner at the hostel.

Sitting back with a cerveza in his hand, Fred asked, "What do you think? The pilgrim menu for tonight looks pretty decent. I say we eat out."

"You always say the same thing, Fred," laughed Miryam. "But, I'll have to admit that I agree with you. There wasn't much choice available in the grocery store."

The chatter and convivial camaraderie continued as René excused himself to go out hunting for photos. It wasn't long before Freya found him wandering in the village.

"Mind if I walk with you?"

"I love to have you walk with me. Here, I want to show you something." René took her to a place called Refugio Vegetariano which had a strangeness to it that was compelling. Inside, they found that they could have a choice of specialty teas, while surrounded by Hindu artifacts and deities. Since neither of them had been drinking beer or wine at the café, the idea of having tea was a welcome thought.

"We have to show this place to Sid and Asha," Freya agreed as she studied the possibilities. "Let's go back and get them, first. Then we can have tea with them."

René felt a hint of disappointment at having to share Freya with Sid and Asha. But, he swallowed that disappointment knowing that it would only cause problems if voiced.

A short while later, the four of them were sitting in the tea house. Sid and Asha were pleased to see signs of their homeland being honoured on the Camino. René made sure to get photos of them in the tea house alongside a statuette of Ganesh. He also took a photo of an animated Freya who was glowing.

Later, in the hostel that night, René wrote:

A few more photos today, people photos – Asha, Sid and Freya in a unique place called Refugio Vegetariano. We were able to find a quiet place on a hillside earlier in the day for our group meditation.

We are staying in a dorm tonight, another night in which I will have to sleep alone. I have to admit that I have come to treasure those nights where I sleep beside the most beautiful woman in the world, the most perfect woman ever created.

Chapter Twenty-Seven – Shadows and Light

The group left La Faba at seven the next morning after having breakfast. By the time they reached O'Cebreiro, only five kilometres from La Faba, they were ready for a rest. They had walked uphill all the way gaining four hundred metres in altitude. And, they had done that walking in the rain which made the trek that much more difficult. They were more than ready for a hot cup of coffee and a bowl of soup in O'Cebreiro,

As they sat by a window, they could see a constant parade of pilgrims, as well as many tourists, who carried umbrellas and cameras, pass by. O'Cebreiro was bustling with more people than any village they had yet seen along the pilgrims' way.

"Wow!" spoke Fred with amazement. "This place is rocking. I'm going to have to come back here again and just hang out."

"Yeah," echoed René, "it's some kind of amazing is right."

René turned from the window and noticed an odd light enveloping his friends. He didn't know if it was a trick of the light, but it held a magical feeling. Taking out his camera, he asked, "Do you mind if I take a group photo?"

A collective smile was given, so René took several shots from various angles hoping that he had somehow captured the glow that surrounded them, something he would only be able to verify when he worked on his photos back in Canada on his large screen monitor.

"Here," said Fred, "give me the camera and I'll take a photo of you with the others. And, how about I get one of the other pilgrims to take a photo of our whole group?"

"Sounds good," René agreed. "But first let me take a few more. I want some individual shots as well, and that includes you too, Buddy."

Shortly after the photos were taken, they noticed that the rain had changed to a light shower. It was time to head back out onto the trail. Occasionally, during the rest of the morning, the sun broke through showing the countryside in sparkling shades of green, painting the Galician world as a land of legends and magic. They passed signs of a spiritual world that had been in Galicia since before the arrival of Christianity, with dolmens, burial mounds that were more than 5,000 years old. The land was still alive with myth and magic. It was in the very air and the light of the land.

In spite of the risk of more rain, the Small Company of Pilgrims found a private little glade not far off the path that allowed them to return to their ritual of skyclad meditation. René was surprised at his body's response to the chill and dampness as he took his seat in the circle. If anything, he felt warmer nude than when he had been dressed only moments earlier.

Sid began to speak:

"This very moment is the perfect teacher, this very moment is always with us – just seeing what's going on – it's right there, teaching us. We can choose to be with what's happening and not dissociate. Awareness is found in both pleasure and pain, in our confusion and our wisdom, and is available in each moment of our weird, unfathomable, ordinary everyday lives."

Later, back on the trail, they easily covered the rest of the distance to Biduedo where they had planned to stop for lunch. They had walked fourteen and a half kilometres from O'Cebreiro, almost twenty from La Faba. All that remained were just over six and a half kilometres until Triacastela, all of it downhill to reach the valley more than five hundred metres lower.

Their lunch was soup and sandwiches, bocadillos y caldo gallego. René found that in spite of having already walked twenty kilometres, he wasn't tired in the least. He felt stronger and more vital than he had felt for a long time, perhaps even in years. Fred had noticed René's animation as he took part in the chatter at the table. Typically René was a listener, only joining in when topics were more serious. Refreshed and energized, the group left the café in the afternoon sunshine and walked on to Triacastela which they reached less than two hours later.

In Triacastela, they headed to the Complexio Xacabo, which Miryam had booked based on Gabe's research. The hostel provided them with the option of separate rooms or dorm rooms for very reasonable prices. Fred volunteered to wash everyone's clothes and dry them in a dryer which was available for their use. The hotel-hostel had it its own bar and restaurant, as well as free Wi-Fi, making it feel like an all-inclusive resort in spite of the fact that meals were not included. In his room, René was busy with uploading photos and responding to e-mails while Freya went out with Miryam for some girl-talk time.

René decided to check the group photos that he had taken, as well as the whole group photo that another pilgrim had taken for him earlier in the day at O'Cebreiro. He wanted to see if the glow he had noticed surrounding his friends had been captured by the camera. He also wanted to post the large group photo to Facebook. When he checked the photos, the glow was indeed there to be seen, but not on everyone, in spite of all of them being positioned in the same light. He couldn't understand it.

Satisfied with the group photo in spite of the uneven light that surrounded some of his friends, he posted it to Facebook. Confused, he had to assume that he had somehow chosen incorrect settings on the camera, which resulted, in what he could only characterise as halos, in the photos taken in the café. He resolved to take new group photos in an outdoor setting to get a better group image for his personal archives.

Curious, he decided to take an indoor photo of the hotel room and another one of himself to see if he could find out what the matter was with indoor settings. When the photos were taken, he played them back and found that both had turned out as expected – normal photos. He decided that he would get Freya to sit still long enough for a few photos when she returned. With the issue set aside for the moment, René turned to do some reading as he lay in the bed. Uncharacteristically, he lay in the bed clothing free.

"Freya, can I take a few photos of you? Somehow my photos at the café of the group didn't turn out very well. Here, let me show you what I mean. I want to make sure that there won't be a repeat of today's pictures in the future," was the greeting Freya received as she came into their private room.

"Sure," she replied. "But wait a second until I get comfortable. I need to use the washroom first."

She emerged from the bathroom wearing only her smile, something that René had thought she would do, as she seemed to be allergic to clothing when conditions warranted.

"What seems to be the problem?"

René showed her the photos that had halo effects over the heads of Mark, Miryam, Sid, Asha and Gabe. There were no halos over Fred, or Freya, or himself.

"You're right," she admitted. "That is weird." Stepping back and leaning against the door to their room, she purred, "How about this pose?"

René took photo after photo of Freya from all sorts of angles, based on changing angles of light. The poses themselves were lost on him as he checked his settings and played back the images. Freya was enjoying being at the centre of René's focus. She then suggested that René set the camera on the cabinet so that they could both be in the photos. So, putting the setting on self-timer at ten seconds, he took quite a few more. Sometimes, it took a long time between photos, as he got lost in her presence. Finally, he squeaked "Enough," and lay back exhausted.

"Let's take a shower and get ready for dinner with the others," suggested Freya. "We can look at the photos later and add more to that collection if inspiration strikes us," Then, she added with a wicked grin. "You wash me and I'll wash you."

They returned to their room late, and tired. Since there was to be an early start in the morning, René forgot about checking the photos. Even his journal was ignored. They fell asleep only moments after slipping into the bed, one folded into the other.

Chapter Twenty-Eight – Skin is Just Skin

After and early breakfast, René and his friends began a twenty-two kilometre walk with the destination being a village called Barbadelo. It would be shorter day than had been the norm for the past few days. They wanted to get past Sarria, which would be crawling with pilgrims, as it was the last official starting point for pilgrims bound for Santiago who wanted an official certificate of completion, a compostela. They decided to not take the alternate route to Samos, as it would have added seven kilometres to their hike, too much for them. As well, going through Samos would have meant that they would have had to stay in Sarria. Because of the heated discussions about the choice of route, René had forgotten all about his intention to check the photos he had taken the night before. There was an excitement in the air that had all them in a grip, an excitement that was growing as they neared Santiago, an excitement that was shared with the other pilgrims around them.

Three hours into the walk, they reached a tiny village called Pintín which had a bar-café where they decided it was time for coffee and a small bite to eat. Later as they made their way from Pintín, because there weren't any sites that seemed suitable for meditation, they pushed on to the centre of Sarria where they stopped for lunch and for a short stay as tourists. With only four kilometres left to reach Barbadelo, they decided that a couple of hours in Sarria wouldn't create a problem in finding accommodations. If worse came to worse, they could always walk the four kilometres back into Sarria where there were always more than enough bed spaces for pilgrims.

A quick lunch was eaten at the bar-café O'Escalinata on Rua Mayor near the Santa Marina church. Besides, the obligatory churches, René took photos of the sixteenth century pilgrim hospital, San Anton, and the Mosteiro de Santa Maria Madalena, a thirteenth century convent. Leaving Sarria, they crossed over the the Río Celeiro to climb up to the village of Barbadelo.

The group had decided against staying at the Xunta chain of hostels feeling that the older albergues, or private hostels, were better choices if they were available. Searching through the village, they chose a picturesque place called Casa de Carmen which had Internet, washing facilities, a restaurant, and beautiful rooms including a few private rooms. They group chose to stay together in a dorm as they wanted to have some together time for meditation.

"We're making pretty good time," commented Gabe as the group sat in the restaurant having pre-dinner beverages and tapas. "I figure that tomorrow we can easily make it to Gonzar even though it is a twenty-five kilometre hike. If we walk another twenty-five the next day, we could stay at O'Coto which would leave just sixty kilometres to reach Santiago, another three days of walking."

"Sounds like you have another great plan, old boy," approved Mark. "I agree that we are all stronger and can handle the longer distances."

"Miryam, do you want to call ahead and book beds at the Casa de Somoza in O'Coto?" asked Gabe. "The next beds are another six and a half kilometres further in Melida. I don't think we want to walk over thirty kilometres in one day if we don't have to. Remember, that's for two nights from now," he grinned good-naturedly.

"Not a problem," agreed Miryam. "Consider it done. Do you have their phone number?"

With the plans for the next two days settled, the pilgrims talked about the countryside through which they had been passing, and the sights and sounds of life in Spain for the rest of the evening until it was time to turn in for the night.

René took advantage of the opportunity later, to write in his journal:

> *Another good day. It looks like we will be in Santiago in five days' time. In one way, I'm not looking forward to it as that will be where I will have to say goodbye to these wonderful people. But at the same time, the achievement of completing the Camino will be its own reward. There is no question in my mind that I will take the time to continue on to Finisterre where I will place "my" stone in the Atlantic Ocean.*

~

René rose early in darkness, as did all of the others, intent on getting out the door as soon as the pre-dawn light allowed. With a twenty-five kilometre walk ahead of them and with increased pilgrim traffic, the last thing they wanted to do was to walk any extra kilometres in search of a bed for the night. Before they had gone too far down the road, dawn began to spread its rays of approaching sunlight, accentuating the few clouds with a vibrant palette of colour. They were just passing the Cruce Baxán when the sun broke free of the eastern horizon. They continued on the trail for another half hour before reaching another cross, the Cruce Leiman, which had a café nearby where they agreed to stop for a quick coffee and toast.

Later they stopped again between Morgade and Ferreios having found a perfect place for their group skyclad meditation, a spot just off the tree-lined path. Meditation was kept short, at twenty minutes. They soon regained the path and walked another two and a half hours to reach Portomarin where they stopped for a late breakfast or early lunch at the popular O'Mirador café.

Two hours after eating lunch, the group arrived at Gonzar where they settled for the night at the Xunta Hostel which had Internet and all the facilities they needed. When post-hiking chores were done, they gathered for a late afternoon lunch feeling good about having completed the days hike in good time. Following their meal, René went for a walk with Fred who wanted to talk about some of the ideas that were swirling around in his head.

"You know, René" Fred began, "we have been meditating nude for so long as a group that it has become almost natural for me. I mean, in spite of being naked. I can feel a collective spirituality that has me question my beliefs about nudity and spiritualism."

"Yeah, I understand what you're saying," admitted René. "It has been much the same for me. At home I have always meditated, and for the past few years, I have meditated nude, but always in private. Meditation has always been a spiritual practice for me, a private spiritual practice."

"Well, as I was saying," Fred continued, "It got me thinking about taking this home with me to my parishioners. But, how would I get passed the barriers we have about nudity as a church community? It's hard enough in our homes to have a micro community sharing life and worship while nude. I know that if it was possible, by building a spiritual community that has each person stand honest, and vulnerable before God and the church community, we could deepen our spiritual practice."

"Well," pondered René, "I guess you'd have to identify the pros and cons of the idea before coming up with a 'why' and 'how' for naked spiritual practice as a group. What are your thoughts on that?"

"Well, I could see how for some, seeing others naked would be a distraction. It's a problem that could only be overcome if personal nudity could became comfortable for them in private. You know, being comfortable in your own skin. I suspect that for nudity to be accept in community, one has to be comfortable with one's personal nudity. Once you have that, then it would become so much easier to be comfortable with others while naked. In any case, branching out to being spiritual with people is not just a question of acceptance of their nakedness, it's also a question of accepting others unconditionally as people. I wonder if mutual tolerance of nudity makes for more acceptance of others."

"Well, that seems to be what has happened to both of us here, hasn't it?" noted René. "I mean, I thought I was comfortable with myself when nude, but when I found myself nude the first time, here with others, I immediately found that I still had some hang-ups about myself, which then made me uncomfortable with the others. It was actually the calmness and unconditional acceptance by Sid and Asha that had allowed something to shift within me. Perhaps we need to have a guide or guides to help bridge that gap in a community?"

"Another problem that comes up for me," Fred continued, "Was that naked group spiritual practice could easily focus on the nudity itself, and have the spiritual aspect become lost in the group. Awareness of their nudity as something holy, and then using it to distance themselves from others whom they would see as "less spiritual" because they weren't naked. You know, in effect being naked spiritual fundamentalists. In other words, they could become filled with themselves as being more spiritual than others who were not nude in their spiritual practice."

"Ha ha," laughed René. "You made me think of some of the Naga Babas I saw in India. Their nudity and spiritual practice seemed to have become street theatre. It seemed that the holy men were more in search of tourist cameras than enlightenment."

"Exactly!" confirmed Fred. "It's that 'look at me' narcissism that feeds off being exposed, rather than a spiritual humility."

"I like that, Fred, spiritual humility. In my Buddhist sangha at home, we have often discussed spiritual consumerism."

"The last thing I came up with," continued Fred, "was about spiritual maturity. For some, there isn't enough spiritual maturity for group practice, whether they are clothed or not clothed. Nudity could just accentuate that spiritual immaturity. In a way, it ties in with what I have already said. Are you mature enough to view nudity as a means of approaching God, and not view nudity as the focus of worship. If not, then it is likely that one needs to approach nudity as a means of approaching God as a way to build maturity rather than simply discard the idea. People do need time to grow into authentic spiritual practice, naked or clothed."

René clapped Fred on the back as he said, "It sounds like you have it all reasoned out. Now, the hard part comes in risking it, Fred."

"Yeah, you're not kidding," he admitted, "Risking it and risking my employment at the same time."

They arrived back at the hostel in time for tapas and a refreshing drink before their evening meal.

"Hi Freya," René said as he hugged her on his return to the hostel. She smiled and pulled him closer in order to hug him back and steal a kiss. Holding hands, they stayed close to each other as they joined in the stories of their Camino family.

> *Fred is a wise man. He has wrestled with the idea of spiritualism for a long time, truly wanting to find a way for his parishioners to enter into a truly spiritual life. I somehow doubt that he will ever find a way to make the path of spiritual nudity happen. I wonder how he will react to that when he has finally experienced spiritualism as it could be – honest, open and fulfilling – through his own nudity.*
>
> *Freya feels so good even when all we do is hold hands. We found some time to look at our 'special' photos together. Technically, the camera showed no issues with indoor light which was my original reason for the photos. However, the photos themselves showed me that she is as in to me, as I am in to her.*
>
> *I wonder and hope if this means that this is a beginning for me. Will this continue long after the Camino is done? I don't want "us" to end.*

Chapter Twenty-Nine – And Two Become One

The next morning they stopped at Casa Mari, in Ligonde for their morning coffee. They had left Gonzar a little more than two hours earlier, and had crested the mountain called Sierra Ligonde. The rest of the morning was taken up in making the journey to Palas de Rei, where they then stopped for an early lunch. The final ten kilometres to reach O'Coto would be walked through gently rolling hills. Between San Xulián and Casa Nova, they passed through an ancient oak forest where they located their communal meditation site for the day.

"Today, it is going to be a special meditation," began Sid. "I think we have become fully trusting of each other allowing us to attempt an advanced form of meditation. However, before I can go any further, I want you all to tell me if there is full trust in Asha and myself as we lead you through the highest level of meditation, a practice that touches the very heart of whatever it is that you believe to be god or spirit."

The question caught the group by surprise. René was the first to respond. "Sid, from the day that I met you on the train from Bayonne to Saint Jean Pied de Port, you have been what I can only call, my spiritual guide. In my Buddhist practice, one trusts implicitly and without question, such a guide. Personally, I trust you without reservation."

Freya was quick to join René in agreeing to follow where Sid and Asha were going to take them in meditation. Mark and Miryam simply smiled and nodded as if they already knew what was going to happen. Gabe grinned knowing in advance what his role in the meditation practice was to be. Fred, was just a bit hesitant to commit, the idea of submitting fully to another was an idea that left him more than a bit nervous. In spite of it, Fred told Sid that he would try.

Sid smiled his usual enigmatic smile. "Fred, I have a special task for you during the meditation." Then turning to René, Sid asked if René would give Fred his camera. René gave the camera to Fred, as Sid continued to give instructions.

"Gabe, as we agreed earlier, you will record on paper what you see, hear and feel during the meditation. Fred, I want you to take photos during the meditation. Don't evaluate or judge what you see, simply record it. There will be time later for discussing the meditation and everyone's responses to the meditation, including yours. Is that okay with you?"

"Of course," replied Fred intrigued by the preamble to the meditation. "I just take photos."

"Of course, at a certain point in the meditation, you will be pulled into your own meditation, and that will be the end of taking photos," Sid added.

"Asha, are you ready?"

Asha stood up and slowly walked towards Sid. As she walked a song filled the air:

> "Sunlight made visible
> the whole length of a sky,
> movement of wind,
> leaf, flower, all six colours
> on tree, bush and creeper:
> all this
> is the day's worship.
>
> Night and day
> in your worship
> I forget myself."

As she walked towards Sid, the words of her song created a golden container of spirt that surrounded her like a golden light. She stood in front of Sid who sat in lotus position with his hands lifted, reminding René of one of the poses he associated with Tibetan Buddhism. While her words continued to pour out, Sid's member rose into the air. Still singing Asha settled onto his shaft and wrapped her legs around Sid. The two had become one.

Freya and René saw that Mark and Miryam were already copying the meditative position modelled by Sid and Asha. Looking deep within Freya, René felt his member swell and stand up. Without the need to speak, Freya took her seat on his lap, letting his member slip into her and then she embraced it with her own strength.

No words of dharma were spoken. It was if something had overpowered the need for words. Meditation embraced not only the breath of the self, but also the breath of the other, making both into one. For a full half hour, lingam stayed erect in the folds of yoni. And then, with an unheard command, lingam was released and one became two.

René came back to awareness of Freya sitting on his lap with her legs wrapped around him and he knew he had just taken part in Tibetan Tantric meditation, Tantric yoga. There were no words he could find. All that he had was to offer. His eyes saw only Freya's eyes, who looked back at him, sharing his wonder.

"What you have just experienced," explained Sid, "is an ancient joining of Shiva and Shakti, the primal god and goddess, the joining of shadow and light, consciousness and the unconscious, man and woman. In this joining, opposites disappear into each other to form a perfection of wholeness."

"Fred," Sid continued, "were you able to take the photos? Were you able to meditate?"

"Yes and yes," Fred replied with awe in his voice.

"Gabe?"

"Yes, Sid. I have it recorded in words."

Standing up, Sid spoke, "We will talk about this later. Now, my good friends, it is time to walk."

The last hour of their day's walk was covered in reflective silence, a quietness which was enhanced by the land through which they passed.

When they checked into Casa de Somoza, they were pleased with their accommodations. All the rooms in the casa were doubles putting Freya and René together once again. In a way, their ease and familiarity that they had developed with each other, evoked a sense of them being a couple who had known each other intimately, for decades, not as two individuals who had met just a month earlier. As they rinsed their socks and hiking clothes worn that day, they talked easily of the day's sights. Unvoiced, was the meditation they had experienced earlier. It didn't take long before they joined the others in the garden area, bringing a refreshing beverage with them.

"So," asked Mark as the last of the group gathered in the garden. "Are we ready to talk about this afternoon's meditation, Sid?"

"I think I want to hear from René first," replied Sid. "René, can you tell us what it was that you experienced?"

"I'll try," he began. "Before I do, would I be correct in suggesting that this was Tantric practice?"

"Yes, you are right. I was certain that you would grasp what was happening. What else can you tell us?"

"Well, as I see it, it fits within a Christian ideal where a man and a woman "know" each other thus creating a bond that is forever inseparable, a holy marriage where two become one, something Fred and I have discussed earlier in our journey on the Camino."

"Yes, that is part of what this practice also contains. And?"

"And within my understanding of depth psychology, it is analogous to the alchemical union of the Red King and the White Queen, the masculine and feminine principles that must come together for the psyche to become whole."

"There, Mark," said Sid, "is your answer. However, we both know that you already knew the answer to your question."

"Fred," questioned Sid. "Any questions?"

"No, I think I need time to process all of this. I am overwhelmed with what I saw. I only hope that the photos will be good enough though I am not sure what they are needed for, to tell you the truth."

Turning to the group, Sid said, "We will meet again, to both look at the photos, and to talk more. For now, it's time to perhaps retreat to our rooms and reflect."

~

"Let's see the photos, René," suggested Freya.

René brought the photos into the viewfinder and saw that Fred had taken quite a few photos, from different angles. "Just a second, I'll just put them on the tablet so that we can see them better."

When the photos were transferred, they looked closely at the photos. "Shit!" exclaimed René, "it's happened again. Look at those auras of light. You can't see Sid, Asha, Mark, Miryam and Gabe at all – just auras of light – just them but not you or me. This is beyond strange. I think that Sid has some explaining to do when we look at the photos together."

"Hmm," smiled Freya as she looked at the photo containing just her and René. "We sure do look good in this picture. Let's practice that position before we go for supper with the others."

~

"What's the plan for tomorrow, Gabe?" Mark asked as they gathered in the dining room.

"Well, it depends on how fast we want to get to Santiago. Now that we are only sixty kilometres away, we could push for two thirty kilometre days or break it up into three easier days. What does everyone think, two or three days?

"Asha and I are not interested in making the rest of our Camino a race," admitted Sid. "Perhaps it's best if we approach these last days more mindfully; and, with the extra time available we could have more intensive meditations on our purpose, as well as our path."

Miryam added her voice, "I agree with you, Sid. There's a lot to think about. After all, it is a pilgrimage, not some episode of The Amazing Race Camino."

"Somehow, I knew that you guys were going to say this," said Gabe, "so here is what I thought we could do. Tomorrow we walk twenty kilometres to Arzua, then then the next day it's nineteen kilometres to Arca O'Pino, leaving a final twenty into Santiago. There's all sorts of places to stay in Arzua and the same can be said about Arca. I doubt that we will need to worry about booking ahead, especially since we aren't walking long distances. We'll be close to the first pilgrims in each town to book beds."

"Masterful as always," complimented Mark. "Sounds like our plans are made."

~

"Come here," invited Freya as she lay on the bed. "This is likely our last night alone together before Santiago. Let's not waste it. I need to practice Tantric meditation with you."

> *What a strange day. We were initiated into a form of Tantric yoga. But more important than that for me was the fact that going through the ritual with Freya has made a transformation in our relationship, one that hopefully with endure until death do us part.*
>
> *But, there is still the issue of photos to deal with.*

Chapter Thirty – Portal To Spirituality

The route to Arzua from O'Coto, began with a trek through woods to a medieval bridge, then into Leboreiro past a thirteenth-century church, the Iglexia Santa Maria. From the church they walked on to cross a second medieval bridge, the Magdalena, before taking the Little Company of Pilgrims onto another senda paralleling the N-547 highway. Four and a half kilometres into their day's hike they came upon yet another medieval bridge called the Ponte Velha Furelos. They then entered a series of suburbs that heralded the nearness of Melide, where they planned to stop for a coffee even though they had only walked six and a half kilometres.

It seemed that every second restaurant in Melide was serving octopus, which wasn't a hit so early in the day, so they walked past the Parque de San Roque towards the other end of the town where they spotted a likely choice, the Meso O'Toxo. Soon everyone had ordered a full breakfast. When the coffee and meal were finished, and feeling satisfied and satiated, it was time for them to continue on their journey.

Before they reached the end of the town, the stopped briefly at the Iglexia Santa Maria de Melide XII for some photos. Another five and a half kilometres later they arrived at the village of Boente, where the local priest was giving blessings to the line of pilgrims who were passing by his church, the Iglexia Santiago.

They found their spot for group meditation just past the village of Castañeda, next to a small river, a tributary of the Rio Iso. Because they were only five and a half kilometres from their destination of Arzua, they were able to enjoy a full hour of meditation.

"René, do you have the photos?" asked Sid when they had finished meditating.

"Yes," said René as he took out the tablet onto which he had kept the photos. "I also have a question about them."

Sid passed the tablet to Fred who studied the pictures he had taken, closely.

René spoke as Fred examined the results, "There is a distortion of light in the photos that have, you, Asha, Mark, Miryam and Gabe. I went back to some of the other photos I had taken and have found the same thing," he explained. "Can you tell me what that is about?"

"I can and I will, but not right now," replied Sid. "Now, I want Fred to tell us about what he saw, and what that brought up in him. Fred?"

"Well, to begin with, when I began taking the photos, I felt like a voyeur, as I saw all of you coupling. In a way, my first reaction was to turn away and not take any photos. I felt betrayed because I trusted you, Sid. However, that judgemental attitude began to change as I saw, I mean I "saw" halos envelope you and Asha. I knew that these halos were signs of the grace of God, signs of holiness."

Fred continued, "Then I began to take the photos, trying to see if I could capture that holiness. As I looked around, I saw the same auras of holiness envelop Mark and Miryam. I knew I was in the presence of something heaven-sent. My eyes then turned to Freya and René and was surprised to see that they weren't enveloped in halos which then confused me. I turned and saw Gabe sitting in a lotus position writing, surrounded by what I can only describe as a living halo of light. I couldn't help shifting the camera and my eyes from one couple to the next and then back to Gabe. Then, I felt drawn to take my meditation position and share in the meditative energy that pulsed. I don't know how to better explain it," concluded Fred.

"That was perfect," pronounced Sid. "Thank you." Then turning to René, Sid added, "René, I will explain more about this later, okay?"

The group decided to stop at the Albergue Los Caminantes, the Walkers' Hostel for the night. The beds were in a dorm. As usual when provided with bunk beds, the women and Mark took bottom bunks while the rest took the upper bunks. The hostel had washers and dryers, as well as Wi-Fi. With restaurants so close by, they decided that there was no need to try cooking a communal meal. That left our small company of pilgrims with time to spare for being tourists in the town of 7,000. Only Fred was willing to walk with René as he went in search of the elusive perfect photo. And as in the day before, Fred had another motive in mind as he wanted to discuss his ideas on René.

"You know," Fred began, "What I saw, and what the camera caught seems to defy everything I have taken for granted about spirituality, about what is good and what is evil. And it wasn't just what the camera recorded either. I mean, the holiness of that moment was burnt into the very core of my being."

"I know what you mean," René answered in agreement. "It felt like perfection, like whatever it is that heaven might be. But it is also surprising in what wasn't captured in the images. Perhaps there are some things that are only observable from the soul, and not through the lens of a camera."

Fred was struggling to find the right words as he continued, "I mean, I did believe that nudity was a portal to spirituality, but I would never have imagined that sexual coupling – yes, that is what it was – could be spiritual as well. But more than that, in Sid and Asha, as well as with Miryam and Mark, it was more, wasn't it? More than spiritual. It was what I could only call holiness. I'll never be able to bring this back to my parishioners."

René considered his words carefully before responding, "I don't think that you should either, Fred. I have been a Buddhist, well sort of a Buddhist, for a good number of years. I already intellectually knew about Tantric yoga, but I had never personally moved from the basic path of meditation and learning of Buddhist dharma. If I had been brought face to face with Tantra before now, I would have run from Buddhism as if I was running from the Plague. The nudity, the engagement – all of it – I was too hung up with my own shame of body, my own negative attitudes towards sex."

Fred paused for a few minutes as they walked on before shifting the conversation, slightly, "Christianity hasn't always been so negative towards nudity and sex. You only have to look at certain forms of monasticism through the centuries and Christian art to know that nudity has not always been looked at as a negative force in Christianity."

"I agree," said René. "Michelangelo's picture of Adam and God in the Sistine Chapel, the nude Christ on the cross, and the baptism of a nude Christ by John the Baptist are some of the art pieces I have seen."

"Naked baby Jesus, Mary breast-feeding, and this list goes on and on," added Fred. "Nudity in modern Christianity has always been problematic, particularly in the United States. Mostly this is because American Christianity has a hard time with new concepts in general and nudity in particular. Many American Christians can't make a distinction between nudity and sex."

"I have to admit, though I stopped being Christian decades ago," admitted René, "I also have had the same problem in making that distinction – well, with the exception of nudity within my marriage, and in relation to my children and grandchildren. It's not so easy to change the scripts we grow up with."

"That is perhaps the bigger issue here," Fred went on to explain, "the issue of our whole culture, our society having strong, negative responses to nudity. Until there is some resolution at the societal level, as far as I see it, there will be a need to pursue spiritual nudism in private settings, undercover so-to-speak."

The conversation continued until their return to the hostel when René went in search of Freya. He found her with the others just a few doors down from the hostel sitting outside a bar-café, enjoying a glass of wine with the rest of their group.

"So, did you get any photos?" joked Gabe. "I know, what a dumb ass question to ask."

"A few," grinned René, as he sat in the chair beside Freya. She reached for his hand and gave him a smile that filled his spirit with a sense of completion. The thought of their parting ways once they had finished the Camino was now unthinkable. He couldn't imagine a life without Freya being in it, at the centre.

"We were just talking about Santiago and life after the Camino," mentioned Mark. "I was telling these guys and ladies, that the pilgrimage never ends. I've been wandering on my own pilgrimage for many years. It's as though the door back home had been locked and the key had been thrown away."

Gabe added his voice saying, "There's an old expression about leaving home and never being able to go back."

"You can only be in the present which is a constantly shifting reality based on a constantly shifting awareness of self," added Sid. "There is no past, no future as far as consciousness is concerned, just an eternal now."

"That's pretty deep," said Fred. "Philosophy and psychology aside, I will be returning to my home and to my ministry in the U.S. of A."

"Going back to a place doesn't mean that the place is the same place you left," Miryam added, surprising the others as she rarely offered her inner thoughts to others. "I don't think the place you left exists any longer. You know, like a river is forever changing, like even a mountain changes though ever so slowly."

"Nicely said," Mark praised Miryam with a smile as well as words.

"You know," Sid went on to explain. "Even if you could return to the physical space you had left with everything and everyone in that space completely unchanged, it would still be different for you. Each of us has changed every day we have been walking here on the Camino, and we will continue to change with the hours and days that remain to us. We could no longer see, hear or relate to the world, as it was before our Camino. In effect we end up recreating the place and the relationships based on our new, expanded consciousness."

The conversation swirled around the idea of how each of them had changed over the past month. The group decided to head back to the hostel for a rest until it was time to go out for an evening meal. It was time for reflection, time to check messages and perhaps write in their journals. René wrote:

> *This pilgrimage is getting weirder and weirder as the days go by – halos on some and not others – tantric meditation, Fred's struggles with finding peace with nudity and spiritualism. The one thing that makes the most sense, is Freya's presence in my life.*

~

The café Tia Doleres appeared at the seven and a half kilometre mark the next morning, perfect timing for a change of socks and a cup of café con leche. With thirst quenched and dry socks on, they continued the walk to Arca. It wasn't long after Salceda when they spotted a woodland opening as a likely place for meditation, a meditation which they kept to a short twenty minutes. Then, back on the path, they stopped for a second breakfast at the fifteen kilometre mark at O'Ceadoiro. In spite of two stops and a pause for meditation, they arrived in Arca before one in the afternoon.

They wandered around a bit with their backpacks before settling on staying at the Albergue O'Burgos for their last night on the Camino route. They were able to choose between rooms with double beds or in the dorm with others. Mark and Miryam, as well as Freya and René chose to take separate rooms. The hostel didn't have a bar or restaurant, but since they had seen several while searching for their accommodation, this wasn't seen as a great concern.

In their own room, René and Freya stripped off their clothes to wash in the sink before taking a shower. Freya took out René's camera to get a photo of René washing his socks, shorts and top.

"I suppose you're going to blow up the photo to put on your wall at home," commented René.

"Who said this photo is for me," teased Freya. "I was thinking of showing it to all the eligible women I know back home. You know, with a caption that reads something like: Desperate Canadian looking for a woman to wash his dirty clothes."

A while later, the two sat in their bed saying very little, simply satisfied with being together. René was writing in his journal while Freya read though the last pages of the guide book.

"René? Have you been thinking about what you are going to do after getting to Santiago?"

"A bit," he admitted. "I decided that I'm not ready to be finished, so I'll be walking a few more days to reach Finisterre. What about you, Freya? Would you come with me?"

"Of course."

Freya's words had answered an unspoken question that had been brewing within him for a few days now. Her answer caused as many problems as they solved. How was he going to fit her into his life? How was she going to fit him in her life? How could he not have her in his life?

"Now, get your clothes on," commanded Freya. "It's time to go meet the others for our dinner. We can talk more, later."

As they prepared to leave the room, René said, "Wait, I want my camera. I want another group photo."

While at the table in a nearby restaurant, René made sure to take quite a few photos including individual candid shots of each of his friends. He had Fred take a photo of him and Freya together as well.

The food could have been good, however the excitement in the air made it impossible to truly taste the various courses that arrived at their table. Wine was plentiful enough, though no one drank to excess, as no one wanted a hangover to spoil their entrance into Santiago the next afternoon. Almost reluctantly, they called it a night and retreated back to the hostel and their respective rooms.

"That was good," said René as he prepared to upload the photos to his tablet where they would then be uploaded to his Flickr account. "You know, I'm going to miss all of them when the Camino is done. Mark told me that he is going to head south and do the Portuguese Camino backward and of course, Miryam is going wherever Mark goes. Sid and Asha are going back to India the day after tomorrow. Gabe says he is flying back to the States as he has an interview about his work on mythology that is going to be on television. Fred mentioned that he was seriously thinking of skipping out on going to Finisterre. I could tell that he is homesick."

"I'm sure that it won't be the last we will hear from all of them, at least some of them. Somehow they will pop back into our lives when the time is right. It's good that Fred is going home, good for him and his wife. I think you have made a valuable friend in Fred, one that is a true, life-time friendship," added Freya.

"Here," said René as he drew Freya close to him on the bed. "Let's look at the photos together."

René stared at the monitor of his tablet and again saw halos of light as he had seen in all the other photos that had been taken of Mark, Miryam, Sid, Asha and Gabe. Of the photos he took at the restaurant, only the photos of Fred, Freya and himself were without halos.

"I just don't understand?" he said in disappointment. "You saw me take the photos. There's something here that needs to be explained."

"Um, René, I have something to tell you," confessed Freya. "Remember I once told you I was a witch?"

"Yes," he answered a bit puzzled by her question.

"Um, well, I think the reason the photos didn't turn out is because except for you and Fred and me, I think it is because they don't really exist in the outer world. I sense that they are not like us, but are more like spiritual beings, maybe our spiritual guides."

"But we can see them, others can see them and talk to them. Are you sure?"

"I have a feeling that they are manifestations. What did you call such things, archetypes? You told me that archetypes were inner presences that are part of who we are. I think Luca was one as well."

"Archetypes? You've got to be kidding. Is that what you're telling me? Next thing you'll tell me is that you're not real either."

"You're not crazy and I am real. Remember, there was no halo surrounding me."

"So now what?"

"We talk to them and ask them to tell us who they really are and why they are here. Okay?"

Chapter Thirty-One – Coming Clean on the Camino

Sleep was hard to come by as René lay in the bed beside Freya who was peacefully sleeping. He was struggling to make sense of what she had told him, stuff he had theoretically known about as a psychotherapist with decades of study based on Carl Jung's work, as well as those who came after him. What Freya told him was nothing he didn't already know intellectually. But, that was all theory and mythology, not about the real world, or so he thought.

"René?" called a voice from the shadows of the room. "Come sit with me."

René lifted his head and opened his eyes to see a glow of golden light within which Sid was sitting. "Sid. Siddhartha, right?"

"Yes, you finally know who and what I am, don't you?"

"You're my Buddha nature?" whispered René hoping not to disturb Freya.

"Yes. You know that it is important to realise that the nature of reality is as a construct of the ego, an illusion that creates duality. You know that what is within, is as real as what is without, and that both form the divine light of consciousness."

"Yes, I remember those lessons though I didn't really know what they meant."

"Your ego didn't know, but your Buddha nature has always known this. All knowledge is within you."

"Thank you, Sid. I think I can sleep now. Will I see you tomorrow?"

"If you are willing, yes. Remember that it is you who creates the portals that allow light to enter, and you who closes the doors to remain in the darkness, seemingly alone."

"Good night, Sid."

"Good night, René."

~

The next morning, the sun was about to make its presence as René walked behind the rest of his Small Company of Pilgrims. Already the path was busy with others making the final surge towards Santiago. Fred walked just ahead of him, with Freya and Miryam just in front of Fred. René took a photo of the group then checked his viewfinder in playback mode. Strangely, he had a recognizable Fred and Freya, but not of the other members of his Little Company of Pilgrims. Shaking his head, he faced backwards to get a sunrise photo with the long line of pilgrims walking towards him, almost as silhouettes against the merging light of day.

"Fred, hold up a bit!" called René to the American pastor.

Over the next two and a half kilometres which took almost three-quarters of an hour, René struggled in silence with the thoughts that raced through his head. What was real, what was illusion? As they passed through a Eucalyptus forest, René saw a likely location for meditation. Pointing out the opening just off to the left to Fred, he veered off to engage in the last meditation before Santiago. It was as if he didn't even have to tell the others of his intentions, as they were already moving to the spot. Obviously there was a level of communication that was intuitive and non-verbal that connected him to all the others. In the privacy of the trees, clothes were neatly placed beside each pilgrim before each took their seat facing Sid.

Once they had rejoined the throng of pilgrims heading west, René began to tell Fred his situation, how these others who were in the group, the ones that had halos in the photos, were manifestations of the unconscious, that they weren't real people. The suggestion that they were walking with spirits seemed to upset Fred. When they reached San Payo, seven and a half kilometres closer to Santiago, they stopped for coffee and toast.

"René tells me that you guys aren't real," Fred told the others in their group. "I think that he is getting quite stressed about the Camino coming to an end."

"Well," began Mark, "it's not as simple as that. We are real, but in a different kind of way. You can see us and touch us and talk to us and we can do the same thing back to you, Fred, Freya and René. Reality as you define it, is the problem, well the definition of reality is the problem."

"I don't get it," frowned Fred in confusion.

"I think I have to tell you who I am and then we can go from there. My name is Mercury, some people have also known me as Hermes. Yes, the same Mercury you have studied about, René, as an agent of transformation in alchemy. Fred, I exist in you as I exist in René and Freya. That's what René calls an archetype. I am the eternal pilgrim in each of us, always on a journey to the holy land but never quite getting there. I guess you could call me a pilgrim's guide to the holy land through the wilderness."

"Miryam here, is Mary of Magdalene. You may have noticed that when we pass chapels, churches and markers that bear her name, she seems to glow. You may have also noticed that she is good at taking care of all of us like a good wife and mother – the wife of Jesus and the mother of his child. You also know of her story as a harlot, a shameless woman who had little use for clothing in her trade. She knew men before Jesus, and after him as well. That's the thing about her is that she is the eternal contradiction in each human, the inner harlot and saint."

"Sid? He is Siddhartha Gautama, sometimes called Buddha. He would be the last person to accept that title, as Buddha isn't or wasn't a person; it is a nature or state of mind-being. He is the source of all enlightenment that is wrapped up in generosity and compassion within all humans. In spite of his denials about being a Buddhist, the philosophy or psychology of Buddhism comes from his teachings, as he has shared with each of us"

"Asha is a saint, a saint that praises the purest of the pure without shame, the Eve from the Garden of Eden, as well as the eternal virgin who resides within the deepest depths of soul. You likely never heard of her presence as the Naked Saint who praised the Lord in poetry and song. You might want to look up her historical name, Akka Mahdevi."

"Gabe is a story teller, a presence within us that shows us the map of our journey if you would trust him. His story is both old and new. He is known by other names such as Homer and more recently as Joseph Campbell. Ah, I see that rings a bell for you, Fred."

"Luca? Well he has been around a long time as well, a man who dances with darkness like Faust and Dostoyevsky. He is the link, a portal of sorts through darkness into light. You might also know him as Carl Jung."

"There was another man that René met for a few days when we weren't with him, David. Yes, the biblical King David. Who put in an appearance to both explain and to redirect René back onto the path before he could be swallowed by a dark, empty path."

René then interrupted Mark, "Thank you, Mark. These eternal presences are something I can understand, have understood intellectually. But now, I am coming to see much clearer as not being dependent upon me. I was struggling with a conceit that I somehow created all of you, that you were illusions not the universal presences with every one of us humans. But what about Jason? I don't see his archetypal role."

Mercury smiled and then answered, "Jason is, as you are, a man. Of course archetypes don't generally run around in control of human bodies, at least not in sane humans, but that's another story that you might explain to Fred at some point. Jason is Jason, the man you had met a few times before as you told us. Call it serendipity that he was here walking with you, especially at a time when you needed his counsel."

"So, Fred," asked Mark. "Is that any clearer?"

"A bit. But why the nudity?"

"Fred, why have you been blogging about nudity for these past number of years? These experiences are in accordance to your need which parallels René's needs – another neat coincidence don't you think? Part of the agenda for what has happened while we've been on the Camino together is for your validation as a minister and as a man in God's image. Remember that man and woman were conceived as naked beings in the Garden of Eden. The only way back to that Garden is by the light of awareness that Sid and Asha represent, a light that cannot be hidden behind clothing. One has to risk everything to regain the garden."

"Uh, one more thing, Mark, I mean Mercury," asked Fred. "You didn't mention Freya."

"No need to be formal, Fred, Mark is good enough. Freya is Freya, flesh and blood like you and René. Serendipity has brought her to the Camino at the same time as René. Perhaps you want to call it fate, but it is more than that. Both have suffered a loss of faith and life partner, and both were in need of trust in their opposites. The combined needs of the three of you drew all of us onto your path here in Spain."

Two kilometres after San Payo when they stopped again at a small river by Lavacolla. Mark led the group to the bank of the river which looked somewhat brackish and foul. He removed his clothing though they were in plain sight of the passing line of pilgrims, walked into the water and washed himself. Without asking why, each of the others did the same. To enter Santiago, tradition demanded that one becomes purified in the waters of this river.

Putting their clothing back on, not paying attention to the stares and odd photo being taken by voyeurs on the path, they rejoined the line of pilgrims walking into Santiago.

Chapter Thirty-Two – Endings Are New Beginnings

Santiago. In what appeared to be a gathering hundreds of other pilgrims, Fred, Freya and René made their way to the Pilgrims' Office, Oficina del Peregrino, where they handed over their pilgrim passports which attested to their journey from Saint Jean Pied de Port to Santiago. Their reward, a certificate of completion, a Compostela, was placed into their waiting hands. The reality of their journey hadn't yet sunk in as they looked at each other's certificate and congratulated each other as well as other pilgrims in the office receiving their certificates. They left the office and returned to the square where the others waited.

"It's not over," remarked René in a voice that seemed far away, almost disconnected from his body. "It's never going to be over, is it?"

Mark looked at both Fred and René with compassion before responding with his usual humour, "And ain't that just grand? Welcome to my world you young 'uns."

"Now about a place to stay for the next two nights," suggested Gabe. "I've got an idea. Of course, it's up to you to make the decision."

"Okay, let's hear it," asked René.

"The hotel, Hesperia Peregrino, is just a few blocks away, and it's available at a great deal for what you get, about sixty Canadian dollars a night for a room. It's kind of a bit luxurious, but it is time to celebrate, isn't it?"

"What do you think, Fred? Go for it?"

"Sure," he agreed. "Let's go and dump these backpacks and find aa rowdy place for a good stiff drink."

The walk had taken more out of René than he had realised. Now that the compostela was in his possession, and the Camino Francés was done. He felt drained. He was glad that he was alone with Freya in their room. There was no plan to get together with the others until seven that evening when they would go out for tapas and a drink before having their evening meal.

Tonight wasn't going to be the typical Pilgrim Menu that had been their basic choice for most of the evenings on the Camino. Tonight was time to celebrate. But for now, all that was important was taking a bath with Freya and then resting together in their bed, perhaps even taking a nap if that was possible. René had come to accept the reality of Freya's presence in his life, her presence which he now saw as a gift.

Freya was becoming as familiar to René as any woman could be said to be known. He couldn't claim to know himself all that well, so he accepted that even with a mortal woman, some mystery had to remain. René realised that Freya wasn't going to go away, she wasn't going to abandon him. The most problematic part of that realisation was the fact that he knew he couldn't ever control her. She had her own locus of energy and power. He had learned that when they became one. René would have to settle for what she would give him whenever she decided to give it. Two who became one, yet continued to be separate.

~

As they waited for the last of their group to arrive in the hotel's bar, Fred began to talk to René and Freya about his thoughts on the pilgrimage, which for him was as much about spiritual nudity as it was about getting to Santiago.

"As I see it," Fred explained, "most nudists seem to be always heading somewhere so that they can find a place to be naked."

"That's understandable," remarked Freya. "Fear. Everyone is afraid of being outed, of being exposed, of being vulnerable. And, for good reason as you North Americans seem intent on making nudity something evil, rather than natural."

"Whether it's for spiritual reasons, or simply a place for a safe retreat for communion with others and with nature, the need to make any intentional journey is a pilgrimage, even if it is to go to a nudist venue hidden in a forest in America."

"I see where you're coming from," admitted René.

"I am beginning to wonder about this actual pilgrimage we've taken to Santiago. I thought it was a spiritual pilgrimage in the traditional Christian sense. But, my pilgrimage was both blessed and challenged with the problem of nakedness – my nakedness as well as yours. I can sure tell you that this wasn't in any way, shape or form, my intention. I was certain that I had basically set it all down in my blogs and that I was moving on to something deeper, perhaps thinking more ethereal which would then become my new point of departure at my blog site."

"Fred," challenged Freya, "Did you really think that writing it on paper, well cyber-paper, would be enough to set to rest what has been bubbling inside of you?"

"Erm, well, yes, I guess I did."

"Something tells me that you have just begun your pilgrimage. Like René, you're going to have to plunge into your quest with heart, body and soul. You know, get vulnerable and naked with yourself. By that I mean open the doors and let your shadow out. It's a risk to finally meet your core self. But then again, maybe you aren't really ready for that, what with your need to pastor your parishioners and their need to have you fit into their limited frames of reference. Something for you to think about."

"Okay," interrupted René, "let's go have a drink or two with the others."

The next evening as they gathered again for a final meal, it came to René that this was time to say goodbye to most of his pilgrimage companions. Their work had been done for now, a work that curiously was for himself, Freya and Fred. Only Freya had planned to stay with him as he walked on to Finisterre. Fred had decided to fly to Paris, and then on to the States the next afternoon. Would they continue to talk in the months and years to come? René hoped so, but he knew that it would ultimately be Fred who would make the decision to re-engage. For René, the door was open and that was all he could do, all that he should do.

As for his other Camino friends, René knew that he would eventually meet them, archetypal presence, again when he needed them. That door had been opened like some kind of Pandora's Box. The opening would radically change the way he would relate to others, and with himself, for the rest of his life, a life he now began to look forward to with Freya at his side.

That night as he lay in bed writing in his journal, the words of Carl Jung came to him that talked of his pilgrimage experience with archetypes:

> "This is the primitive way of describing the libido's entry into the interior world of the psyche, the unconscious. There, through its introversion and regression, contents are constellated which till now were latent. These are the primordial images, the

archetypes, which have been so enriched with individual memories through the introversion of libido as to become perceptible to the conscious mind."

'Hmm, that sounds suspiciously like my journey, this pilgrimage,' he mumbled to himself before turning to his journal:

> *We're in Santiago, well I am in Santiago with Fred and Freya. The others have now retreated into the depths from whence they came. I think I am ready to return to work and to living a full life. But first, Freya and I will journey on to Finisterre and then on to Paris. We have a life to plan together.*

Epilogue

Freya stood in front of her husband, in the throne room in Valaskjalf in Asgard. "It has begun, Odin. The human, René will be ours."

"I was sure that like always, you would able to weave your power to ensnare him for our purposes," Odin spoke with assurance. "No man stands a chance against the goddess of love, sex, beauty, fertility, gold, war, and death."

"There is just one problem," Freya added with a hint of frustration tinged with anger. "The Celts are trying to add the human, René, into their plans."

"It doesn't surprise me," Odin gritted. "I guess you are right, it has just begun. Just do what you have to do to get this mortal to serve our needs. We can't have the Tuatha Dé Danann get this prize."

"Don't worry, husband. No man can resist me. I will succeed in this. René will be ours in the coming showdown.

Afterword

This novel is a blend of fantasy, Jungian psychology, Buddhism and naturism. The journey follows a real path called the Camino Francés – the French Way – of the Camino de Santiago. Every town, village, hostel, café and geographic feature that the Small Company of Pilgrims pass through are real places. However, these characters on the journey are fictions.

That said, the characters in the novel sometimes borrow words and ideas of historical people such as Buddha, Akka Mahadevi, Joseph Campbell, and Carl Jung. A few contemporary people are also adding their voices in the story. The poetry of Asha is taken directly from the original poetry of Akka Mahadevi. The character Sid, speaks with paraphrased words from Buddha, Chogyam Trungpa and Pema Chodron. Jason Johnson speaks with the voice of James Hollis, an American Jungian analyst. Even though their voices are brought into the story, it in no way suggests that they agree with the story as presented. No voice presented in any way, attempts to distort their original words and ideas.

It is the opinion of the author that every word spoken or written and held is personal, and is in fact arising from the collective consciousness and the collective unconscious that has been experienced by all of us in the process of living.

Acknowledgements

Like others who have written, there are many people that I need to thank. In order for this novel to come into existence, I have to thank my wife for her patience as I got caught up in the fantasy world of this story.

I also have to thank Pastor Ed Raby Sr., for his comments at various points in the story, as well as a few trusted readers such as Paul Z Walker and Bill Rathborne, who were kind enough to highlight errors in structure and spelling and general confusion.

As well there are so many others who deserve thanks for their valuable insight and critical eyes. I also must thank my many friends and family who have consistently encouraged me along the way.

Made in the USA
San Bernardino, CA
24 April 2017